PRAISE FO

"Tattooed hero fans!! You're gonna love this book!! So for anyone looking for a really freaking good, deliciously swoony, non-frustrating, sexy, fun romance with a dash of suspense all mixed together with a generous helping of protective, heart-melting, and tattooed Alpha male, THIS IS IT. This is the mac & cheese of contemporary romance." —*Aestas Book Blog*

"Cole has a winner in this debut novel and series opener . . . steamy romance, body art, and a little intrigue will keep readers up well past their bedtimes."
—*Library Journal Xpress Reviews*

"Cole delivers a thrilling tale of new beginnings. The chemistry is as electric as the villain is creepy. This fast-paced read will leave you eager for the rest of the series." —*RT Book Reviews*

"One of those books that will hold you captive from the first word to the last. Author Scarlett Cole has penned an amazing story . . . . you will feel empathy, anger, warmth, fear, hope, and love with every word. *The Strongest Steel* is on my TRA (To Read Again) shelf and I can't wait to get my hands on the next Second Circle Tattoos novel." —*Fresh Fiction*

"Scarlett Cole truly knows how to get readers invested in her characters and in the story. Her writing is excellent, and I'd love to read more from her. I'm definitely waiting with bated breath for the next book in this series." —*Romance Reviews*, Top Pick

"For her debut title, Ms. Cole has mastered suspense and complicated characters that you pray get that HEA. Well done!"

—Violetta Rand, author of the Devil's Den series

"Poignant and intriguing. Scarlett Cole wrote a wonderful story full of emotion, mystery, and second chances. Make room for this on your keeper shelf."

—Sarah Grimm, author of the Black Phoenix series

"After reading *The Strongest Steel*, Scarlett Cole has definitely been added to my list of must-read authors. I loved the instant connection between Harper and Trent . . . Swoon!" —*Life with Two Boys*

"I AM IN LOVE!!!! That is all I can say about *The Strongest Steel* by Scarlett Cole. I am in love with Trent Andrews. I am in love with Harper Connelly. I am in love with this book. I am already in love with this series and this is only the first book released and I am in love with this author . . . my NEW FAVORITE book that I have read this year!"

—*Everything Books by Heather*

"Harper is probably my new favorite female character now. Put it on your TBR. I cannot say enough wonderful things about this book!" —*Book Disciple*

"Wow . . . I [can't] even sum up appropriate descriptors to tell you how much I loved this book. Pretty sure I've found myself a new series, because I'm already over here wanting to jump on a couch like Tom Cruise in excitement for the next book." —*Wild Heart Reviews*

"A beautiful story about letting go of the past and healing . . . Cole hit this one out of the park."

—*Avid Reader Amy's Reviews*

ALSO BY SCARLETT COLE

THE SECOND CIRCLE TATTOO SERIES

The Strongest Steel

The Fractured Heart

The Purest Hook

The Darkest Link

THE PRELOAD SERIES

Jordan Reclaimed

Elliott Redeemed

UNDER FIRE

Scarlett Cole

St. Martin's Paperbacks

This is a work of fiction. All of the characters, organizations, and events portrayed in this novel are either products of the author's imagination or are used fictitiously.

UNDER FIRE

For information address St. Martin's Press, 175 Fifth Avenue, New York, NY 10010.

ISBN: 978-1-250-12844-7

Our books may be purchased in bulk for promotional, educational, or business use. Please contact your local bookseller or the Macmillan Corporate and Premium Sales Department at 1-800-221-7945, ext. 5442, or by e-mail at MacmillanSpecialMarkets@macmillan.com.

Printed in the United States of America

St. Martin's Paperbacks edition / August 2017

St. Martin's Paperbacks are published by St. Martin's Press, 175 Fifth Avenue, New York, NY 10010.

10 9 8 7 6 5 4 3 2 1

To Greg, Ted, Gaz, Joel, and Rob.
Thank you for being heroes.

ACKNOWLEDGMENTS

To the military men who helped with the details of this book, from gun choices to enacting the final scene live on video while wearing board shorts so I could understand it better, thank you. I couldn't have written this without you. If I have misrepresented any detail, the fault is mine. You are the definition of courage, and I am honored to have met you all. And special thank you, CDR Greg Geisen, USN Retired, Naval Special Warfare Command Public Affairs (2005–2010), for helping the hero of the story with his explanations about medals. Your fantastic one-liner made it into the book as promised!

Barb Devlin—Thank you for walking me through the complicated relationship between the police, CIA, and FBI, and for being one of greatest writer friends I have. Your willingness to share your knowledge is rare and wonderful.

Lizzie Poteet—Book number seven, baby! Thank you for believing in this series, and me! I learn more from you each time we go through this process.

Beth Phelan—For continuing to be the best agent a girl could wish for. I am unbelievably grateful for you.

To my Stars—For being uniquely you. You make me laugh so hard, and usually when I most need it. Thank you for being my happy place on the internet.

To Sidney Halston—For being a rockstar author, my writer BFF, and partner-in-crime.

To all the bloggers who have supported me. I am grateful for every one of your tweets, posts, and shares. A thousand thank-yous.

To Louise Rees—Thank you for picking up all the scattered bits of me and putting them back together in an organized way.

To Amanda and Michelle—Thanks for being such wonderful friends . . . and for always bringing alcohol!

To T, F, and L.—You three are my everything. Thank you for continuing to support me as I undertake this crazy author ride.

CHAPTER ONE

Sixton "Six" Rapp parked his truck but left the motor running, taking a long moment to stare at his first civilian workplace since a lifeguarding gig in college. Never had a nondescript warehouse with peeling paint looked so incredible.

There was no sand here to work its way into every crevice known to man. Just good old American black asphalt and some brown grass in desperate need of the elusive San Diego rain. There was no gunfire, no screaming, and no whirring aircraft propellers. Instead, the sweet sound of Nina Simone singing about sugar in her bowl blasted from his speakers. Most importantly, the building was his. Well, a third of it.

He checked his watch. He was late—a new habit he'd subconsciously developed in the last two weeks since he'd left his Navy SEAL career behind.

"Shit," he said, pocketing his keys and grabbing his gym bag and garment bag from the passenger seat. He threw them over his shoulder as he got out and winced as the straps crossed over the four lines of scratch marks that Lauren . . . Lori . . . whatever her name was . . . had left on his back after an impromptu heated farewell against his front door. Some things were worth being late for.

With a gait borne of over a decade of military conditioning, Six jogged into the building. The smell of still-drying paint lingered in the air as he made his way past the empty reception desk. Hiring somebody for the post had been Mac's responsibility, but he was out on their first real two-week job, finding and retrieving a child who had been abducted by her biological father and taken to Mexico. It was nasty case involving years of abuse and a restraining order that was as useless as the paper it was written on.

It was hard to believe that what they had been working on and saving so hard for over the last few years was finally about to be realized. Five years earlier, when Cabe had floated the idea to start planning and saving for a business of their own for when they were done with the military, Six and their best friend, Mac, had thought Cabe was getting ahead of himself. Still hardcore committed to the SEAL brotherhood, retirement had been far from their thoughts as they'd scoured the dusty, barren foothills of the Hindu Kush for signs of a terrorist cell suspected of using the Wakhjir Pass to gain access into northern Pakistan.

But now, at thirty-three, with a Purple Heart and a healed bullet wound to the stomach, Six appreciated Cabe's foresight. Cabe had invested the money they'd saved from salaries, reenlistment bonuses, jump pay, and special-duty assignment pay. The guy was such a freaking genius when it came to playing the stock market that Six wondered why Cabe didn't just stay home and play Warren Buffett all day. Their modest savings had grown enough to make Eagle Securities a reality, if not a particularly wealthy one.

It was going to take time to build their special-ops reputation and grow their business, and Six stopped to look at the large board that listed events and names, an idea Mac had had to fill the gap. High-end, discreet security services. Nobody would ever call it exciting work, but it would help pay the bills in return for minimum effort until they were fully booked.

"Hello," he shouted into the empty building. There was a slight echo as his voice bounced off the tiled floor and undecorated hallway.

"Down here," a voice shouted from a corridor to his left.

Six followed the sound and found his best friend and former kindergarten carpet partner, Cabe Moss, on his knees underneath the table, fiddling with wires running into the floor.

"I swear to God your ass gets uglier and uglier," Six said, walking into the room.

Cabe crawled from underneath the table. "And I swear to God, your face gets uglier and uglier. Better my ass than your mug." He jumped to his feet and hugged Six. "How've you been, Viking?"

Six laughed at the old nickname. A family project during high school had uncovered the origins of his tall frame and blond hair. His family was descended from the original fierce raiders. And though the guys had always teased him about it, knowing that fighting was in his blood had been a source of incredible motivation in the hours before getting the go on a mission.

"Glad to be back in San Dog. Spent most of the weekend on my board instead of unpacking. Surfing Seaside was one giant welcome home."

"Well, I'm glad you're here, finally. We've got shit to do, man, to get this place ready for business. Let me show you around."

Six followed Cabe out of the room and into a wide-open space the size of a small plane hangar.

"Fitness center is over there," Cabe said, pointing toward a bank of strength-training equipment and some cardio machines. Two treadmills, a rower, a couple of spin bikes, and a recumbent. Six had plans for those later. "Showers are down the corridor to the left. There's a dorm with three bunks in it to the right. Can double as medical. Got basic supplies in there for now."

The guys had obviously been busy. "We doing training in here too?" he asked. The space would be great for it.

"Yeah, folding desks and chairs are in the storeroom over there. And we can project onto this wall over here. Black out blinds and shit." Cabe lifted his chin to the narrow windows that ran along the upper wall. "For when we need to do briefings, unit level training, specialty training, etc."

Six could see it. Teams, missions, debriefings. Their own chain of command, with them ultimately in charge. "Did we end up hiring any of those resumes I screened?"

Cabe led them back down the hallway they'd come from. "We got five on the books and a couple more starting over the next week, including an ex-SAS guy from the UK. Will intro two of them later. Mac took three of them with him to Mexico to retrieve the child. The job only needed two, but he wanted to test them out."

"Good plan," Six said as they stopped in front of a steel cabinet. "Armory?" he asked.

Cabe nodded. "Electronic code lock. The date Brock died, followed by the date we enlisted," he said quietly, entering the number on the keypad.

They didn't talk about Brock often. Especially not with Mac. But the two dates went together, one having led to the other. It had been Brock's dream to become a SEAL, but when he'd died in their final year of college, everything had changed, even their own career aspirations.

"We look a little light because the guys flew out privately with their weapons. Had to fight to get all the permits. We should have set up in the OC. Would have been easier. Or somewhere we're allowed automatics as well as semis."

Six could only imagine the paperwork Mac had had to take care of, and he felt shitty that he hadn't been there to help out. But their separation dates were never going to line up properly, especially with different quantities of terminal leave due, so he'd done what he could from Virginia. "It's good to be home, Cabe."

Cabe looked at him and grinned. "Sure as hell is. Over there you've seen. It's a conference room for meeting with clients. One that still doesn't have reliable Internet. And we also have a smaller one that's completely blacked out for security," he said, taking them down a small corridor. "This is my office, and Mac's is next door." Cabe pointed to the left of the corridor. "And this side is the secure conference room. And, finally, your office."

A sign hung on the door. SIX RAPP.

A phone rang in the distance. "Gotta get that," Cabe said, heading back down the corridor. "But you and me, security detail tonight at a big fundraiser. I'll catch you later with the details. Settle in for a while."

Six stepped into his office. Black shelves and cupboards lined one wall. A large glass desk with chrome legs dominated the space. On it were two large monitors and a laptop with a sticky note.

User id: sixtonrapp
Password: #i<3unicorns
(You can change that->8 characters, 1 number, 1 symbol)

Six laughed. "Asshole," he said. He ran his hand over the cool glass, walked to the other side of the desk, and took a seat in the chair that was probably ergonomically designed, given that Mac had picked it. It was sturdy for his large frame, though, which was all that mattered to Six. He turned to face the window looking out over the parking lot.

Home.

He'd not only made it, but he'd survived.

So why did he feel so lost?

Someone has touched my files.

Louisa North blew her bangs out of her eyes and flicked through the folder one more time. There was something wrong with her notes, but she couldn't put her finger on exactly what it was. If she didn't know better, she'd swear someone had been through them. It wasn't anything obvious, but she was anal about lining up the corners of the pages before she closed any binder, and the pages were out of alignment as though someone had hurriedly flipped through them.

In the largest privately funded medical laboratory in San Diego, it wasn't unusual for researchers to collaborate, consult, and borrow information from one another in their quests to find answers to global problems as quickly as possible. But usually people asked permission.

She closed the file and pulled up her notes on her laptop. She bookmarked the article she hadn't yet finished reading on gene silencing and its possible effects on clustered regularly interspaced short palindromic repeats. CRISPR for short. While the findings were crucial to her research into treating Huntington's disease, the acronym always made her think of the salad drawer in her refrigerator.

Everything about her computer files and email looked normal. The *last modified* date matched the date she could last remember opening them. No emails were marked as read that she hadn't opened. While it was possible that her lab partner, Ivan, who was also the lab owner's grandson, had taken a look at her handwritten notes, it was very unlikely. After all their time working together, he knew better than to mess with her things.

She looked through the glass-fronted cleanroom walls to the two labs across the hallway that faced hers. Six to eight people shared space in each of them, a thought that made Louisa shiver. It had been a condition of her mother's investment in the laboratory that

Louisa be given her own lab to avoid having to deal with people on a daily basis. It was a good thing too, because some days it was almost more of a drain than she could bear having only Ivan around. Cognitive behavior therapies had only gone so far in helping her overcome her chronic anthropophobia, but her extreme shyness still took over her life at times. While all the breathing and modifying thoughts enabled her to get out of bed in the morning and come to work, daily challenges like looking someone in the eye remained an issue. It was part of the reason she'd let her bangs grow so damn long, even though it aggravated the hell out of her mother.

Diligently, she straightened all the corners of the pages so they lined up and placed the binder to one side. She couldn't spend more time worrying about it right now, because there were other things that needed tackling.

Louisa pulled up the presentation she was supposed to give at tonight's fundraiser. Her palms began to sweat as she paged through it. It wasn't so much the presentation that made her feel ill, more the crowds who usually came to listen to what she had to say. And she knew she was a double whammy. Researcher who'd dedicated her life to understanding Huntington's—check. Potential carrier of the disease—check. She'd buried her beloved father, Isaiah North, a decade ago, when he'd finally succumbed to the disease, and she was well aware that there was a fifty-percent chance that she, too, was a Huntington's disease gene carrier. Like most potential gene carriers, she'd chosen not to be tested, a decision that those who were not in the line of fire rarely understood. In her mind, there was no point living under a storm cloud when she had the chance to dance in the sun.

The slide with her credentials popped up on the screen. Usually she hated talking about herself, but she knew that if she wanted to stand a chance of convincing some of the attendees at tonight's gala to part with even more of their money, she needed to prove that she knew what she was talking about. Thanks to her parents' generosity, Louisa had been afforded an education most people could only dream about. With an undergrad degree from Harvard University and an MD from Yale, she'd been on the fast track as a neurology resident and ultimately fellow in neuro-therapeutics and movement disorders at Johns Hopkins—until her phobia got in the way. When people asked why she'd chosen to bury herself in a lab, she offered them a vanilla answer about dedication and focus.

She wished she could tell the attendees tonight that her quest for an alternative to Tetrabenazine, the drug that had been developed initially to treat schizophrenia but had proven useful in treating conditions with involuntary movements, like Huntington's disease, had proven fruitful. It would have been wonderful to share with the audience that she'd found one with potentially less-harmful side effects, that her research was on the right track, but in truth, the drug she'd been working on had ended up being more poison than medicine. She'd been convinced that she was on the way to creating a drug that would reduce hyperkinesia, the uncontrollable muscle spasms, without increasing the risk of psychiatric conditions such as depression, paranoia, and suicidal ideation. The same psychiatric conditions that caused her prone-to-depression father to succumb to his despair and hang himself in the garage of their estate in Torrey Pines. But instead, the drug she'd tested had gone too far, causing paralysis in rats while leaving them fully aware of what was happening to them. They'd been unable to eat or drink or help themselves.

Louisa studied each slide in detail. The audience wouldn't have the patience to hear long scientific proclamations, so she used layman's terms, like genes and chromosomes, and explained how everyone's fourth chromosome produced a protein called huntingtin, and faulty genes caused mutant huntingtin, which could ultimately kill. She'd learned over the years to avoid phrases like "basal ganglia" and "C-A-G repeats" because, in truth, no one really cared. People were attending the fundraiser for her work because her mother had asked them to. Because other rich people would be there. Because they needed to be seen doing good. Cancer they worried about because it could affect them at any point in time, but a hereditary disease that they knew their family didn't carry . . .

Her eyes caught the clock on the wall.

Crap.

It was already four in the afternoon. She normally didn't leave the lab until eight or nine in the evening. Fewer people in the lab, fewer people on the roads, fewer people, period. But Highway 5 to her home in Mission Hills was likely to be as congested as a nasal infection, and if she wanted to get home, get ready, psych herself up, and get back into the city for the fundraiser, she needed to get going now.

She grabbed the folders and made her way around the

lab, turning off lights and locking up as she went. On her way to the exit, and the small room where they stored their files, Louisa stopped in front of the laboratory refrigerators and looked at the sample, trying to think dispassionately about what had happened on the last test.

But the trays drew her eye, and the same feeling crept over her skin as she'd had when she'd opened her files.

It was impossible to tell if anybody had tampered with it. Were the trays a little off-center? Maybe. Had the doors been opened? Impossible to say. But was it safe to assume this was all in her head? To do nothing?

If someone had been messing with the sample, they'd either found what they were looking for or hadn't finished searching. She pulled out an earlier sample drug that had been equally unsuccessful but had had nowhere near the same kind of side effects as the sample she had just finished testing. Carefully, with her back to the lab across the hall, she removed the labels from both of the samples, switched them, and replaced the samples on the shelf. It was her laboratory, so she could manage the samples any way she liked. Even in a way that might seem—or worse, *be*—paranoid. Paranoia had been one of her father's earliest symptoms at the onset of the disease.

Louisa closed the door and tried to ignore the way her heart raced. She reminded herself that fear was simply a signal for the body to engage, a command for adrenaline to flood the skeletal muscles in preparation for some kind of physical activity to avoid disaster, and that while it was one of the most adaptive emotions, she wasn't in any real danger right now.

She squared the microscope so its edges matched up with the corner of the desk and turned all the Erlenmeyer flasks so the measurements faced toward her. Then she hurried over to the autoclave and grabbed a clean beaker, just to make sure there were an equal number of beakers lined up with their spouts at forty-five degrees.

Relieved that the lab was in order, Louisa inhaled a deep breath in preparation for the battle to get out of the building. She left through the cleanroom air blower, allowing the hard jets to blow any chemical residue from her before she stepped into the small hallway where she kept her coat and purse in the locker.

Keeping close to the wall of the corridor, she hurried from the building. *I'm fine*, she reminded herself as she thought about the samples.

If only she could command her trembling hands to agree.

Six took another tour around the ballroom, eyeing the exits and balcony while trying to avoid the not-so-discreet glances of some of the female attendees and a couple of the men. He tugged the cuff of his crisp white shirt beneath the sleeve of his black tux. Maybe it was years of conditioning, but his head was running multiple scenarios. There was a truckload of money in the room. Not that he'd been to too many fundraisers hosted by the ultra-rich, but this one seemed to be swimming in a sea of diamonds. Sure, it was all for a good cause, but he couldn't help but imagine how much impact that money could have on the lives of injured veterans.

"Sixton Rapp. I didn't know you were back in town." Ivan Popov held out his hand and Six took it, politely greeting his old school friend even though he couldn't stand the guy.

"Just two weeks. How've you been, Ivan?" he asked, trying to sound like he actually cared. After all, Ivan and his grandfather were the ones paying their bill for the night.

"I'm good. Just bought a new place in La Jolla and picked up a McLaren 650S. Pharma always did pay better than fighting. Still serving our country, man?" This tool had the audacity to talk about serving America in the same breath as he gloated about his wealth. Rumors abounded about huge multipliers on the prices of the most basic drugs. The guy was gouging Americans, not helping them. Six should kick his ass just for that.

"Out two weeks. I'm actually working." Six pointed to the earpiece and mic.

Ivan laughed. "No shit. This is a fundraiser for my project. You remember my grandfather owns VNP Laboratories? This is to fund our research."

That Vasilii Popov, a billionaire who could probably find between his sofa cushions the kind of change these rich jet-set rollers were handing over, was fundraising instead of giving only reinforced Six's view that these things were a crock of shit. Rich people had no idea how privileged they were.

"Small world," Six said politely, but it was time to disengage before the thoughts pinging around inside his head came out through his mouth. "Look, I gotta get back to work."

"Yeah. Good seeing you, man," Ivan said, shaking his hand again.

Six began another circuit, walking carefully to ensure he looked everywhere for the possibility of trouble. A loud crash sounded behind him, and without a moment's hesitation, he turned, the palm of his hand wrapped discreetly around the handle of his holstered Sig Sauer P220, a gun he carried legally, in spite of San Diego's tight gun laws. He relaxed his grip when he saw two servers picking up broken china from the floor.

Why was his heart rate way up over broken plates? He didn't do jumpy. He did cool under pressure.

He began box breathing. In for four, hold for four, out for four, hold for four. His brothers would laugh if they knew he'd been spooked by silver serving trays and china. And if he told them the truth—that it was a fairly regular occurrence—they'd start some kind of well-meaning outreach program like he was a charity case.

"Next time Mac has a good idea to make money, remind me to tell him to go fuck himself," Six said into his microphone, looking for some way to release the pressure he felt. Banter between the brothers had been the one thing that had kept his naive, idealistic ass sane on his very first tour and the ones that followed.

Cabe's laughter crackled through the earpiece. "It's not all bad. See the red dress over by table eight. I'm calling dibs."

Six shook his head and turned to look over at the blonde wrapped in a bandage dress. They always looked sexy on, those dresses, but trying to help a girl out of one was like wrestling a gazelle out of the jaws of an alligator. "In that case, I'll take the white dress at the bar and the green dress over by the third exit, preferably at the same time."

"Good to see you haven't lost your appetite," Cabe said. "The presentation is up soon. Daughter of the main fundraiser is some med-geek researcher who works at the lab. Probably going to be as dull as dishwater."

Six made his way over to the podium, checking the surrounding area thoroughly. It was already beginning to feel highly unlikely that anything out of the ordinary was going to happen tonight, but if anything *were* going to happen, it would likely be when all the guests were definitely in the room for something like a presentation.

"Do we know what's behind these?" he asked Cabe, taking a step toward the closed, rich blue velvet drapes behind the temporary podium.

"Yeah, I checked it out earlier." A crackle cut through his earpiece. "A small balcony."

Curious, Six took the few steps over to the curtain and wiggled the handle of the doors. Unlocked, it swung open on to a small space.

"You can do this," a soft voice whispered in the half light. "It's nothing. Go in. Get it done. Get out."

"You okay?" he asked, spotting the woman seated doubled over on a white chair. She was half-hidden by the ivy that crawled up the brick wall next to the door.

"I'm fine," the woman replied, in the most unfine tone he'd ever heard.

He took a few steps closer. All he could see was the top of her head, messy brunette waves fluttering in all directions as a breeze came in off the bay. The hem of her aqua tulle skirt danced around her calves. Toenails that matched the skirt peeked out through tall-heeled silver sandals. He crouched down in front of her. "Can I get someone to come out to you? Get you some water maybe?"

The woman lifted her head. He could barely see her

eyes through her bangs, but the snatches he could see were as brown as the Negra Modelo beer he'd drunk by the bucketload in Mexico the week before. Plump lips and defined cheekbones, both with minimal makeup, added a softness to a strong nose and brow. Not hot, like the women he usually went for. More *interesting.* And he got the feeling she'd hate that word.

"Crap," the woman said and lowered her head to her hands, not quite putting her head between her knees.

"You sure you aren't going to pass out?" he asked. At a loss, he placed his hand on her back, wanting to bring her comfort. She was definitely shaking.

"You need help, Six?" Cabe whispered in his earpiece.

"Nah. I got this," he replied.

"You got what?" Her words were mumbled.

"Oh. No. I was just talking to my partner," he replied. "I'm Six. I'm part of the security team tonight."

"Louisa," the woman said. "I'm part of the dog-and-pony show."

The med-geek researcher. "You're the presenter who's up in a few minutes?" Six placed his finger under her chin and raised her face until he could just about see under her bangs to her eyes if he crouched low enough.

Her eyes found his for a moment, and then they looked away quickly. "Shit. Is it time already?"

"It's getting close. I'm sure you are going to do great." Though he was pretty certain he was going to have to crane her out of the seat when it was showtime, he needed to say something to encourage her. Abject fear pulsed from her, and he could have sworn he felt the chill of it.

Louisa stood suddenly. "Hardly," she said, walking to the balcony.

Now that she was standing, he could see that she'd topped the tulle, knee-length skirt with a fitted white waistcoat with very little underneath as far as he could see. It was quirky and so unlike anything he'd seen inside of the room. Part of him assessed her as outdressed by the attendees, but there was something very unique about her.

"The last time I did this, on the way back from the stage I puked into a large, potted *Dieffenbachia fortunensis*."

Six laughed, and she turned to face him.

"It wasn't funny," she said, but her pout turned into the makings of a grin.

"I wasn't laughing at the puking. I was laughing that you knew the plant and its . . . make or whatever."

The sound of someone testing the microphone drew Louisa's attention to the door, and she shook her head. "Its species and genus," she said casually before taking a deep breath and squaring her shoulders. "And I guess it's showtime." She walked toward the door and reached for the handle, but turned back before she opened it. She blew her bangs out of her face, and he finally got a good, straight look at her. "Pretty" was the first word that came to mind. "Compelling" was the second.

"Thank you for rescuing me, Six," she said.

The door opened and the lights shone brightly through her skirt, making it ever so slightly transparent. From the silhouette, he could see she had legs that went on for days.

"You're welcome," he said as the door clicked shut.

CHAPTER TWO

Goddamn. Why couldn't she get that blond hair and those eyes that were the color of a frozen lake out of her mind?

Louisa pulled her car to a stop outside the lab and rested her head on the steering wheel. It had been five days since she'd survived her presentation, and he was still there in her head, front and center.

In high school, she'd laughed at the girls who'd gotten distracted by boys. The ones who'd spent their lunch breaks pretending to be Britney Spears running through a high school gym as they'd practiced their dance moves, or debating the relative merits of *NSYNC versus the Backstreet Boys while sitting on the bleachers hoping to attract the attention of their latest crush. Instead, she'd sat in the shade and focused on the relationship between the DNA polymerase binding site and start and stop codons. They'd called her a geek, a nerd, and often, a loser. But her father's symptoms had been getting worse, and she had been determined, even back then, to find the cure that would fix their once-perfect family. Plus, she was simply happier in her own company.

Confusion over a man was a new thing. Louisa had tried dating when she was younger, but the calling of her laboratory had always felt more interesting than going to the movies or dinner to waste two hours of her life getting to know a man she had no intention of staying with for the long term. It was time that could be spent doing something important, and eventually the relationships had fizzled out. Any remaining desire to date had been killed by her dislike of being around people. Social outings, family gatherings, and getting to know strangers took so much effort.

So obsessing over Six, which couldn't possibly be his real name, and who was quite literally the most handsome man she'd ever seen, was disconcerting. At the presentation, he'd slipped back out onto the stage moments before she'd started speaking and moved down the stairs to stand to the left of the podium. It was nice to see those broad shoulders as he turned his face out to the crowd. As she'd spoken to the audience, his head had turned from side to side as he'd observed the room, and focusing on the steady metronome of his movements had helped keep her calm. When she'd finished her speech, he'd offered her his hand to help her down the steps and then had mischievously whispered that there was a potted palm to her right if she felt the urge to barf. It had made her laugh and had loosened the tightness in her stomach.

As she'd been forced to listen to her mother gush about her latest boyfriend, she'd watched Six from beneath the safety of her bangs. Given his handsome face and incredibly confident posture, she knew she wasn't the only woman watching. Toward the end of the evening, she'd seen a beautiful woman in a green dress approach him and hand him a slip of paper on which Louisa imagined she'd written her phone number. Six had glanced at it and then looked straight back at the woman and grinned, nodding his head as if in agreement. Later, though, she'd also seen him slip his wallet out of his pocket, take out some bills, and hand them over to Valerie, one of the foundation members who had been collecting money from the attendees. Most people flashed their credit cards, or brought checks, so the sweet gesture had warmed Louisa's heart. Her mother's latest boy toy, Lucan, who had accompanied her to the event, hadn't opened his wallet once, and Louisa had struggled to contain her frustration when he'd asked her mother to bid on their behalf in the silent auction for a luxury trip to the Galápagos Islands.

Louisa gathered her bags and stepped out of her Audi A3, a car her mother had called "pedestrian." As if she had the right to judge—or had any judgment herself—these days. She'd been on a self-destructive kick since Louisa's father's death, dating men way younger than herself who were, unfortunately, out for one thing only—the gifts the North family millions could provide. Gigolos, charlatans, call them what Louisa would, her mother just wouldn't listen and was routinely getting her heart broken after a lavish trip or expensive item had been paid for. How she could be so clueless about these men was unfathomable.

Using her pass, Louisa let herself into the building and discreetly hurried down the corridor to her locker. No one really understood her acute terror at being around people. Even experts who professed to be able to cure her failed to understand how debilitating it could be. She planned her journeys around the paths of least resistance, which meant she arrived at places either before they opened or just before they shut for the day. The hallways were empty as she slipped her purse into her locker and closed it.

She and Ivan had been working through a complex revised formula the previous day, but she still felt as though they were missing something. Today, Ivan was attending the company board meeting with his grandfather, Vasilii, a job Louisa didn't envy. Accounts, balance sheets, committee meetings, and action items all made Louisa shudder. Give her an opportunity to develop models of pathological dynamic activities in neurological disease, and she was all over it, but corporate objectives killed her brain cells faster than cerebral hypoxia.

She put on her lab coat and gloves, passed through the air blower, and stepped into the cool embrace of her lab. Her sanctuary. It felt more like home than home. There were some cultures growing that she needed to check on, and she was excited to have been asked to review the results of a brain slice out of the Baltimore Huntington's Disease Center over at Johns Hopkins. Who got results first or made the biggest strides in the race for the cure really didn't matter to Louisa, just so long as somebody did, and soon.

A cold blast of air washed over her as she opened the refrigerator to grab the cultures. She grabbed them off the shelf and was about to close the door when she noticed that one of the samples she'd put in there the night of the presentation was missing. Sliding the cultures in her hand back onto their shelf, she stood on her toes to see if the samples had been pushed back into the deep unit. But it was empty. She thought through her steps five days earlier when she had deliberately switched the dangerous sample with an innocuous one because of her paranoia that her papers had been messed with.

She gazed across all of the shelves and all of the samples. It was obviously possible that Ivan had been in the lab while she hadn't been there, but he'd always been an incredibly thoughtful and thorough lab partner and had graciously humored her need for order. Until he got out of his meeting, she couldn't ask him in person where the sample might be, but she could step outside, grab her phone, and send him a quick text in the hope that he would check in some time before the end of the day, however unlikely that was. Vasilii, who was old school, had limited patience with digital interference during meetings.

Bracing herself, Louisa left the lab and walked across the hallway to where research for a cure for Alzheimer's, as well as medicine to delay its onset, happened. VNP Laboratories, under Vasilii's leadership, was focused on brain disorders, though for reasons quite different from her own. Unlike cancer, which had a fifty-percent or more ten-year survival rate and a series of treatment options, nobody had found a way to stop neurological disease. So medication to manage symptoms was the only option. To Vasilii, this research was about profits and balance sheets; to her it was life or death. She looked left and right along the corridor. The only people in sight were heading to the stairwell to take them to the second level. With a sigh of relief, she crossed to the other lab and knocked on the window to get the attention of Aiden, one of the few people she could talk to. He understood her drive and had become a wonderful mentor who respected her social boundaries.

They met in the air shower at the entrance to the lab. "What's up, Louisa?"

"I'm sure this is probably Ivan's doing, but I had some samples in the refrigerator since Friday, and one of them isn't there today. I wondered if you or any of your guys had been in the lab to borrow something and maybe moved them around."

"Certainly wasn't me, but give me a sec and I'll go ask."

Aiden stepped back into the lab, and she saw most of her colleagues shake their heads. "Sorry," Aiden said when he returned. "Nobody's been over there. Like you said, it's probably just Ivan."

Louisa felt her stomach drop. "Cool," she said, way more casually than she actually felt. "Sorry for bothering you guys." She hurried back to her laboratory. This time, though, she didn't feel the same sense of safety there. She was certain someone had removed the sample from her lab. Her head was filled with nefarious reasons why it could have happened. Which wasn't like her. She was usually rational. Well, unless she allowed the little voice inside her head to remind her that she could just be being paranoid.

Like her father had been.

The Beach Boys had had it right. In all of his travels, he'd never seen anything quite like California girls.

Andie, the girl in the green dress, had been more than willing to wait for him to finish his job, but instead, he'd gone home alone, thoughts filled with a quirky brunette in tulle. Toward the end of the night, he'd looked for her, wondering if he should make sure she got out okay. He'd wandered to the table she'd been seated at, and found no sign of her barring three origami elephants made from what looked like pages of her speech, one of which now sat on his kitchen table.

Six stepped out of his truck and cricked his neck from left to right. One thing guaranteed to shift thoughts of Louisa North from his mind was a long run along the Los Peñasquitos Canyon trail with its waterfall, volcanic rock, and forest of majestic California oaks that he'd sorely missed while he'd been deployed. He secured his earbuds, and set The Boss to play. Couldn't beat a bit of Springsteen to get you through time-trial running. He locked his truck and set off along the trail. All in all, retirement was looking like a good choice. He still had the camaraderie he'd loved about the military, even if they all came from different places. Most of the day had been spent getting to know his new brothers in arms. Gareth, a proud Welshman who'd served fourteen years in the Special Air Service, also known as the SAS, was the joker of the bunch but was also as fit as anyone he'd ever met. Gaz was a third-generation SAS member whose father had been involved in the Iranian Embassy siege in the early eighties, and Gaz had shown them the crazy-ass footage on YouTube. Then there was Joel Budd, call sign Buddha, graduate of TOPGUN and qualified civilian pilot for just about every type of aircraft that existed. His was a great hire that would enable them to rent their own private equipment to get them in and out of more remote places. Turned out the guy really knew his shit when it came to combat too. Cabe had put them through their paces earlier, and they'd nailed it.

Stepping up his pace, Six began to sweat. His mom had always said he'd been born with too much energy. Most of his school reports had said the same thing. He didn't know what to do with it all when he was young. College had been less about his future and more about celebrating his present, and there'd been no shortage of sorority girls willing to join the line for a piece of him. He had no idea what he would've ended up doing after that if Brock hadn't died the way he did the year before they graduated.

Becoming a Navy SEAL had been Brock's dream, and for all of them, signing up after his funeral had felt like the right thing to do. Mac, who'd blamed himself, and still did, for Brock's death, had been the most passionate and driven to do it.

But the decision Six had made had taken him from reasonably in shape and aimless to an elite level of fitness and focused. As he ran up the next incline, Six wondered what it would be like to go through BUD/S again, the rigorous basic training all SEALs went through, including the notorious Hell Week, now a distant memory.

He stepped up his pace in an open stretch of trail, determined to hit a personal best on this route, and remembered the realities of the six months spent at the Naval Special Warfare Training Center where he'd had his ass handed to him on a daily basis. Even at his age, if he were to start all over again, he'd kick the butts of the newbies, because he knew something they didn't yet know. That being a SEAL was ninety percent mental.

The trail ran close to the road as he turned the corner, and he could see traffic racing by. Another runner passed him, and then he noticed a woman walking up the hill toward him. For a second, he thought she was Louisa, but he shook his head. So much for a run clearing it. It was funny how she had stuck in his mind—

There was a loud crash, the sound of metal on metal like a tank hitting an IED, and he imagined bodies blowing into the air. On autopilot, he scrambled for cover, hitting the dirt and pressing himself up against the shrub line, but he almost immediately realized what he'd done. Motherfucker. His hands shook, and the acrid sting of adrenaline coursed through him.

"Are you okay?" a female voice said.

Shit, the woman who'd been walking toward him. "I'm fine," he mumbled, trying to control his breathing.

"I think that was my line, wasn't it?"

The woman crouched down next to him, but he was too stunned by the whole thing to figure out exactly what was going on. "By the looks of it, there's an accident on the road over there," she said.

Six looked up to find Louisa staring back at him through that thick hair of hers. "I don't know what just happened," he blurted. For a moment he questioned why he hadn't made up some kind of excuse like tripping over a branch or needing to stop and tie his shoelaces.

Louisa blew her bangs out of her eyes, and he noticed that her cheeks were really pink. "Did you fall down, or did the sound of that car crashing scare the shit out of you?" She got to her feet and offered him her hand. He took it and received a shock of static electricity. Louisa shook her head and helped him to his feet.

Maybe it was the way she said the words so bluntly, like it was no big deal, but he felt the need to answer her truthfully. "It's just loud noises out of context," he said. "Ex-military and all that." Six dusted off his shorts, doing his best to play down whatever the hell had just happened while the blood rushed around his body so quickly that it felt like he was going to pass out.

"I hate being around people," Louisa offered casually and picked some grass off his arm. "Walking up the hill toward you, I suffered anticipatory anxiety. Panic at the thought of walking past you. So I get it. I study neurology, yet I can't figure out how to make it stop."

"Your presentation on Friday was great," he said, not wanting to talk further about what had happened.

"Case in point," she said. "You had your back to me the entire time. You just couldn't see the way I was white-knuckling the podium. The way I didn't make eye contact with a single person in the room."

"Well, you don't need to worry. You were amazing. Even I understood what you were saying."

"Didn't stop my amygdala from firing glutamate into the region of the brain that made me freeze, the same way your amygdala flooded glutamate into the region of your brain that makes you involuntarily jump. In both cases, our hypothalamus triggered our autonomous nervous system, which elevated my heart rate and prompted adrenaline through my body, just like it's doing to you now."

Six took a deep breath and looked out across the

canyon. Medical descriptions he could deal with, but if she veered anywhere close to something that smelled like sympathy he'd be pissed off. It was no big deal, and he didn't want her making it one. He looked in the direction he'd been running and then back in the direction of the parking lot where he'd left his truck and where Louisa had been headed.

"Anyway, I'd much rather be alone in my lab or home, which is where I should head back to. Are you okay?"

Finally, he looked at her directly. In the daylight, the hair that he'd thought to be simply brunette had strands of spun gold through it. She wore ink-blue denim jeans that fit her like a second skin and were cuffed at the bottom, aqua-colored Converse, and a simple white T-shirt that hugged her curves. And yet none of these were the reason he wanted to spend a little more time with her. She intrigued him, the two sides of her—the scientist and shy human—seeming at odds.

"I'm good," he said. "Seriously, but I don't feel like running anymore. Will you let me walk with you for a little while?" Unable to resist, he reached toward her and pushed her hair to one side. There was something compelling about her. Perhaps she wasn't traditionally pretty, but she was arresting in her own way.

Her cheeks became even more flushed, and she stepped away from his reach.

"I'm sorry, Louisa. I shouldn't have done that." *Shit.* He hadn't meant to make her feel bad, but just being around her was bringing his heart rate back under control. "Look, I'll leave you to your walk. I'll even give you a head start so it doesn't look like I'm stalking you."

Louisa shook her head. "Nope," she said. "You were . . .

fine. I mean, I didn't mind, I just stepped back because . . . Well. I don't know what it is about you, but somehow I don't feel quite so weird around you compared to other people."

The words tightened his chest, and while he wasn't sure how he felt about that, he was more than willing to go with it. "Does that mean we're walking?"

With a smile that completely transformed her face, she turned herself in the direction in which she'd been walking and kicked her toe into the dirt. "I suppose it does," she said, and started off.

It felt like the most natural thing in the world to walk alongside her, and he wasn't prepared to question why.

"You want to race there, Louisa?" Six teased as she marched them toward the parking lot.

The confusing thing about stress response was you couldn't always be one hundred percent certain what had caused it. Certainly if someone pushed you off the top of a tall building, it was a reasonable assessment that it was being caused by the fact you were hurtling to your death at chronically fast speeds. But having a borderline pathological response to shyness while walking alongside a now shirtless and sweaty Six, with abs, and tattoos, and . . . Urgh, who the hell knew why the adrenaline was flowing? All she knew was that it was telling her *flight*, even though she was intellectually willing herself not to listen.

Louisa forced herself to slow down. To enjoy the experience. To take in the nature around her rather than how low Six's shorts hung on his hips. She noticed a large scar on his stomach that had long since healed.

"What branch of military were you?" she asked, hoping he'd believe her breathlessness was a function of exertion, not . . . well, whatever it was.

"Navy, ma'am," he said. "A proud member of the SEAL brotherhood."

Holy shit. There was no military in her family. Spending Friday evenings at home watching movies like *American Sniper* and *Lone Survivor* constituted her only brushes with it, but even she knew that SEALs took on the toughest jobs in the toughest places. "That's pretty badass," she said, lamely. It wasn't like she was known for her witty *repartee* on the best of days, but around Six, even her most basic conversationalist skills withered like the shrubbery that lined the canyon path. "Wait. This is the part where I am supposed to thank you for your service, right?"

Six laughed. "You're funny, Louisa, and no, you don't have to thank me. It was my pleasure."

Shit. She'd spent the last five years in particular avoiding small talk for this very reason. "Well, I do thank you. Seriously, I do."

His hand slipped around her wrist and he pulled her to a stop. She turned to look at him . . . up at him. Christ, the man was tall.

"You're welcome," he said.

Her attempts to avoid eye contact failed miserably, and she was drawn to his face. *Damn.* It all felt a bit too close. Suffocating. She turned and started to walk down the other side of the hill. Suddenly going for a hike to wind down, to take her mind off the missing sample in the lab, didn't seem like such a great idea.

"What are you doing now?" she asked, more in an

effort to kill time until she could dive into her car and retreat to the safety of her patio with a glass—no, bottle—of pinot. Then she'd fire up her laptop and chat with some of her online friends.

"I own a private security firm with two of my buddies from school who were SEALs too. It's called Eagle Securities. We have a building not too far from here."

"So you do things like last night? Protection, bodyguard-type stuff?"

From the corner of her eye, she could see Six nod his head. "Yeah, that and other things," he said vaguely.

Louisa felt her phone vibrate in her pocket, and out of habit, because it was her preferred method of communication, she pulled it out and checked it. It was a message from Ivan.

Didn't move any of the samples. Too focused on post-mortem of failed test, and board meeting. Sorry. Check with Aiden.

First thing in the morning, she was going to orchestrate a thorough search of the lab. Top to bottom they were going to check every shelf, not because the missing sample was dangerous, but because it was the innocuous one with the poisonous one's label on it. They couldn't afford to have something like that happen ever again. After all, what if an *actual* dangerous sample disappeared?

"Everything okay, Louisa?" Six asked.

She looked around and realized that she had stopped walking. "Yeah. Just some lab stuff that's going on. Sorry." Louisa started to walk again. "So what made you leave?"

"In all honesty, I'd always thought I was a career

SEAL. But two of my friends decided they wanted to be out by our mid-thirties and that we should start saving to open a security firm. So we did. And that time we spent saving just flew by. Before I knew it, I was packing up my bag and moving back home."

"You're from around here originally?" Now that she was paying attention it made sense. He had that laid-back vibe about him.

Six nodded. "Yeah. Born and raised in Encinitas. Drank more seawater than milk growing up. Spent more time in the ocean than out of it. That, and being on the swim team in college, gave me a huge advantage during training."

Their hands brushed against each other as they walked, and it was hard to miss the way Six quickly retreated from her. His hand had been warm against hers, and she wondered what it would feel like if she took the plunge and linked her fingers with his. But she'd obviously scared him off when she'd stepped away as he'd brushed the hair from her eyes, not realizing that her bangs were her shield.

"Sounds like you were made for the navy," she said.

"What about you, Louisa? How did you end up doing what you're doing?"

She considered taking a step to her right and putting them in closer contact so she could possibly feel her hand brush against his one more time. It was one of those things, however, that felt relatively simple as a thought but was impossible to put into practice. "My father died when I was twenty as a result of having Huntington's disease. He'd been living with the symptoms for a while longer than that. So I made up my mind quite young that I was going to go into research to see if I could find a cure. After getting my MD and spending time as a neurology resident and then fellow at Johns Hopkins, I moved into private research because I found the bureaucracy of the big hospitals tied my hands." She left out how she'd blown through her degrees, doubling down on courses, always scoring the highest GPA.

Six placed his hand on her lower back, his palm warm through her T-shirt. "I'm sorry, Louisa. That really sucks."

Feeling uncharacteristically brave, she pushed her bangs to the side and looked at him. "Thank you," she said quietly. Time could only be stopped, she knew, if the body was traveling at the speed of light, and even then it was only a perception of the body itself, relative to space and time. But when Six's eyes caught hers, she could have sworn that it happened.

She sighed deeply and turned into the lot where her car was parked. "I'm over here," she said. She dug in her pocket for the key and pressed the button to open the locks.

"That's me." Six tilted his chin in the direction of a silver truck. "Look, about what happened back there. Can we keep it to ourselves?"

Unable to resist, she reached out her hand and rested it on his arm. "That goes without saying. It's nobody else's business but your own. But I know a thing or two about the brain. And whether the damage is neurological, psychological, or anything at all pathological, it is very rare that it just heals itself."

Six looked back out over the canyon and sighed. The sunset was beautiful, rich shades of orange, red, and purple all painted into a fiery sky. She wondered whether he saw the pretty colors, or whether he was so lost in thought he didn't see them at all.

"I know I said it already today, but thanks, Louisa. And I hear what you're saying. I just . . . I don't know . . . I guess I just want to see if this'll fade with time first."

It wouldn't, she was certain, but it wasn't her place to tell a man she barely knew how to live his life. "Wait here," she said as a crazy idea took shape in her head. She jogged over to her car and opened the trunk, where she'd put her purse. After rummaging through it for a business card, she hurried back to him. "I'm sure you've got tons of friends and family, or a girlfriend or wife that you can talk these things through with," she said, extending the card to him and willing her hand not to shake. "But if you ever need someone to talk to, I do great motivational pep talks through whatever app you like to use."

Six swallowed hard. He studied both the back and front of her card. "Louisa North," he said, "you are quite the woman."

The moment needed humor, she knew, but it had never been her strong suit. "I do better Internet conversation than I do in real life. And however fast you type, I guarantee I'll be faster."

"I'll remember that, Ms. North, as long as you remember . . ." His words trailed off as he wrapped his arms around her, pulling her against his chest. She tensed at the action, every muscle more rigid than steel rods as she fought the urge to step away, until he placed a kiss on the top of her head. The action caught her so off guard, it was over before she could formulate a response. Soft, light blond chest hair brushed her cheek as her heart raced.

"Remember what?" she whispered against his chest, not trusting the strength of her own voice or her own feet if she attempted to move.

Six stepped back and winked. "That *I* do real life better than the Internet."

CHAPTER THREE

Six waited for Louisa to get into her car and pull out of the parking lot. She beeped her horn, and he flashed his lights in her direction. All very cute, especially when inside he was dying of mortification. What the hell was going on?

A car crash had freaked him out. How was that even possible after he'd spent months doing almost daily patrols in Kandahar without batting an eye?

The constant throng of chaos had surrounded them as they'd driven through the crowded streets, horns beeping, people shouting. They'd never stopped. It had been too unsafe. Too uncertain. Plus, they hadn't been able to tell friend from foe, so better to keep the show on the road. He'd been back on US soil for a couple of months, so why the hell was this happening now? How was he supposed to do his job at Eagle when he couldn't guarantee that he wouldn't lose his shit?

He drove north up the coast to Encinitas. Focus. That was all it would take to overcome whatever he had.

Mind over matter had always worked for him before as a philosophy. There were guys who had it so much worse than he did. Guys who had come home with their legs blown off or had carried their friends off the battlefield. Yeah, he'd seen some shit, but as SEAL careers went, there was no way he could have PTSD. And he most definitely wasn't going to ask Mac whether Eagle's non-existent healthcare plan covered psychologists.

It was just a few flashbacks. He'd manage them on his own.

Finally, he relaxed as he saw the sign for Encinitas. That had to be a good thing, being in a place where he felt at peace with the world. The vibrant beachside community of Old Encinitas, his home since birth, was buried deep inside his soul. When he'd lived out east, he'd missed it. As he pulled up in front of his home on top of the steep incline of E Street, he remembered the time when he was twelve and he'd thought he'd broken his wrist skateboarding away from this very yard. There were so many memories attached to this house. His parents had loved flipping and selling homes, so as a family they'd lived on just about every street in Old Encinitas. This house, however, had always been his constant. Every time he stepped through the front door, he was certain he was going to smell his grandmother's apple cobbler or hear his grandfather trying to convince someone to join him in a game of Scrabble again. Just about every Christmas had been spent here, his own home usually in the middle of some huge renovation. When his grandparents had died within five days of each other during his second tour, he'd been devastated. They'd left the property to him, and he'd held on to it.

With his parents' help, he'd rented it to a low-maintenance couple ever since. He'd felt like an asshole serving notice to tenants before he returned, but it was, in his heart, his home. Once Eagle started to make some money he was going to do the place up. For a while, he'd contemplated having a roommate, as the extra monthly income would be helpful, but he'd soon realized that he needed his space more than he needed the money.

Six let himself into the small, bright home. It needed a good coat of paint at a minimum, but he loved the bones of the place. Long linen drapes that he left closed hung from the window in the living room. A large array of plants grew in the bay window, left by the tenants when they'd moved out. They made him think of Louisa. She'd probably know how to look after them beyond just watering them when the soil became more arid than the trails in Afghanistan's Badakhshan Province.

He grabbed his phone from his shorts before he dropped them and his briefs to the floor. He kicked off his shoes and socks and left them in the hallway, closer to the laundry in the garage, and walked to the guest bath to fill the tub. He'd refitted his own bathroom with a large walk-in shower, but some days he just needed a soak. Just as he was about to step into the hot water, his phone rang.

"Six," he said.

There was a crackle on the line.

"Hello. Is there anybody there?" Six pulled the phone away from his ear and checked the caller display. Unknown number.

"Six, man. It's Mac." The line was severely distorted, but he was thrilled to hear his friend.

"Yo, Mac. How's it going?" He turned the tap off and wrapped a towel around his waist before he wandered back into his room to lie down on the bed.

"Good. Sorry I haven't been around, but this was a quick and dirty job, good pay, and it seemed stupid to turn it down."

"Dude, I'm living in a house that needs a shit ton of work. Anything that pays the bills is priority. How's it working out? Did you find the father and daughter?"

"Took us too long to track the girl down. We need more unit-level training for it to come together and a better intel network, but I know Cabe's working on that. I'm pretty certain that the guy doesn't know we're hunting, but he keeps moving her around. I'm not sure he has anywhere permanent lined up for them to live, which tells me he abducted her on a whim rather than with a well-thought-out plan. Anyway, we're going in tomorrow. Quick in and out."

Six remembered the calm he'd used to feel the night before an extraction, the way he could still his mind until he was almost meditating. Perhaps he should try that now. Regain some control. He'd been slacking lately. If his mom and dad weren't out of town, he would have gone to spend some time with his mom. She was a great sounding board and wouldn't judge what he was going through.

"Take care, brother," he said.

"On it! Speak to you when it's done."

The phone disconnected.

Six returned to the bathroom and studied his face in the mirror before sitting on the edge of the bath. Perhaps he should shave, throw on a shirt, and head out for a drink. Call up a couple of buddies . . . Wait, scratch that . . . Call up one of the girls he knew was happy to have a good time, and go out for dinner. But for some reason a quick hookup didn't appeal. Instead wavy dark hair and expressive eyes hidden behind bangs flashed through his mind.

Louisa. He'd seen the way she'd bitten back a grin when he'd teased her and he liked how he'd felt with her. And she hadn't judged him for hitting the ground, at least not as far as he could tell. It had been a long time since a woman had done more than interest him, but Louisa had intrigued him. Made him curious. Now he wanted to know more about her.

But she probably lived in the city, and the idea of fighting traffic was more than he could deal with. Plus, he'd just left her a few hours ago.

The clock on his phone told him it was nearly eight. There was still enough half light to get a surf in, and he stood, seriously considering the idea, but for some reason he just didn't feel like it.

Why couldn't he decide what to do?

A soak for his tired muscles, a night in, a mindless movie, pizza, and a cold beer. He'd make lousy company in this frame of mind.

Six grabbed his phone and hit the kitchen for a cold beer. Once he'd taken a sip, he grabbed Louisa's card. He wasn't sure why he suddenly felt the need to contact her, but he did. If he didn't, he'd probably end up pulling on some clothes before hitting the highway to find her and convince her to go out to dinner. Five more minutes with her would surely answer his questions about why she was on his mind so much.

Wanted to check you got home okay? 6

There was a pause, the little dots bouncing in the corner of the screen, and he was surprised to find his heart rate elevated a little in anticipation.

I did, thank you. Did you?

He laughed. Usually girls wrote him freaking essays when he texted them. But Louisa spared nothing.

I did . . . Now what should he write? *What are you doing?*

Really original. Good job he wasn't particularly trying to impress her.

Reading a book on the top medical advancements of the twentieth century.

Six laughed. *Of course you are.*

He waited for a response.

Hey, if you needed insulin, you'd be pretty excited by it. What are you doing?

Unable to resist, he was honest. *Drinking a beer.*

Of course you are. Good night, Six.

Good night, Lou.

Louisa stepped into the lab and looked around. Everything was exactly as she'd left it the night before, but she was starting to think that appearances didn't mean a damn thing.

In spite of logic telling her there must be a rational explanation as to why the sample was missing, it felt as though someone was squeezing her chest tightly. She took some deep breaths anyway in the hope they would deal with the tiny flicker of fear she felt in the pit of her stomach. Even though she could recite the details of the sample in her sleep, Louisa hurried to the file on her desk to remind herself of its composition. While she was reasonably certain it was innocuous, it was definitely worth double-checking. Flicking through the pages, she confirmed what she already knew. Nobody was at risk from the missing sample if it had been taken for erroneous reasons, which was most certainly a relief.

Her mind went to all kinds of places. Logically, she knew she was overreacting. Samples got moved around all the time, which was bound to happen in a laboratory jammed with researchers and scientists. Yet she'd asked in all of the labs, and nobody had set foot in her domain. Even Ivan had confirmed he hadn't moved them. But her gut told her that somebody wanted the toxin they'd created, a poison that didn't just limit hyperkinetic movement disorders through its anti-chorea properties but also reduced the user's ability to move at all while remaining fully conscious, leaving them open to pain receptors. She'd obviously watched one too many thrillers, because a nagging voice told her it would be the perfect drug to torture somebody with. They'd felt so confident when they'd moved on to animal testing, and she'd been crushed when it had resulted in paralysis.

Louisa flicked through the file to find her handwritten notes from that day. She'd typed them into files on her computer later that evening, censoring out words that revealed her true frustration, but she'd kept the originals. Every page she turned tightened the band around her chest until she got to the end of the binder and still hadn't found them. *Breathe, Louisa.*

"More haste, less speed, Louisa. You will find it," her father used to say to her in encouragement, even as his symptoms had deteriorated, along with *"I'm confident*

in you, chickpea." She went back to the start of the binder and carefully flicked page by page. When she got to the back of the binder again, her hands started to shake.

She flipped open the laptop and entered a password, *NaClCH3COOH*. Usually she found entering the chemical formulas for salt and vinegar, her favorite flavor of chips, entertaining. But today it was just a waste of time as she hurried to see whether the notes still existed. Her fingers flew across the keyboard as she accessed file after file. There were no records. Everything she had entered was gone. She checked other versions, other iterations of the same experiment, and they were all there. So there hadn't been some kind of file failure or computer malfunction. It was just the one experiment.

Louisa looked out of the window to the laboratory across the hallway. Aiden waved, and she returned the gesture halfheartedly. Somebody was lying. Somebody had taken all the information, and somebody thought they'd gotten the sample. In the spirit of discretion, Louisa decided to take it straight to the top. Vasilii would want to know and would be best placed to handle it. Watching a green strip on the otherwise gray linoleum gave her the opportunity to avoid talking to anyone as she hurried up the staircase to the luxury offices and approached Vasilii's assistant.

"Hey, Liz. Is Vasilii in his office?" As one of his most senior researchers, she had the perk of being able to get time on his calendar.

"Hey, Louisa. He's just between calls. Is it quick?" Louisa nodded, even though it wouldn't be. She was certain, though, that once Vasilii knew what she wanted to talk about, he'd defer whatever meeting he had next. Espionage between drug manufacturers was a real issue. It was the reason they weren't allowed to take their phones into the labs or their laptops out. As somebody who just wanted to do good and develop medicines that would help people, it irritated her how much money was made from owning patents.

She was equally certain that Vasilii would be concerned about the reputation of the lab. Louisa considered how to handle the fact, though, that she'd switched the samples. Ivan would be pissed that she hadn't told him, and it was poor lab etiquette to deliberately mislabel. She'd make sure there was a thorough investigation first, and then tell him it wasn't as damaging as it could have been.

"Okay, go in, sweetheart."

Louisa hurried to the door, knocked twice, and pushed it open. "Hey, Vasilii. Liz said it was okay to pop in for a word."

He was seated at his desk, looking at real estate photos on his computer, and he quickly shut them down. "Of course, of course. Come in. I was about to email your mother. The fundraiser was a huge success."

"It was," she agreed. Her mother had told her the final tally and it would most definitely enable her to continue her research for at least another eighteen months. "I'm sure she'd appreciate hearing from you. And I'm sure she'd love to see you for dinner one evening." Her mother had once dated Vasilii's son, Ivan's father. In another world, she and Ivan could have been siblings instead of lab partners.

Vasilii nodded his agreement. "I'll have to go see her

soon. I'm thinking of moving, downsizing. My place is too big for an old man like me. Your mother has a good eye for real estate."

"She does. I think living with an architect all those years helped," Lou said, thinking of her father fondly.

"So, what can I do for you, Lou?"

"I have a sample missing in the lab. We've searched for it, but more frighteningly, all my notes that go with it are gone."

Vasilii stood and walked around the front of the desk. "You think somebody has stolen it?"

She knew that would be the first place he would go. "I'm not sure. But I think it's odd that the sample and all of our notes would go missing."

"Let me call Ivan."

She waited as he carried his cell phone toward the window and muttered something to Ivan she couldn't hear, and within a minute, Ivan bounded into the room.

"Hey, Louisa, Vasilii," he said, coming to stand next to her.

Louisa had always thought it odd, yet understandable, that Ivan usually addressed his grandfather by his first name.

"Ivan," Vasilii said. "Louisa has concerns about a missing sample."

Ivan turned to face her. "What sample are you talking about, Louisa? The one you texted me about?"

"Yes. That one. The one we had just moved to live testing. The one that led to paralysis."

Ivan sat down in one of the chairs opposite his grandfather. "Have you done a thorough check?"

"I did. All the other labs have checked their units.

Everybody has been asked whether they borrowed anything from the lab. I've gone through our units four times, and always get the same answer. The sample is missing."

She was about to add that she had switched the samples, but something made her hold back. Something niggled the back of her brain. But she trusted these two men. They'd been good to her, provided a safe place to continue her research, but something . . . what. Irked? Itched? She couldn't put her finger on what had her so unsettled.

"Just to be doubly cautious, I'll do a check," Ivan said. "You know how it is, sometimes you can't see for looking. Happens to me all the time with my car keys, and they are usually right there in front of me."

"Of course, that's a great idea," she replied tactfully. "But that doesn't explain why all the notes are missing. They're gone too. I looked this morning, but they aren't there. Someone removed the working notes from the file and the full reports from the system. It's as if the sample never existed."

Vasilii stood. "Tell me more about the sample. What is it? What are the risks?"

"It had been looking really positive until we started live testing," Ivan answered. "It paralyzed the mice yet kept them alive and fully functioning mentally. They could feel pain but not respond."

"Look," she said, standing. "I know we have protocol for this kind of thing, but I think there is a quick way to figure this out. We can use the security footage of the lab to see who went through the files. We keep the footage for a while, right? Or maybe somebody in IT can help figure out who accessed the data. They'd have to have put in a user ID, right?"

"Louisa," Vasilii said, calmly, "the cameras in your lab haven't worked in over two months. We trusted you and Ivan, so it wasn't a priority to fix them."

The news hurt like a kick to the stomach. The wind left her.

"But there are things we can do," Vasilii continued. "We can look at which cameras near your lab work, maybe we can see someone heading to your lab who had no business there. And you are right, we can get IT to take a look and see if the person who deleted the files left some kind of trace behind them."

"We should call the police as a precaution," Louisa said, feeling anxious.

"Let us conduct our own internal investigation, first. If the samples turn up in the lab, it will be a significant embarrassment for all. And even if they don't, we need to handle this carefully. Losing a dangerous sample is not something we would want to get out there if we can avoid it. Let us check those things out first, then I promise you we will call in the police if there are no answers."

"Great idea, Grandfather."

Vasilii held out his hand toward the door, and Louisa turned toward it. "You and Ivan should return to the lab and begin your search while I start the wheels in motion. Trust me, Louisa. You know I take things like this incredibly seriously, and the perpetrator will be punished to the fullest extent of the law."

As she walked toward the lab with Ivan, who was chattering on about how it was likely nothing, and how they'd be laughing about it by lunchtime when they found the sample in a silly location, thoughts flashed through her mind at high speeds. She felt like Dr. Susan Wheeler in the old movie *Coma*. What if she had stumbled onto a conspiracy? She shook her head. Those were the rambling thoughts of someone who was paranoid. It was a missing sample, and Vasilii was taking steps to find the culprit. She had to have faith in the process.

Louisa pulled on her lab coat and hurried back inside her lab. She unlocked the refrigerator and made a show of looking at all the samples in there with Ivan, just in case Vasilii had been lying about the cameras not working. The failed sample was still there, tucked away at the back of one of the lower shelves. With security and bag search on the way out of the building, she couldn't exactly smuggle it out. Plus, she didn't have the means to dispose of it at home. She had to trust that nobody would realize what it was until she came back into the office after the weekend.

By then, she would have a plan.

"In two weeks, we're going to be so busy we won't know which side is up," Cabe said over the loud music as he threw a twenty-kilo slam ball against the wall of his cousin's gym in the Gaslamp district. The neighborhood would be the perfect spot for dinner after their end-of-week workout before he headed home for a quiet evening. Cabe had been threatening a big night, and Six was at risk of caving. He could always crash at Cabe's for the night, but really, he just wanted to head home after a few drinks feeling pleasantly relaxed.

They'd decided to leave the office and head downtown, meet up with Cabe's brother, Noah, a sergeant with the major case squad of the San Diego Police Department, who was busy flirting with a young woman while he *assisted* her pull-ups. Two inches higher and the guy would be gripping her ass, but he couldn't blame Noah. It was a cute one. He wondered if Louisa worked out. A gym like this would probably be hell for her.

He looked around. There were people everywhere, some there to work hard, some there to try to look good while they got a workout in. She would struggle with the volume of people she'd have to avoid.

"You going to throw that ball or just stand there like a goldfish," Cabe said, throwing the towel he'd just wiped his face on straight at Six.

"Fuck you," he said good-naturedly, tossing it back. Six shook his head to clear it. Nothing good was going to come from his keeping thinking about Lou, despite the fact he'd pulled his phone out several times to text her, call her maybe. If he was honest, it was part of the reason he was at the gym at seven on a Friday night instead of getting ready to meet up with friends for beers. "Sorry, man. Miles away. It's good it's gonna ramp up. I had a look at those financials you sent over. Hadn't realized our monthly outgoings were going to be quite so high, and there is still a ton to do with the building." He lifted the ball, turned sideways, then pivoted to throw the ball against the wall, catching it without moving his feet when it bounced back toward him. One down, nineteen to go. He felt the tightening through his abs and obliques.

"There are five major jobs next month. We need to talk about who is taking which one. Was thinking I'll do the training of the aid-route security down in Sierra Leone. I've been home longest. And that is pretty much all of September. I'll take two guys with me. That will leave you, Mac, and three guys to tackle the other four. Plus, all the fill-in work of security."

Six finished the set and changed sides. "If that works for you, it works for me. While we're building up, we should keep the security guard training side of the business going. Offer courses during the down weeks, take on one-off security engagements. Build some cash." He threw the ball and began his twenty-rep set on his left side as Cabe followed suit and finished off the exercise.

Without discussion, they moved over to the pull-up stations. "Race you to fifty," Six said, jumping up quickly.

"Asshole." Cabe laughed and joined him. They'd egged each other on since those early days in boot camp. When he'd received his SEAL pin two years later, he owed it as much to Cabe and Mac as he did to the million dollars the US Navy had invested in him.

Noah wandered back over to them. "You know you guys are in your thirties now, right?"

Six finished first. He always did. Pull-ups had always been Cabe's nemesis, which was weird given how fit the guy was. Didn't stop the guy trying though.

"How are things with you, Noah?" Six asked as he dropped to the floor. He opened his water bottle and took a large gulp of cool water.

"Still waiting for an opening in homicide," he replied, and lowered to the ground. Push-ups. Noah started counting, and Six joined him.

"Don't listen to him," Cabe said. He wrapped his

towel around his neck. "He's like a freaking all-star and hasn't even hit ten years' service yet."

"You could leave, come join us," Six said, only sort of joking. Someone with great detective skills would be an asset. He shifted to his back for crunches.

Noah laughed. "Yeah. Can't see myself doing that anytime soon. I found my home with the force. Now I just got to wait my time for a position in the department I want most. Special Investigations is pretty varied, and I get to work with the *feebs* which is always a barrel of laughs."

They were coming to the end of their workout, and Six began to stretch. If he didn't, he'd walk like an old woman in the morning. He rested his left hand on the wall, kicked his foot up to his butt, and gripped it with his right hand. His quad groaned in disagreement at the move, but he knew it would thank him within a minute.

"Hi. Are you new to the gym?" A cute woman with bright blue eyes and blond hair piled up in a messy bun on top of her head walked into view. She wore neon leggings that showed off a very defined ass and a sports bra that highlighted her saline-filled assets. Usually one of his favorite combinations, but now she seemed a little . . . obvious. At least when compared to Louisa. But it took guts to walk up to a guy you didn't know, so he humored her.

"I'm an old friend of the owner. Been out of town for a few years. What about you?"

She pursed her lips, suddenly looking very confused. "The owner has been out of town for a few years?" she asked.

He couldn't imagine Louisa confusing what he'd said.

He'd put money on it that she wouldn't have mixed things up. "No, I have," he explained patiently. "I've been overseas. The owner hasn't been anywhere. I'm Six." He offered her his hand, and she shook it.

"Ha ha," she said, as if she got the joke. The one he hadn't made. "You are way older than six."

Six shook his head and looked around for one of the guys. "No, my name is Six, short for Sixton."

"Huh. I'm Poppy which isn't short for anything. I mean, my dad used to call me Popsicle. But then that's actually longer than Poppy, so . . ."

He couldn't help but laugh, but he thought of Lou. She had her own kind of awkward, but she was engaging and smart. Someone you could go on a hike with and not run out of things to say. If you'd asked him a week ago who he would have preferred to take on a date, Poppy would have won by a mile. But suddenly he found himself attracted to brains and quirk.

"Noah," he said, and waved his friend over. "This is Poppy, which isn't short for anything."

He slapped Noah's back and let him take over.

"What's with you?" Cabe asked, following him to the locker room.

"What do you mean?" Six asked, grabbing his shower bag.

"Poppy with the tight ass. That's what's wrong with you," he laughed, grabbing his own supplies.

How to explain that a totally different kind of woman had grabbed his attention? Once showered, dressed, and packed up, they wandered outside with Noah, who'd arranged a date with Poppy for the following evening.

"You sure you don't want to join us? We're meeting up with some of Noah's cop friends," Cabe asked

Six shook his head. "Thanks for the offer but I'm gonna head. See if I can't actually act like an adult and start to unpack all the boxes sitting around my house."

"Okay. Cool. Talk to you tomorrow about the Mexico job, right?"

Working on a Saturday was nothing new. "Sure thing."

All the talk of Mexico gave him an idea for dinner. He walked in the direction of the truck with plans to stop off at a Mexican place he knew in the Gaslamp district first to get some food so he didn't need to bother when he got home. As he crossed the street, he caught sight of a brunette, and did a double take. Lou was walking with an older woman on the opposite side of the street. She was wearing a pale blue sundress and brown ankle boots. The kind that made him think of country songs and stolen kisses behind hay bales, although the way the dress skimmed her body gave him the urge for a little more than simple kisses. He should just let her go about her business, but he wanted to talk to her again, and *accidentally* running into her was a whole heck less risky than calling her up. Hurrying across the street, he tried to catch them, but as they stepped off the sidewalk to cross the street, the older woman fell down heavily to the ground. A taxi screeched to a halt inches in front of her and Six began to run as the woman tried to scramble back toward the curb, crying out in pain as she put weight onto her ankle.

"Oh, Mom," he heard Louisa say as he jogged closer. She offered her hand to her mom to help her up. "Are you okay, what did you hurt?"

"Here, let me, Lou," he said, anxious to help her mother off the road where an irate taxi driver was already gesticulating to them. Six flipped him the bird and told him to cool his heels. Lou looked at him in shock and he wasn't sure whether it was her mom's fall, his sudden appearance, or the fact that he had just yelled at a cabbie.

But it didn't matter. His heart raced, and it wasn't the adrenaline of the woman's fall.

It was the fact that Lou was looking at him. And he loved it.

Six gently placed an arm under her mom's legs and around her back and scooped her mom up as if she didn't weigh more than a bag of apples. Louisa was certain that it was very wrong to study the way his biceps stretched his pale gray T-shirt as he carried her mom onto the sidewalk where an industrious server from the restaurant on the corner had delivered a chair from their patio. With care, he lowered her mom onto the seat, and in a rush, she returned her focus to her mom's injuries instead of the man who stood next to her. "Oh my gosh, Mom. Are you okay?" She crouched down in front of the chair, and Six joined her.

"No," her mom whimpered. "I really hurt my ankle. I can't put any weight on it."

Louisa touched it gently, and her mom winced. It was already starting to swell rather nastily.

"Should we get you to a hospital?" Six asked. He

placed his hand on the small of Louisa's back and rubbed it gently.

"I think I need to go," her mom answered, tears filling her eyes. "Let me call Lucan. He can take me."

Oh dear lord. Louisa could only imagine how caring the guy would be when faced with a Friday evening spent in the ER. "Mom, we can take a cab," she encouraged. They could grab some food to go so they didn't starve at the hospital.

"Please. Just let me call him," her mom begged.

Louisa watched as her mom pulled her phone from her purse and dialed. She couldn't bear to listen to the pleading conversation, so she stood and stepped away.

"You okay, Lou?" Six asked, and placed his hand on her shoulder. It felt warm and comforting.

She nodded and looked up at him. "Lucan is my age, as have been most of my mom's friends of late. We were meant to meet him for dinner."

There was a sadness to her voice, and he hated that it was there. "I could drive you both. My truck is only another block that way. I can help your mom get in."

"Oh, thank you. But I wouldn't want to interrupt your plans for the evening. You're probably late for your . . . whatever you were heading to. I'm sorry."

Six placed his arm over her shoulder. "The only thing I'm late for is a plate full of tacos, alone. I got nowhere else to be."

"Louisa. Lucan is on his way," her mother called from behind her, and Lou rolled her eyes.

"Of course he is," she mumbled, just for Six to hear. "He'll be worried his allowance will get cut if he doesn't come."

The server came out with a bag filled with ice, and Lou helped her mom place it around her ankle. They attached it with her mother's Hermès scarf and tied it tight to reduce the swelling.

Within a few more minutes, the roar of a powerful engine disturbed the peace and a sleek black sports car pulled up by the curb. It was the one her mother had bought Lucan for Valentine's Day, and Louisa felt a little ill at such a vulgar display of their wealth.

"Toni, sweetheart," Lucan said as he leapt out of the car and walked to where her mom sat. "What happened?"

"I fell off the curb and think I broke my ankle. I wondered if you could take me to the hospital."

Louisa watched as Lucan looked from her mom's foot to his car to his watch. "We had reservations at eight thirty. Are you sure we can't perhaps go eat, rest your foot on a stool maybe, see how it feels in the morning?"

He was trying to worm his way out of it, just as she'd known he would. She was about to step forward, torn between giving Lucan a piece of her mind or simply demanding that her mother went to the hospital with her instead, when Six placed his hand on her shoulder and stepped forward.

"I'm gonna mark that bullshit answer down to the stress of finding out your girlfriend was nearly killed when she fell down in front of a moving vehicle," he said, stepping into Lucan's personal space, completely dwarfing him.

Despite her mom's injury, Louisa covered her mouth with her hand so Lucan wouldn't see the grin she was trying to stop.

"So given you are still clearly shaken," Six said, "I'll lift Toni into your car while you cancel those reservations."

Lucan nodded, mutely.

Once her mother was safely in Lucan's car with promises to keep Lou posted on her diagnosis, Lucan pulled away from the curb. She watched the flashy taillights as he braked at the first set of lights.

"Thanks again, Six," Lou said, turning to face him. "Your timing was perfect." She looked at him for a moment, then her bangs fell back in the way.

"Always a pleasure. You can make it up to me by preventing me from eating alone. Have dinner with me, Lou."

Dinner with Six felt like a trap. Restaurants, people, servers she'd need to answer. She hadn't wanted to eat out with her mother or Lucan either, but they'd reserved a table at a spacious restaurant, and her mother had assured her it wouldn't be overly busy.

"Don't worry, Lou," he said, taking her hand. "Just stay with me and we'll figure this out."

She could always hop in her car and head back home. It would take less than ten minutes given the traffic at this time of night. She could call in an order to her favorite deli in Little Italy. They'd even pop outside and hand it to her so she didn't need to go inside. But she couldn't tug her hand away from his. For some reason, staying with him seemed the most compelling of options.

"Want to join me for tacos?" Six asked playfully. "I know a great place just south of here that does incredible seafood."

"I'm pretty much a vegetarian," Louisa said, ready for the awkward comments about her choices, but Six didn't even blink.

"Well. I'm sure you can find something on the menu that works. If not, we'll just head somewhere else instead. There's Café Gratitude. They do a really good vegetarian Indian curry bowl."

Louisa grinned.

"What?" Six asked, looking at her curiously.

"Nothing," she said, shaking her head. How on earth had she ended up going to dinner with Six? Was it a date? Or was it just an act of mercy? If that was the case, someone should put her out of her misery now.

"So do you live locally?" Six asked, leading them purposefully. His hand was wrapped tightly around hers. It was an anchor to hold on to as she navigated the busy street.

"About ten minutes away. I'm in Mission Hills."

"Nice neighborhood. One second," he said, leading them into a Mexican restaurant that had bright yellow umbrellas and tall wooden tables. There was a large crowd of people around the bar, and most of the tables were full. Six placed his mouth close to her ear. "Does outside work for you? Or is it easier for you inside? And if it's too busy for you, we can just go somewhere else."

It *was* too busy for her. She glanced back through the window and noticed a couple leaving a corner seat on the patio. "If we could sit there it would be fine," she said, gesturing toward it.

Six spoke to the hostess, and within moments, they

were seated in the corner, Louisa with her back to the crowd. The only thing to focus on was Six, and at moments like this, she really wished she wasn't quite so . . . inept. She'd noticed the way the hostess had looked up at him and done every enviable girl trick to flirt with him, from twirling her long ebony ponytail around her finger to fluttering eyelashes that had to be fake. Because nobody's eyelashes were that thick naturally. Yet Louisa could barely look at him. It was taking every ounce of energy she had just to deal with the crowds around her.

"What were you thinking?" Six asked, and she realized she hadn't even looked at the menu. "I'd recommend the mahi-mahi tacos normally, but I have no idea what's good vegetarian-wise."

His blond hair fluttered in the warm breeze, making him look even more . . . gah. Food, she needed to focus on food. She picked up the menu and hid behind it. Quickly scanning the menu, she chose the first vegetarian thing she saw, a mushroom, spinach, and avocado quesadilla. It sounded perfect, but her stomach was so squeezed with nervous excitement, she wasn't sure she could eat it. She returned the menu to the table and looked up at Six, who looked concerned.

"Are you okay, Lou?" he asked, quietly.

Louisa looked around behind her. "It's just . . . a lot," she said, not feeling the need to hide behind her stoic mask.

Six reached across the table. "Do you trust me?" he asked.

She nodded. "I do."

"Hey, I'm Carrie. Can I take your order?" the server asked as she approached them.

"Yeah. Can we get it to go? We just found out we need to leave."

They told Carrie what they wanted and she hurried away to deal with their order.

Relief battled with disappointment. She wasn't certain how much longer she could have sat in such a busy restaurant, although it had felt nice for a millisecond to act like a normal person. But disappointment washed through her. Going home to eat her Mexican alone instead of sitting outside and enjoying Six's company sucked.

When the food arrived at the table in one big bag, Six settled the bill and led Lou quickly away onto one of the quieter side streets. "Breathe, Lou," he said as he walked toward his silver truck. He grabbed a blanket from inside the truck, then handed her the bag of food before he pulled down the tailgate.

"Hop on up," he said, slipping his hands around her waist to give her a boost up. The move caught her off guard.

"What? Why am I . . . ?"

Six hopped up alongside her. Literally hopped. He placed one hand on the bed, then before she could figure out how he did it, he was standing behind her and offering her his hand.

"I want to eat dinner with you in a place you are comfortable. There's nobody here in this side street," he said, turning in a circle and gesturing with his hand. "And this," he said, laying the blanket down on the bed of the truck, "is our own private restaurant."

The tightness in her chest that had been plaguing her since she'd first seen him on the street relaxed. He still wanted to have dinner with her. And in a tiny, small way, she loved him for that.

CHAPTER FOUR

Once upon a time, Monday mornings had been the greatest thing ever. It was the opportunity to wake up and start a whole new week of experimentation and research. But today, Louisa wanted to hide under the quilt. Rules were her thing. They'd gotten her through her SATs. They'd gotten her through college. Science and mathematics were filled with rules. The circumference of a circle would always equal pi multiplied by the diameter. The inferior vena cava would always carry deoxygenated blood to the heart. And Louisa North adhered to every rule. *Every* rule.

So why was she contemplating heading into the lab like a bad Bond villain to secretly discard the dangerous sample that still sat, mislabeled, at the bottom of the refrigeration unit? Although she was more of the good guy. More Moneypenny, less Oddjob. Louisa threw her arm across her eyes. Whoever wanted the sample already had all the notes on how to make the damn thing. Except sometimes, it was better to use a base solution to test from and run more tests on the sample before it headed into any kind of mass production. Though who the hell would want to mass produce a drug that didn't work and that had horrid side effects?

Louisa shoved the covers out of the way with a huff and got ready for work. In the shower, it occurred to her that she might have watched way too many Jason Bourne movies. Not everything was a conspiracy to be thwarted. While eating homemade banana and oatmeal muffins covered in peanut butter, she decided against doing anything. First, she'd check in with Ivan and Vasilii to see what the internal review had found and what the police had said. If this was just some grabby-hand lab tech who wanted to try to make a few bucks by taking an unsuccessful lab sample to another lab, then the sample was fine where it was. Although she was pretty certain that the police would have to notify the FBI if that had happened, and she most definitely didn't want to hand the sample to the government.

Damn. She was back to conspiracies again.

On the way out of the door, she grabbed Six's sweater, the one he'd loaned her as the night had dropped cooler as they had sat in the back of his truck. He'd leaned back on one side of the truck, she'd rested against the other. They'd talked for hours. Well, mostly he'd talked, and she'd asked questions and listened. Talking about herself wasn't high on her priority list. He'd told her about his company and the kind of work they were hoping to do. She wondered if he realized just how animated he became as he talked about Cabe and Mac. It had been entertaining to listen to the mischievous stories of their youth.

Long after they'd finished their meal, they'd stayed in the back of the truck, even though her butt had gone numb. He never touched her again. Not even once. Well, except to help her down out of his truck. He'd insisted on driving her to her car, and they'd listened to Nina Simone, an artist she'd only ever had a passing interest in but he seemed to know a lot about. Now Louisa had her greatest hits on her phone.

Once she got in her car she set it to play. Maybe Nina could help her screw her head on straight. She hated the idea that her lab had been violated and was disappointed that Vasilii had allowed the cameras inside to remain broken. They'd have to discard everything in there if they couldn't guarantee it hadn't been tampered with.

Traffic cooperated, and she found herself at work early. After she'd dropped her bag into her locker, she headed upstairs to Vasilii's office. He was the ultimate early riser and was often the first person to reach the building in the morning. Liz was already seated at her desk.

"Morning, Liz. Is Vasilii in?" she asked.

Liz smiled softly. "He is, and I just took him coffee. Can I get you one, dear?"

Coffee was such a good idea. "Only if you are getting one for yourself. You don't need to go to that effort on my account."

"My pleasure. Go on in. I'll bring it to you."

Louisa knocked and pushed the large wooden door open. "Hey, Vasilii. Can I bother you for a moment?"

Vasilii wrapped up the large blueprints on the table to make room for her. "Of course. Come and sit down. Your mother mentioned she took a spill. Is she okay?"

She was fine, if you ignored the fact she'd spent a large percent of the weekend complaining that Lucan hadn't been overly companionable. He'd only shown his face once over the weekend and had stayed the sum total of twenty-three minutes. Louisa knew because she'd timed him. "It was a pretty clean break. She needs six to eight weeks in a cast. We hired a nurse to help her with day-to-day things like bathing."

"If you need some time off to go be with her, we can most definitely arrange it. If you feel you should be there . . ."

"Thank you, Vasilii, but I think it is better for both of us that she has help and I go see her every day."

Vasilii squinted his eyes at her. "Are you sure? I feel like this would be a good idea. Yes?"

Louisa shook her head. "No. Thank you. I came to see about the missing sample," she said, changing the subject. "Were you able to find the person who took it?"

Abruptly, Vasilii pushed his chair away from the desk and stood before putting the blueprints on his shelf. "We are still working on it," he said. "We have some suspects."

"But if you haven't found anyone yet, should we call the police?"

Vasilii returned to the table and sat back down. "Of course we've informed all the relevant parties," he said. "Our reputation is paramount, and I won't have anybody mess with it. Listen, you have enough to worry about, Louisa," he said. "With your mother and all. Please. Leave this to me to deal with. I'll let you know if you can be of help."

Liz bustled in and gave Lou her coffee. "Enjoy, my love."

"Thanks, Liz."

Liz picked up a stack of mail from Vasilii's desk and walked out again.

"Louisa. I'm grateful that you care so much about this. But it is probably nothing for us to worry about."

She stood and picked up her coffee. "I certainly hope so."

The lack of progress was a concern. Without knowing why the sample was taken, it was impossible to know whether someone had messed with other samples. She hated the thought of having to dispose of the brain slice she'd been sent; the very idea squeezed at her chest. It was hard to find donors for medical research, and the body parts were treated like gold once they were. A highly valuable commodity, and a once-in-a-million chance to figure out in real time what had caused the condition they suffered from.

Louisa wandered into the break room, which was still quiet. She sipped her coffee while looking out over the parking lot. The gray sky would soon be brilliantly lit by the late August sunshine. Perhaps it was time for her to go see a doctor. Her mind was telling her that there was something strange about the way Vasilii had answered her question about the police. He'd never said yes. All he'd done was tell her that he'd called the relevant authorities. But the man had been a friend of her family's for years. He treated her like a daughter. Her heart was telling her there was nothing strange about the way he was handling it . . . but her mind. It was on fast-forward. She could barely keep up with the doubt and paranoia it was creating.

Louisa rinsed her mug in the sink and placed it into the dishwasher. No closer to understanding what was going on, she knew there was one thing she could do. It was small, and it might not even reduce the risk.

Determined, she returned to the lab. Ivan wouldn't be in for another hour. Not such an early riser. She hurried into her lab coat and protective clothes and entered the air unit. Once inside the lab, she grabbed the sample from the fridge and a large bottle of bleach, then headed to the sink they disposed of biomedical waste in. She mixed the sample and bleach together, neutralizing its properties and destroying it forever.

"What are you doing?"

"Oh my God. Ivan." She placed her hand over her chest. "You made me jump."

Ivan picked up the sample bottle. "Clearing out? What was this?"

Thinking quickly on her feet, she said the only plausible thing he would buy. "With the lab being compromised, and us not knowing what was tampered with, I thought we should clean house. It sucks to get rid of some of this work, but what good is continuing if we aren't a hundred percent certain what we are working with."

Ivan studied her at length, and she got the sneaking suspicion he was testing her. "Don't you think that is a little premature?"

She shook her head. "We don't have any footage in here of what they touched, even if whoever took it was only in here for a few moments." God, it was ridiculous to doubt Ivan.

He stared for a few more seconds. "Okay. I'll go get more bleach."

Louisa let out a huge breath as she watched his back disappear out of the lab. She needed someone to think this through with, and the only person she could think of was Six.

Six put the phone down and leaned back in his office chair. One of his old CIA contacts was eager to know when he might be able to call on Eagle for support, especially for more sensitive operations on US soil. The politics of navigating the CIA's growing powers to manage terrorism with the role of the FBI and local law enforcement aside, that was exactly the kind of work they wanted to get into, and Six had told his contact that they were willing and able to jump in. But today he had a class full of wannabe security guards who he needed to put through their paces. It was another one of Mac's ideas. Eagle Securities–certified guards, with the attendees paying a thousand bucks for a three-day training course. Gaz and Joel had spent the prior day with them, teaching modules on the basics—setting up, preplanning, how to conduct perimeter checks, etc. Today he would present modules on everything from tactical identification of threat to close combat and restraint. Friday was on Cabe.

He'd also had two interviews for new operators and a long to-do list that involved finding a reputable lawyer in Iraq, as contractors there were subject to Iraqi law. If they were going to do any kind of work for the CIA overseas, they'd need legal representation in most of the countries they operated in, just as backup. No point waiting until an op went to shit, or a brother was arrested on trumped-up charges. He'd started by reaching out to a friend of his in the Naval Special Warfare Development Group who'd ensured that kind of thing was in place for the SEAL teams in the past.

"Yo, Six," Buddha shouted as he walked into the training area. "There's a woman looking for you out front."

"On it. Thanks." He walked toward the reception area and pressed the green button at the side of the door to unlock it. With a shove, it opened, and there in the lobby was Louisa, her hands clasped tightly in front of her. She was looking toward the floor as always, and he felt for her. Usually, he was drawn to people who oozed confidence, but his own issues were making him more sympathetic.

"Hey, Louisa. Are you okay?" he asked, walking toward her, waiting for her to look up at him. That moment when she'd made eye contact on their walk had been as powerful as anything he'd ever experienced, and because he realized she wouldn't do that for everybody, it felt special.

When she did, he saw a whole heap of worry and stress in the lines of her face. "Wait, no. Hey," he said, pulling her into his arms without thinking. "Come here." Her body leaned into his and her shoulder slid under his arm. She fit against him perfectly—though right now was the least appropriate time to think about that. Except, damn, he loved the feel of her body pressed up against his.

"I'm not upset," she practically snarled, but she wrapped her arms around his waist all the same. "I'm mad. And a lot confused."

Okay. They stood there for a moment in silence until he stepped back and took her hand. "Let's go to my office, and we can talk."

He buzzed them through the security door, not entirely sure why she'd come to him, but happy that she had nonetheless. Friday night had been a new experience, just hanging out and talking, and on Saturday, when he'd been out in a bar over on Coronado with a whole bunch of SEAL brothers, shooting shit, he'd found himself wondering what Lou was doing.

He offered her a seat and perched himself on the desk in front of her. Louisa sat for all of two seconds, then huffed and stood and started pacing back and forth in his office. She went to his bookshelf where he'd thrown all of his binders and books haphazardly, just happy to have them out of boxes, and started to organize them as she spoke.

"I have a problem, and I didn't know who to ask for help. I think something is going on at the lab," she said as she pulled the binders off one shelf and put them back onto another, grouping them by height and color. He'd have thought it was cute if what she'd just said hadn't been so damn serious. "I don't know what to do or whether I should go to the police."

"Knock, knock," Cabe said, poking his head around the door.

"Hey, Cabe. This is Louisa, the presenter from the fundraiser last Friday. Louisa, this is Cabe. He's the one I told you about on Friday." Six took note of the way

Cabe's eyebrow raised at him, but Cabe was polite nonetheless.

"Hey, Louisa, your presentation was awesome. Nice to finally meet you," Cabe said.

Louisa looked up briefly, but quickly returned to what she was doing, which appeared to be reorganizing the books that were left on the shelves into alphabetical order. Cabe glanced over in his direction, a what-the-hell-is-she-doing? look on his face. Six smiled and shook his head slightly.

"Louisa was just telling me that she was having some problems. You want to continue, Lou?"

She finished the shelves and made her way over to the window and started to untangle the cords for the blinds, which were full of knots. "My medical research focuses specifically on finding a drug to combat the involuntary movements of Huntington's disease," she said, threading a cord back on itself. "It used to be called Huntington's chorea because chorea is the Greek word for dancing, but that was a really limiting title because there is way more to the disease than those abnormal jerky movements. Some trials work, some trials don't. We just developed a treatment that we were really confident was going to work, but it ended up paralyzing the rats we tested it on. What was doubly frightening was the way it mutated. We hadn't gotten around to doing the full postmortem on both the experiment and the rats, so we held on to the sample we'd created. When I saw you out on the trail last week, I was waiting for an answer from my lab partner because I couldn't find one of the samples. Then on Friday, I went straight to the lab to check the files to confirm what the chemical makeup of the missing sample was, because any way you looked at it, that sample was dangerous and could quite possibly be used to do harm. My handwritten notes and my electronic files are all gone."

The hairs on the back of Six's neck stood on end. He usually had a pretty good radar for detecting bullshit stories, and his gut was telling him that Louisa was telling the truth.

"So, report it to the police," Cabe said. "Feels like a civilian thing rather than the kind of thing we do."

"Technically you're right. It would become an FBI issue. But . . . *gah.* See, I can't even explain it to you. It's a feeling. My lab partner and my boss, who happens to be my lab partner's grandfather, are just acting . . . strange . . . cagey."

"So your fear is what?" Cabe asked.

"What we'd created had all the makings of a chemical weapon," Louisa said, finally looking up at them as her hands kept busy.

"Is that possible?' Six asked.

Louisa dropped the cord, and he noticed there were no knots left in it. "Do you know the history of chemotherapy?"

Six looked over at Cabe, and they both shook their heads.

"It came from two doctors at Yale University looking at the medical records of soldiers who had died from mustard gas poisoning in the Great War. They were trying to find an antidote for the weaponized poisonous gas because World War II was on its way, but instead they noticed that many of those who'd died had had a very low number of immune cells. So they figured that if mustard gas could kill good cells, it could probably kill cancerous ones too. It's a bit more complicated than that, obviously, but that was pretty much the start of chemotherapy as a cancer treatment. In short, it's not uncommon for many of these cures to walk a very fine line between medicinal brilliance and poison."

Talking science calmed her. It probably wasn't a conscious thing, but he noticed the way her voice lost its uncertainty as she spoke. "I had no idea," Six said. The whole time they'd been in his office, he'd remained perched on the desk while she continued to roam around and move things. It might drive many people nuts, but he found it quite endearing.

"Most people don't realize the connection, but that's what makes the sample so dangerous. It's not uncommon for there to be occurrences of espionage between one lab and another. Or for someone to get the smart idea to steal a sample and attempt to either sell it to another lab or blackmail the lab it came from to deliver it back to them. Neither of those things ever work, because everybody assumes the sample is compromised. But it's just weird how Ivan and Vasilii are acting."

"Ivan Popov?" Six asked, becoming more and more intrigued by her problem, especially now that it involved somebody he knew and didn't particularly like.

"So, why did you come to Six?" Cabe interrupted before Louisa could answer.

"I can't decide whether going to the police is the right thing. Will I get fired if I go around my boss to the police to ask them directly for an update? Is there a way for me to figure this out a little more before I make a career-ending decision to push Vasilii and Ivan? I don't know."

She looked straight at him, a rarity. "I just thought you might be able to give me some advice."

"It isn't the kind of thing we do. You need a private investigator, or in all honesty just call the police," Cabe said. Six ran his hand over his face. He wanted to help her, he really did, but as much as it annoyed him, Cabe was right. This really wasn't the kind of work *they* got into. But he could definitely help her think it through some more.

"Hey, Cabe. What did you want when you popped your head in?" Six asked, shooting him a look that he hopefully understood as *"Fuck off, you asshole."*

Cabe looked between Six and Louisa. "Fine," he huffed. "I just wanted those files on the job we have coming up at the start of next month." Security for an energy company's engineers in Venezuela. Six reached behind him, grabbed the folder off his desk, and handed it to Cabe, who promptly left the room.

"It's okay," Louisa said, head down as she walked to the door. "It's fine. I'll get out of your hair."

"Louisa. Wait," Six said, jumping to his feet. "I can talk this through with you. Isn't that what you came here for?"

"No. You know what, I'm overreacting. It's okay," she said, attempting to square her shoulders but then letting them fall in defeat. "Just saying it out loud to you guys made it sound silly."

"Well, call the police right away if you get worried." He reached for her wrist and realized how small it was in his hand. "Or even better, call me. You've got my number."

She turned and left his office, and he heard the soft click of the security doors.

Screw Cabe.

Fuck the rules.

It was partly his company. And he'd decide for himself what kind of work he took on.

"I can't believe he left me after I bought him a car. He said the hospital trip had been a wake-up call about our age gap, and that he didn't want to be a caregiver. I'm only fifty-five for goodness' sake." Her mother, Antonia, poured a small measure of port into the vintage cut-crystal glass that she'd had Louisa carry out on a silver tray. "Are you sure you don't want one?" she asked.

Louisa shook her head and focused on the roar of the ocean as waves crashed onto the shore that ran along the front of her mother's Torrey Pines Road home. The large patio that ran the full length of the property was accessed through the living room and was shaded by a large pergola that was covered in large, sweetly scented violet blooms of wisteria.

"I'm going to have to drive home soon," she answered, turning to face her mom. After three strangely quiet days in the lab, as they took stock of where they were after disposing of everything in the lab, she'd asked Ivan about updates, but he had no new information to share. So she'd come to get her mom's opinion on the situation, but as soon as she'd arrived, her mother had started in about her latest romantic disaster, so she'd decided to save the conversation for another day. "Mom, I have to ask, are you really surprised that Lucan left?

And I'm judging him, not you, with that question. Daddy wouldn't want you to be alone—that isn't what this is about—but some of these men are twenty, perhaps thirty years younger than you. It's almost like you're not mutually dating them. You get to take them out, but they never take you out with their friends or families."

Her mom sat back in her chair. "I'm not some naïve old woman, you know."

"I know, Mom. But you are incredibly generous. And have a big heart. And somehow these men are getting under your skin."

Antonia took a sip of port. "The dating world has changed so much since your father and I met. Somebody suggested that I should use a dating website because I'm lonely, Louisa. I really am."

Louisa thought long and hard about how to answer, because in a strange dichotomy, since meeting Six, she'd felt very faint pangs of loneliness herself. "I get that, Mom, but loneliness isn't a good enough reason to settle. And it's never going to work if you have to buy their attention." Every single man her mother had dated was perfectly handsome, all with pretty faces and smooth tongues. They'd flatter her mother and flirt. But a handful of them had shown their true colors. One of them had made a pass at Louisa as her mother was in the kitchen while they celebrated Christmas two years ago. *"I wasn't aware there was a younger option,"* he'd said as he slid his hand along her thigh and up her skirt. She'd slapped him, and he'd left. At first, her mother had been distraught at his sudden disappearance, but once Louisa had explained exactly what had happened, her mother had been more concerned that he'd left wearing the

Breitling Navitimer watch she'd given him only hours earlier.

She thought of all the pretty faces that had passed through the house since her father's death. Every man had been a slick con artist who'd been with her mother for no other reason than what she could provide.

"I'm sorry, Mom. I'm sorry that so many of these men are total shitbags. Maybe you *should* join a dating site, but I have to believe that joining a discreet high-end matchmaking service might be the better way to go."

Her mother sighed and took another sip. "Are you sure I can't convince you to join me for dinner at the Hansens' house tonight? I know they would love to see you."

A night with the Hansens was absolutely the last thing she wanted. Especially if their newly divorced quantum physicist son was home. As much as she loved science, after hours of listening to him go on and on about the superposition of states and quantum decoherence and their effect on reality as we perceived it, she'd be ready to poke her own eyes out with one of the ridiculous wooden toothpicks he insisted on chewing after dinner.

Louisa stood and took another deep breath. There was something about the ocean that just did her soul good. "I have a date with some work and some great horror from the fifties," she lied. Well, apart from the horror, which was her usual Thursday-night routine.

"When are we going to talk about you and dating? We should talk about that handsome young man who came to my aid," her mother said good-naturedly.

"I have plenty of time to worry about dating," Louisa said, her usual stock response. Not ready to talk about her messy feelings toward Six, she pushed the thought to the back of her mind. She stayed a little while longer, listened to her mother's endless gossip, then kissed her good-bye and jumped into her car.

Her phone vibrated as she started the engine, and she checked her message.

Where do you live? Do you mind if I swing by later? 6

Six. Even though she was still embarrassed that she'd thrown herself at his mercy two days earlier, she quickly typed her response.

Why are you swinging by?

Wanted to discuss a couple of things with you.

Well, that told her the sum total of nothing, but she texted her address before she changed her mind.

He responded immediately. *It'll be late. Don't wait up if you get tired—just text me and let me know.*

With traffic in her favor, it only took her half an hour to get to her Mission Hills home. The first time she'd seen it, she'd known it was the one for her, even though her father had offered to buy her a significantly larger home in La Jolla, purely because he could afford it. He'd invested heavily in the dot-com bubble, having gotten in early on companies like Google, Amazon, and eBay, and while he'd suffered some losses when the bubble had burst, he'd been smart and dumped most of his stock before it happened, making the family well over a hundred million dollars. But the ultra-rich lifestyle wasn't really her. She had no desire to sit on the boards of charities or attend society weddings. There were days when she could only just stand her own company, let alone anybody else's.

She pulled up in the driveway of her half-brick, half-blue-sided home, which had white windows and wooden doors. Under the front window was a wooden bench with two pretty blue-and-white cushions she'd bought from one of her favorite online stores, and a terra-cotta planter filled with lavender stood next to the door. Odor-evoked autobiographical memory was a proven fact, and every time she smelled lavender, it reminded her of entering into the safety of her home.

Louisa stopped the engine, grabbed her bags, and stepped out of the car. She let herself into the house, switched off the alarm, and walked straight upstairs to her office. Unpacking her bag was a ritual. It symbolized being home. She pulled out her notebook and phone, set her purse in its spot on the bookshelf, and then turned to walk toward the bedroom. Two wooden sculptures that sat on top of her filing cabinet caught her eye. They were abstract, but in Louisa's mind, there was a back and a front to them. And one faced the wrong way. The thudding of her heart and the rush of blood whooshing through her temples sounded horribly loud.

Quickly, she hurried over to the filing cabinet and looked around for signs of entry, but the lock was still tightly sealed and there were no other signs of disturbance. Louisa scanned the room thoroughly, looking for the slightest sign of movement. She searched the pile of the soft cream carpet for footprints, but couldn't see any other than her own. Silently, she slipped her shoes off and made her way through her home, checking the windows, looking in cupboards, and even peering under beds.

When she was finally satisfied that she was alone in her home and that only the wooden sculpture was out of place, she padded into the cobalt blue kitchen, the terracotta tile cool on her feet, and pulled open the fridge. A half-full bottle of Pinot Grigio would help scare away the jitters. The only explanation for the sculpture was that she'd knocked it somehow. She grabbed a white wine glass from one of the open shelves that ran along the wall and poured herself a generous measure. There was no point in dwelling in anxiety. Instead, she ran through the things she could do to take her mind off it. Catch up on sleep, read medical journals, jump into her pool.

She rustled up some sweet potato and black bean enchiladas and sipped on her wine while they were baking in the oven. Nothing comforted her quite like home cooking. Thirty minutes later, she'd changed into shorts and a tank, put her hair up, poured another glass of wine, and was seated in front of the television watching the 1957 classic *Night of the Demon* by Jacques Tourneur.

It was dark outside by the time the movie had finished and she took her plate down to the kitchen. Usually the dark wasn't an issue. Normally she'd take her glass of wine out onto the wooden deck and watch the stars for hours on end. But tonight felt different. Tonight it felt edgy. The safety she usually felt inside her home was missing. Desperate to make it feel normal, she followed her usual routine. She set some popcorn to pop while she rinsed her dishes and filled up her wine glass. As she was pouring the finished popcorn into a blue glass bowl and was just about to head back to her TV, she heard a car door slam and jumped. But then she remembered Six's text. It had to be him. A giddiness she hadn't felt since high school trickled through her. She stood on her toes and leaned over the sink to look out at the driveway, but the automatic lights weren't on, and there was no sign of his truck.

Louisa shook her head and laughed. Too much drama at work, too much alcohol, and watching a horror movie were spooking her unnecessarily. Maybe she should watch one of her favorite nonhorror films, like *Chocolat* or *Shakespeare in Love* or something.

Anything to chase away the panic.

Six hummed along to Nina singing about being misunderstood. All the important mile markers in his life were tagged with one of her songs. "Ain't Got No, I Got Life" had blasted from the speakers as he'd been separated from Mac and Cabe when he'd been transferred from their West Coast unit to the East Coast. "I Think It's Going to Rain Today" had played as he'd gotten dressed for Brock's funeral. He'd even lost his virginity to Jessica McKade in the back of his dad's truck to "Do I Move You?" The whole thing had been over before the end of the three-minute song. He grinned at the memory. His skills had certainly improved since then.

When others had reached for the roughest and toughest rock music to get them in the mood for war, he'd reached for "Sinnerman." And while he'd never publicly confess it, "Here Comes the Sun" had seen him through his spell in military hospital. There was a simple pleasure in listening to her on American soil for once with the windows of his truck down, even though the hour was late.

Getting a business off the ground was a whole different ball of wax from what he was expecting. He felt kinda shitty about all the work Mac and Cabe had already done in the months they'd been out. Now it was all guns blazing as they battled to build their business. Over breakfast, he'd prepared a proposal for a contract supporting an aid convoy through Colombia. On the way into work, he'd participated in a conference call with an old CIA friend of theirs about potential coverage for an off-the-grid group in Syria. Lunch had included a meeting with a potential candidate for an office manager. In between, he'd written modules for their security-guard-training business, put an hour in at the gun range, and finished painting the medical room. Their to-do list was never-ending, and for a moment, he yearned for the days when he was just given orders to follow. His body ached in a good way, ready for a soak in a hot bath with a cold beer.

When they'd started Eagle Securities, he'd imagined being on constant missions somewhere doing something adrenaline-filled all on their own dime and with their own rules, but for now, the days blended into a never-ending pile of paperwork. The calendar on the wall was beginning to fill up with work, though, and come October, they'd be busy. Probably busier than they could handle, but they would embrace it.

Despite the pile of work on his desk, Louisa was on his mind. After she'd left, he'd studied his neatly organized bookshelves and wondered if she'd even realized what she'd done. She'd barely looked at the books as she'd put them back in place, but he noticed she'd sorted them by type before alphabetizing them. Which meant she'd either read every book in his collection, which he found highly unlikely, or she'd read the backs in a millisecond to categorize them, which was equally crazy unless she was an epic speed reader.

But it wasn't just the books. It was her eyes. He recognized the look in them. The one that said they'd seen more than they should. The one that pleaded with him to help her, even as she'd told him she'd handle it on her own.

He turned the truck onto her street and lowered the volume on Nina. It was a pretty neighborhood. Even by the light of all the little solar lamps that illuminated the pathways up to front doors, he could see that the lawns were greener than should be possible with the drought watch in effect. *Wealth.* It made people feel like they were above the restrictions and laws the common man faced. It irritated him, like it had the night of the fundraiser he'd attended. Yet he'd felt compelled to donate after Louisa's persuasive presentation. Finding a cure for the disease was more important than worrying about who was donating the dollars. What did people's motivations matter as long as the charity benefited?

His tension eased, though, when he saw Louisa's yard, which was filled with plants that he'd bet his ass were drought resistant, given her clear knowledge of plants. Louisa North was a complicated woman.

He pulled his truck up onto the curb and killed the engine. There was an outside light turned on by the front door, but he didn't see any lights on inside. Perhaps she'd taken him at his word and gone to bed. For a moment he considered texting to see if she was awake, but he decided to hop out of the truck and knock first. The wooden door was weathered beneath his knuckles and the sweet smell of lavender greeted him.

Silence clung to the air until he heard feet pad across a tiled floor. There was the sound of a chain being unlocked.

"Six," she said breathlessly, looking at him through those long bangs of hers.

Okay, the whole tightening in his chest could go away because there was absolutely nothing sexy about the loose gym shorts she wore. And yes, it was clear she wasn't wearing a bra underneath that tank because, Christ . . . nipples . . . but he could be professional. He tried to convince his cock that there was nothing to see here, like a Jedi mind trick, but it didn't work. Acting independently, it had fully decided there was plenty to take in.

"Hey, Lou," he said, his voice a little gruffer than normal. He coughed to clear his throat, and Louisa kicked out a hip as she waited for him to pull his shit together. The move raised her top an inch, revealing a narrow band of skin that looked soft enough to lick, which really didn't help the discomfort he felt in his jeans. "I wanted to come out and check on you. Learn more about what's going on, see if there isn't something I can help you with."

"I appreciate that." She stepped back and ushered him into the hallway. "I'm not particularly good with . . . company," she said quietly.

He couldn't imagine what that must be like. His own

outgoing nature had been the only thing he could count on when he'd had to move as often as he did, fit in with new teams, and make friends in the places he was deployed. "You're doing just fine," he said as he entered her home.

The hallway was large but sparse. Pale yellow walls were decorated with framed pictures of vintage technical drawings of insects. There were lithographic plates of butterflies, bees, and grasshoppers. They were unusual yet strangely compelling. Kind of like their owner.

"Many of them are from Otto Staudinger's *Catalog der Lepidopteren des palaearctischen Faunengebietes.* It's the standard work of reference for Lepidoptera."

The random stuff this woman knew. *"Lepidoptera?"*

"You know, the groupings of nearly two hundred thousand species of moths and butterflies. It's a highly organized insect structure. Carl Linnaeus, a Swedish botanist, came up with the term from the Greek words—"

"How do you know all this shit?" he asked.

Louisa tensed, and he wished he'd just let her talk. "Sorry," she said with a shrug.

"No, seriously. How on earth can you remember all this stuff?"

"Eidetic memory, I guess."

"Eidetic?"

"Never mind," she said, and headed toward a closed door. "Can I get you a drink? Beer? Wine?"

Well, crap. That had gone well.

"Sure, beer would be good if you have some."

He followed her into a kitchen of the brightest blue. Wooden shelves lined one wall. He was no expert, but china that looked like it came from one of those expensive stores lined the shelves, like the kind Cabe's fiancée had placed on their wedding registry before . . . well . . . he shook his head. China rimmed in silver sat next to plates like the ones he'd picked up for nothing at IKEA. And mixed in were pottery-style plates in vibrant colors that could have come from any street market in Mexico.

Without wasting movement or words, Louisa efficiently went to the fridge, grabbed a beer, and cracked the cap before handing it to him. Popcorn sat in a bright blue bowl on the counter. Next to it, a glass of white wine, the condensation on it telling him that she'd only recently poured it.

"Sorry, am I interrupting something?" Alcohol and popcorn seemed like such a date thing to do.

Louisa smiled. "Not unless you count scaring myself to death with vintage horror. I was just about to put something else on." She looked up at him, and with her head tilted to the side, he could see her eyes clearly again. "You want to come watch something? I mean, while we chat, we could . . . never mind. You probably have stuff to do, and I have some reports I need to—"

"I'd love to," he said, unable to hide the grin at her awkwardness.

"Really?" she asked, those coffee-colored eyes of hers as wide as the stash of Christmas plates he'd seen displayed on her shelves. In August.

"*Really*. Unless you have chronically bad taste in movies, in which case I'm out, beer or no beer," he said, picking up the bowl of popcorn.

"Oh-kay," she said, drawing out the syllables as if

he'd just given her an instruction she didn't understand. It sounded more like a question than an answer.

It was impossible to ignore the subtle sway of her hips as she walked ahead of him. He was such a sucker for hips. And ass. And tits. Especially ones with responsive nipples under thin tanks. *Goddamn.* Focus.

Louisa set her wine down on the table and opened a door in the built-in unit around the television.

Six couldn't help but laugh as he put his beer and the popcorn down. "Lou, I don't get it," he said. He stepped closer to her and ran his fingers over the spines of movie after movie that were not only organized by category, but also had laminated cards stuck to the shelf telling him where each section started.

"Don't get what?" she asked, the look on her face one of genuine confusion.

"This," he said, gesturing his hand up and down the shelf. "Your kitchen shelves are an eclectic mix of stuff, all piled randomly, yet you organized the shit out of this."

"Well, I don't get this," she said, gesturing up and down him the way he had at her shelf. "Tell me again why you are here."

She was cute when she was prickly. He reached forward and pulled *Ocean's Eleven*, the original one, from a category titled CAPERS, and handed it to her.

"I heard it's movie night at the North house, so figured I'd come hang out." He moved to the sofa, flopped down, and placed his boots on the glass coffee table.

Once the movie started, she came and sat by him, and he did his best to ignore the way her shorts rode up her thighs. He spent more of his time with company in his bed than not. And that company, whoever she was that given day, usually had no issue whatsoever dropping her clothes the moment she stepped through his door. So naked skin he was totally down with. Yet somehow, just that tiny bit of extra flesh had him feeling giddy, like he was the boy who'd lost his virginity in less than two minutes giving it to Jessica McKade.

Louisa slapped his thigh. "At least take your shoes off," she said before she stuck her hand in their popcorn.

"Yes, ma'am," he said, sitting forward and toeing his boots off.

A week ago, he couldn't have imagined himself ready to take orders again so soon, but back then, he hadn't met Louisa North.

CHAPTER FIVE

Missing someone she wasn't even in a relationship with because she hadn't seen them since Wednesday, and it was now Saturday, was ridiculous. With a capital *R*. So instead, Louisa drove to Torrey Pines to collect her mom, then drove them back to Coronado so they could have lunch at the Hotel Del, her mother's favorite spot. The fact that she'd listened to Nina Simone all the way there and back had nothing to do with it. For the first time in her life, it felt good to be out of the lab and away from the invisible band she felt around her chest when she stepped inside.

There'd been no progress, and Liz had advised her that Vasilii was becoming irritated by her constant requests for information. Louisa's gut told her that what had happened mattered, but she'd begun to consider that it was her ego speaking. What if it got out into the research community about her failure? Sure, research was all about test, trial, revisit. Failure was as much a part of a researcher's life as white coats and biohazards. But she didn't want the world to see her dirty laundry. Plus, she'd begun to wonder if it would reflect badly on her personally as head of that specific lab that the sample was stolen from.

Before driving home, they'd headed south down the island. All her life, she'd known that Navy SEALs trained along the beach. Hell, before they'd closed access to that part of the shoreline, she may have even seen them a time or two. Hauling logs up and down the dunes, or diving in and out of the water. But it felt different knowing that this was a place Six had spent a large chunk of his life, and she'd never met him. In fact, if he hadn't approached her on the balcony at the presentation, their paths would likely have never crossed. As she'd dropped her mom off at home, she'd commented that Louisa had seemed distracted. It was nothing less than the truth, and she knew she needed to do *something.*

By the time she turned her car onto her driveway, she was exhausted, but she knew she needed to make a list. She took a deep inhale of the lavender she'd planted in the container by the front door, letting it soothe her as she turned the key in the lock and stepped inside. Louisa took her purse upstairs and placed it by her desk before she kicked off her shoes. Thankfully, the wooden sculptures were where she had left them. Quickly, she grabbed a notebook and headed to the kitchen. Once seated, she turned the page in her notebook and started a new list. *SIX.*

Her pencil hovered above the page as she replayed Wednesday evening's events in her mind. He'd stayed for nearly three hours and had switched to water after his first beer. As they'd watched the movie, he'd asked her questions about what had happened, and she'd explained how she'd truly believed Vasilii would do the right thing for the sake of the lab's reputation. Once Vasilii had completed his investigation, he'd call her up and apologize for being so short with her, she was certain. He wouldn't tolerate that kind of mess in his lab.

Six had challenged her to call the police, but she owed it to Vasilii to trust him that the right people had been involved, let him carry out his own investigation in his own way first. Plus, despite Ivan's suspicious behavior, hovering over her shoulder in the lab all day, there could be an explanation she hadn't considered. Science had taught her not to close off potential avenues of investigation. She'd promised Six, however, that if Vasilii's findings were anything other than the truth as she knew it, she'd call the police immediately.

What should she write on this list? *He was understanding. Was helpful to talk it through with. Has eyes the color of a winter storm.*

Gah. This was useless. She slapped the pencil down on the table. Just thinking about the man was stirring her up all over again. He'd never touched her . . . Well, except for the times when their hands had reached into the popcorn at the same time. At first it had been awkward, and she'd pulled her hand out right away. But Six had turned it into a game, grabbing her fingers when they came within the proximity of his. His reflexes were so quick that she didn't have time to whisk hers out of his reach. Occasionally he'd held on to her fingers for just a fraction longer than she would have held on to his, had the tables been reversed.

Louisa leaned back in her chair. The way he'd looked in blue denim that hugged his ass and the black T-shirt that was so dull yet freaking heavenly in the way it followed the contour of his biceps had been delicious enough. But the way he always led with one side of his mouth when he smiled with the other side following and the way he'd look at her from the corners of his eyes without ever moving his head just added to the tension. He'd probably noticed how . . . aware . . . he made her after she hurried to the kitchen to top up her wine when she still had half a glass left. She'd just needed to leave the room before she imploded.

The sound of her phone ringing made her jump. Six flashed up on her phone. Literally. A photo of him sitting on her sofa appeared on the screen.

"Did you mess with my phone?" she asked.

"Hey, Louisa. I'm good, thanks for asking. How are you?" Six asked, his easy drawl laced with humor.

Fine. She didn't need to be quite so curt. "I'm good. What's up?"

"I'm coming around later," he said. "Will you be home?"

He was what? "Why?"

"Because that third shelf of yours in the kitchen looks like it's going to collapse. I'm adding a middle bracket to all the shelves so they'll bear more weight. So are you in? It might be late. Like nine-ish."

She ran a hand through her hair, suddenly feeling bulldozed, and studied the shelves. He was correct. They *were* bowing in the middle. How come she'd never noticed it before? And was the answer really a man she barely knew coming to her house for some DIY? "Um . . ."

"If you don't mind waiting, I could pick up takeout, or order pizza or something."

Just the thought of him joining her for another evening felt . . . everything.

"Shelves and pizza," he said, without giving her time to respond. "Not a big deal, Lou. Don't overthink it." Why did he have to sound so thoroughly . . . breezy . . . about it? Probably because he did this kind of thing all the time.

"Fine. Thank you," she added quickly.

"No worries, Lou. See you later."

She hung up the phone as she attempted to process what the hell just happened. In the relatively short space of a week, she'd lost a sample and gained a male friend. A male friend who happened to be built like one of those Calvin Klein models she'd seen on billboards.

With the thought of Six posing reclined in his underwear, she needed cooling off. She slipped into her swimsuit, grabbed a towel from the closet, and headed out of the sliding door in the kitchen toward the pool.

Several hours later, Louisa deadheaded the fresh herbs she grew on the large kitchen windowsill. Not that they really needed pruning, but it gave her something to do with the nervous energy buzzing through her. All of her crockery and glasses were stacked on the counters, leaving the wooden shelves empty. She'd wiped the nonexistent dust from them and had begun the process of running some of the dishes she rarely used through the dishwasher.

The closer she got to Six's arrival, the more she felt like calling to cancel. The shelves were fine. Heck, she could even head over to her mom's and borrow the tools that belonged to her father that her mother hadn't been able to get rid of after his death. There had to be time in her schedule to attempt some handiwork herself, in between her research and bed each day.

She heard a bang outside and leaned toward the window to see if Six had parked in her driveway, but nobody was there. Probably one of the neighbors closing a car door or taking out the trash. The scent of mint filled the air as she finished pruning and dropped the scissors into the sink.

The same noise came again, quieter this time but accompanied by the sound of glass clinking against glass. The sound was coming from inside her house.

She wanted it to be Six. Wanted him to be playing some stupid prank that she could be mad about later. Part of her thought about calling out to him to be sure. But she knew it wasn't.

She heard glass hitting glass again. Somebody must have slid her dining room window open, because the sound of glass tinkling was coming from her collection of antique insulators that sat on shelves beneath the window. Louisa's heart raced as she thought through her options. Her phone was still charging in the office, and running upstairs away from exit doors didn't feel like the smartest thing to do. She could escape through the patio doors in the kitchen and scream in the hope someone would hear, realize it was her, and then run to help her. Given that the key to the lock on the rear gate was hanging on a hook in the hallway, the odds of it being a successful strategy were low. Or she could creep toward the front door. It would require walking past the archway to the dining room, but she could grab her car keys and run to her car. That felt like the best option.

Gingerly, she picked up the rolling pin she kept on the counter and the large carving knife from the knife block and crept toward the entrance.

It was a little after nine o'clock when Six pulled slowly onto Louisa's street. The truck could be noisy, and the last thing he wanted to do was aggravate or wake the neighborhood. Six yawned. He'd spent the last few hours with Cabe in communication with Mac to go over all of the final details for the extraction of the little girl in the custody case. They'd located her and had spent several days trailing the family to establish a pattern of life from which they could deduce the best time to grab her. The location for the pickup had been decided. It would take place early Sunday morning from the girl's grandmother's home, before she was returned to her father's home. It would take them approximately eleven minutes to get from the collection point to the helicopter and the beginning of her return to US soil. Hopefully they'd be in the air before the police had made it to the scene. Thanks to a former SEAL with the right connections, they'd be landing at a private airport about twenty miles outside of San Diego. Cabe was to collect the mother once the plane was wheels up out of Mexico.

The details were still buzzing around in his head. It felt odd being purely on the logistics end of an op when his heart belonged in the action of it. It was even harder when his mind kept drifting to Louisa. Lack of focus had *never* been his problem. In fact, his clarity had been one of his enduring traits. But despite the significance of this first op, he was worried. For some reason, he could sense how much it had cost her to come ask him for help, and the way she'd accepted what Cabe had said and had disappeared so quickly made it clear that she hadn't expected them to help her anyway. Now, after spending time with her midweek, he was more committed than ever to keeping tabs on her. He was certain that some people would find her abrupt, standoffish even, but he could see the person beneath all that, and he had a sneaking suspicion she didn't have anybody to lean on. He wanted to check on her again, and the shelves were a good excuse.

Plenty of women showed interest in him, and a solid amount of them followed through, either by slipping him their numbers or simply launching a full-on assault. He liked both approaches equally, almost as much as he'd liked the feel on Louisa's eyes on him, but on Wednesday she'd never moved from her end of the sofa, not even when he'd started messing around when she'd reached for popcorn. What would she have done if he'd reached for her hand and kept hold of it? Six shook his head. Why was he even thinking about this? This was nothing more than offering a friendly hand to someone who'd offered him the same courtesy when he'd freaked out on his run.

A black van was parked across the street from Louisa's. The sliding side door was open and the engine was running, but strangely the lights were off. By the illumination of his own headlights, he could see the driver looking nervously toward Louisa's driveway, straining from left to right as if to try to get a better line of sight.

He'd always believed that the best SEALs had the ability to slow time, could somehow absorb thousands of details in a split second, process them, and make a decision in the time it took normal people to blink. The driver of the van spotted him, sat up tall, and reached his hand toward something on the seat next to him.

Six drove past, deliberately missing the entrance to Louisa's curved driveway. While the rational part of his mind told him he was probably blowing this out of all proportion, something about the van and its driver had tripped his senses. After all, if only half of what Louisa had told him was true, the missing sample was dangerous.

Perhaps things had escalated since their earlier conversation, and he wondered whether Lou would have called him if they had. If that van really was a getaway vehicle of some kind, then there were people in Louisa's house, possibly armed. The last thing he wanted to do was make them jumpier. With absolute normalcy, so as not to draw attention to himself, he drove around the corner and parked the truck. He tugged his white T-shirt off over his head and fished around in his gym bag for his black hoodie. Quickly he tugged it over his head and put the hood up to hide his blond hair. Under San Diego's restrictive gun laws, he shouldn't be able to carry the weapon currently tucked in the glove compartment, but there hadn't been a rule yet that he hadn't been able to find his way around. For that he was grateful.

As silently as possible, he jumped out of the truck and snicked the door shut. He didn't bother with the alarm because the beep was loud. Six crept in the shadows toward the house and didn't even think about holstering his weapon. There was nobody out on the street except the idling van driver he wanted to avoid, so he slipped into the neighbor's driveway and assessed a place to cut through. A border garden separated the two properties. Six looked up to the side of the neighbor's house and saw wall-mounted lights with sensors pointed to pertinent spots like access to the rear gate and the main driveway. He didn't want them to come on. Staying low and tight against the shrubs, he headed for a break between the rows of plants, but stopped short of setting foot on Louisa's driveway. The window at the side of the house was open.

The van he'd seen wasn't big, so there couldn't be too many targets inside, but his primary concern was getting to Louisa. He took a quick picture of the van with his phone and then calmly hurried over to her house and pressed himself up against the wall next to the window. If this was a delivery of shoes or flowers or something, he was going to feel like the biggest idiot on the planet, but something in his gut told him this was all wrong. He'd rather scare the shit out of Louisa by expecting the worst than get them both killed by blindly expecting the best.

One thing he'd always been told was that taking a sneak peek was a surefire way to get killed. Nine times out of ten there was somebody waiting with a gun pointing in your direction. But in this instance, it was dark and they'd obviously been careful to not be seen, so they certainly weren't expecting him to creep up behind them like the bogeyman.

Six dropped to his knees below the windowsill and slowly raised his head to peer into the darkened room.

To the right, he could hear the television playing as it had the previous night. If Louisa was in there, she was a sitting duck. He heard a scream, but it came from the opposite direction, from the kitchen. He pulled himself through the window and rolled across the floor, coming to a stop in a crouched position, one knee on the floor, gun in both hands pointed straight ahead. Quickly getting to his feet, Six pressed his back against the wall and blocked Louisa's screams out. It would be dangerous for both of them if he gave in to panic. Instead, he slipped around the wall that led in the direction of Louisa's cries. The solid door to the kitchen stood between him and Louisa. The best of his training kicked in as it always did, and he dropped low before pushing the door open and rolling inside. When doors opened, people automatically expected somebody to walk through them, so gunmen would always fire high rather than low.

As bullets flew over his head, he caught sight of Louisa trapped behind a table. The two intruders had obviously been about to capture her between them, but the smart girl had armed herself and was going to make it difficult for them.

"What the . . . ?" one of the men cried out. "I thought you said she was alone."

Six dropped behind the kitchen island. He didn't want to shoot because they were too close to Louisa and he didn't have a clear shot, so he crawled to the other side in the hope that he could reassure her in some way to stay calm. Shots ricocheted off the cupboards behind him. "The police are on their way," Six shouted. "You've got maybe three minutes to get the fuck out of here."

One of the men moved in his direction and raised

his gun. Six capitalized on the rookie error and fired low, catching the intruder closest to him in the calf. Out of the corner of his eye, he saw Louisa drop and crawl under the table. Smart girl. Taking cover was the best thing she could do with bullets flying around. The other guy ran for the open door.

The wounded assailant screamed out in agony and shouted something in a language Six didn't understand but that sounded Eastern European. Like his partner, he ran for the door, leaving a bloody trail behind him.

"You okay, Lou?" he called out as he jumped to his feet.

"I'm fine," she shouted as he ran out of the door after them.

Protecting Louisa—getting the thugs away from her and keeping them away—was his first priority. He ran out onto the street where the van was already making its exit. The guy he'd shot was being dragged in through the open side door as the van turned the corner.

Six ran back into the house, locked the front door, hurried to what he now knew was the dining room, and closed the window. When he returned to the kitchen, he found Louisa on the phone speaking to emergency services. He pushed down his hood and walked over to her to place his hand on her back.

"No, I think they're gone," she said to the 911 operator, her voice wavering. "Right?" she asked, looking at him.

Six nodded. "In a black van," he said, and wrote the license plate down on a notepad on the counter.

Louisa relayed the information to the operator. "Yes, that's right." There was a pause. "Okay, thank you," she said, and hung up the phone. She let out a gasp and sagged against the island.

"Holy shit," she gasped. "Holy shit." Her breath came quickly and unevenly. "There were men in my house. My *home*."

"Louisa, look at me," he said, concerned about shock. Home intrusion was often doubly violating because being attacked in the place that was supposed to be the person's safest haven made them feel incredibly vulnerable. She raised her head. Her cheeks were a bit flushed and her skin a little paler than normal, but beneath it all was the spark of anger.

"Now do you believe me?" she asked.

"You think I didn't believe you that something was going on?" Six asked incredulously.

In truth, Louisa wasn't sure what to think. Her head was spinning, seemingly filled with both useful and useless information about what had happened. Kind of like all the extra material in genomes that accumulated over time even though it didn't serve any biological purpose. Two weeks ago, she'd stood in this very kitchen and had eaten breakfast while worrying over a missing sample and planning to tell the head of the lab about her concerns. Now two men had broken into her home, and Six had undoubtedly saved her life. Oh, and there was blood on her kitchen tiles, which she compulsively needed to clean up yet intelligently knew she needed to leave until the police had come and gone. She threaded her shaking hands into her hair and looked around the kitchen that she'd loved, knowing it would never feel the same to her again.

"I don't know." She shrugged. "It did seem like I was overreacting, I guess. But it all adds up to the same, thing," she said. "Anyway, it doesn't matter. The police are on their way, so you should go. I'll be fine. I'm very relieved you swung by when you did." Her voice cracked on the last words, and any attempt to appear brave disappeared faster than the lab sample had. Tears that rarely fell stung the corners of her eyes, and before she could utter the words to excuse herself momentarily so she could cry in the privacy of the washroom, Six had pulled her into his strong arms and wrapped them tightly around her. They felt safe, comforting even, and she pressed her cheek against his hoodie and closed her eyes. While she might know the biological reason why adrenaline was pumping through her veins right now, it didn't make it any more bearable. Her entire body shook with uncontrollable force.

"It's not fine," he said, rubbing her back gently. "It's not okay that somebody broke into your home. And don't attempt to dismiss me again, missy," he teased. "Because while I have a decade's experience of taking orders for my job, I don't take kindly to them in my personal life. Also, if you were thinking straight, you would have realized that the police will probably want to speak to the guy who put a bullet in the leg of one of your assailants."

They stood silently for a moment as Louisa focused on breathing deeply. She gripped Six's waist tightly. She supposed it should be awkward, but it wasn't. It was comforting. She could feel the strength of him, and she knew he wouldn't let anything happen to her.

Louisa tilted her head back to look at him. "Do I want

to know why you have a gun when San Diego pretty much prohibits concealed carry?"

Thankfully he didn't let go of her. In fact, he pulled her closer and leaned back against the kitchen island, placing his legs on either side of hers. "Well, you can thank Sheriff Pike in Alabama for that."

His proximity was confusing her. Her body was still on high alert as her hand shook and her body tried to figure out what to do with the chemical instruction to flee. But then another part of her was highly aware of the way they lined up against each other. And how the fact that he'd slouched a little meant they'd lined up in a way that was too intimate. She needed to focus on their conversation and not the way his inner thigh felt so warm against the side of her leg.

"What does Sheriff Pike have to do with it?"

"Ever heard of the Law Enforcement Officers Safety Act?" Six asked, and Louisa shook her head. "It's a federal law that's over a decade old that allows law enforcement people to carry concealed firearms in any jurisdiction in the United States. So I got Sheriff Pike to deputize me—even got the gold star to prove it. And now I carry a gun."

"That sounds like a technicality to me."

Six smiled. "It kind of is. Now that you've got a little more color in your face, and you've stopped shaking, you want to tell me who those men were, or what they wanted?"

Louisa smoothed her hands down the front of his chest to fix his rumpled hoodie and then straightened the hem. Six grabbed her hands in his and stilled them. His hands were the size of baseball mitts compared to hers.

"I don't know for sure. They beat you in here by a minute or two at most. They told me that they wanted me to go with them, and that was about it. I don't want to think this has something to do with the missing sample."

Thoughts crowded in almost too quickly to process them all. Things like this didn't happen to her. It went against the rules. *Her* rules that said she would spend her life doing research away from all the horrid stuff that went on in the world. And shit like this certainly didn't happen in Mission Hills. She wondered if it was smart to keep the fact that she'd swapped the two samples and disposed of the one they seemed to be after five days earlier from the police when they finally arrived. But this was a golden opportunity to find out where the police were with the theft in the lab. Obviously Six had saved her life, but she didn't want him to get into trouble for shooting one of the men. She wasn't even sure how that would work. It wasn't like he was defending his home. He was defending hers with a gun he'd brought with him which she wasn't sure was even legal. *Crap.*

"It's all such a mess," she whispered against Six's shoulder.

"I know. But I'm right here with you," he said softly.

Her heart pounded again and her head felt groggy, like mud, as though she was hungover. What she really needed was some silence. She tried to pull away from Six, but he wouldn't let her move. "Let me go," she said, blowing her bangs out of her face.

Six shook his head slowly. "I don't know what's going on, but you'll walk the police through it step by step, and I'll tell them what I know. Then we'll figure out how to make you safe tonight. Then in the morning, I'll help you figure out what you can do to remain safe while this gets sorted out."

What if they came back? Oh, God. She hadn't thought that far ahead. She could go to her mother's home, but that might lead the people that were after her to her family. *Damn.* Why had she already decided it was about the sample when it could have been an abduction attempt or an armed robbery, which didn't make her feel less vulnerable but did quash all the conspiracy theories in her head? What if she was excluding options that were important? She was the daughter of a very wealthy widow. Ransom could be a possibility.

Six squeezed her shaking hands, bringing her back to the present. "And just so you know, staying safe means learning to protect yourself, sweetheart."

"I did just fine," Louisa huffed, unwilling to take on the mantle of victim she was constructing in her head.

"You held a rolling pin," Six said, shaking his head at her. "What were you going to do, Betty Crocker them to death?"

She pushed her hands against his chest, and this time he let her go. It had never occurred to her that someone would violate her home, but Six was right. If she looked at it logically, she obviously needed to upgrade every element of her home security. She couldn't even remember when she'd last opened the window in the dining room, but she'd obviously become lax in locking it afterward. And none of her external security lights had come on, which meant they either weren't effective or the sensors were pointing at the wrong places. And her alarm had the ability to be on for just the doors and windows when she was home but awake, yet she never—

"What's going on inside that head of yours?" Six asked. "Because you disappear inside it sometimes and I worry when I see you start messing with things."

Louisa looked down at her hands and realized she was restacking the coasters she had placed on the marble. "I was just thinking through what you said. I guess I've become a little lazy . . . I've stopped worrying about home security because nothing ever really happens here."

"Okay, we'll look at two things. One, how you protect your home, and two, how you protect *yourself* in the event that someone makes it past all of your other defenses." He parted her bangs with his finger, and it made her shiver.

Since her father's death, she hadn't had anyone to count on. Not like this. "Why are you really here, Six? It's not about my uneven shelves, is it?" she asked quietly.

Six studied her face, taking in her forehead, her cheeks, and even her neck before meeting her eyes. It was a moment that felt much longer, filled with . . . something. Potential, maybe. "Because you asked me to help, and—"

He stopped talking at the sound of wheels pulling onto the gravel. Quickly, he shut off the kitchen light, and it became apparent that the exterior lights were on. With a swift jog, gun drawn, he hurried to take a look out the window. Blue and red beams of light flashed onto her kitchen wall. They were the best thing she'd seen all day, well, other than seeing the door to the kitchen burst open and Six rolling in, looking as deadly as any soldier she'd ever seen. In hindsight, now that the danger had passed, she realized he'd looked hotter than any Hollywood action star in a big blockbuster movie.

Even as she wondered what other reason he'd been about to give her for being there, she realized that none of his words, or the arrival of the police, meant she was safe.

"So, you said the lab sample was reported missing by you a week ago yesterday."

"Yes," Louisa said as the police officer made notes on his report. "I'm sure Vasilii Popov, the lab owner, has already filed a report, but I can't tell you when he did it."

"Let me just get the details for that," Officer Meeks said. "Dispatch, can I get a report for a theft at VPN Laboratories?" He added other details, such as the lab address. "Complainant is either a Vasilii Popov or Ivan Popov."

Six listened as the police officer repeated the information Lou had given him via his radio to the dispatcher to ask for details and report number. Six couldn't fault him for this thoroughness. Plus, he'd noticed that Lou was immediately ill at ease with strangers in her house, and the tenured cop had been observant enough to act accordingly.

For Lou's part, she was holding herself together remarkably well, but once the adrenaline began to clear her system, he wasn't sure how she would react. One thing he was certain of was that she wouldn't be alone.

"I don't want Six to get into any trouble," she said.

In everything that was going on, she was still thinking about him.

Officer Meeks's partner poked his head around the

door of the living room. "Forensics are here. I set them up in the kitchen. And I also called Sherriff Pike in Alabama. He corroborates Mr. Rapp's story."

When the police had arrived, Six had exited the building with his hands in the air, identified himself, and informed the police officers of the location of his weapon. In return, they'd been mildly angry about his interference and had lectured him extensively about not treating US soil as a militarized zone, as if they even knew what that meant. But he'd do it again in a heartbeat if Louisa's life was in danger.

Officer Meeks looked at Louisa. "Mr. Rapp won't be facing any charges from us. He is allowed to concealed carry." He turned and looked pointedly at Six. "We just hope next time he takes a second to call us before things go down rather than after."

Six reclined on the sofa and placed his hand on Louisa's back, rubbing it up and down until she sat up straighter. Hopefully the forensic team would work fast, because while blood and empty shell casings on the floor meant nothing to him, they meant everything to Lou. The longer they'd stayed in the kitchen while waiting for the police to arrive, the more Louisa had stared at the blood trail. It had taken every ounce of persuasion to get her to step away from the crime scene and up to her living room. Seeing little yellow plastic triangles with numbers on them covering the tile in the kitchen certainly wasn't going to help. The shock would catch up with her eventually, no matter how hard she fought it. And he wanted the police out of her house as quickly as possible because he could pull a plan together way better than they could.

"G213, that is a negative to reports of break-in at VNP Laboratory," a voice crackled over the radio. "I also ran checks against the names Vasilii Popov and Ivan Popov and returned nothing."

Louisa turned to face him. "Vasilii never reported it. I knew he wanted to save his reputation, but the sample is too dangerous to be ignored."

Everything about this had him on edge. And somehow he needed to figure out how to best help her. This was just getting more and more out of hand. Six gripped her hands tightly between his. They were chilled, and he was starting to worry about shock setting in. "We'll work through this with Officer Meeks, and then I'm going to stay here tonight. We'll figure this out."

Louisa slumped forward in her seat and placed her head in her hands. "I knew this would happen."

"I'm sorry, ma'am," Officer Meeks said. "We can't find any report of that incident, so why don't you tell me what you know, starting from the top?"

Three hours later, they were all gone, leaving behind a buffet of fingerprint powder around the windows, and lines around the blood on the kitchen floor. Job one was to get Louisa into bed. He saw the police officers out of the house and returned to find her slumped on the chair arm, fast asleep. Her bangs had fallen off to the side, and he could see her long eyelashes resting on her cheeks. She reminded him of the riptide he'd been caught in when he was fifteen. The water had been a little energetic, but the waves had looked amazing. Great swell, a little choppy, but he'd been feeling confident. His third ride of the day had gone a little off course, landing him right in the middle of the rip. He'd lain flat out on his board and tried to paddle in, but the tide kept whipping him out. He imagined that that was what every day felt like for her, an exhausting struggle against a tide that was always pulling her in the opposite direction, and he wanted to help her, keep people away from her.

He carefully slid one arm around her back and his other under her legs and lifted her into the air. She turned her head into his shoulder and wrapped her arms around his neck. "Did everybody leave?" she mumbled.

"Yeah, sweetheart. They did. What's your alarm code?"

"The Fibonacci sequence," she said through a giant yawn. ". . . 0-1-1-2-3-5-8-13."

As gently as he could, he took the stairs up to her room and quickly decided which bedroom was likeliest to be hers based on which looked most lived in. He laid her down on the bed, and even though she'd pretend to hate him for it in the morning, he slipped her bra off without removing her tank to protect her modesty. It was as important to him as it would be to her that he could look her in the eye and say he hadn't seen anything she'd be embarrassed about. As much as he wanted to be a gentleman, he couldn't resist checking her out a little though. He'd forgotten the charm of natural breasts. His type could usually give Barbie a run for her money in the plastic and silicon stakes. But Louisa's were perfect.

He slipped the band out of Louisa's hair so she wouldn't have a headache when she woke and tugged the comforter from the other side of the bed over her so she wouldn't get chilled. When he was certain that she was comfortable and sleeping peacefully, he jogged back downstairs and checked every door and window. He found a set of house keys in the hallway and tested them in the front door before he quietly let himself out and ran to his truck, which was thankfully still where he'd left it. With a roar that couldn't be avoided, he started the truck, turned it around, and then drove back down the street to pull it onto her driveway. It wouldn't stop a determined assailant, but it might give someone pause if they thought Louisa had company.

Thankfully his gym bag was always stocked with clothes, as staying in shape was a huge part of his life. At seventeen years old, he'd realized that having a six-pack and biceps ensured he'd spend the summer surrounded by girls in tiny bikinis. Through college, it had been about anything that would give him the fastest swim times. But it was when he'd decided to enlist that he'd gotten serious about complete functional strength. Now he trained every day and felt kind of grumpy if he didn't. He grabbed his bag, hopped out of the truck, locked it up, and let himself back into the house.

Once inside, he bolted the door and moved to set the alarm. What the hell was the *Fibonacci sequence* anyway? He pulled out his phone and looked it up. Typical. Some sort of mathematical formula that appeared a lot in nature. It was actually kind of interesting. While he had his phone in hand, he dropped Cabe a text. The guy was on the hook for pickup of the hostage retrieval, but he'd feel better if at least one more person outside of the police knew what had happened to Louisa.

With his bag over his shoulder, Six walked back up the stairs. It would be safer for them both if they slept in the same room, just for tonight, but as Louisa hadn't been awake long enough to ask if she'd be cool with his sleeping on the bed next to her, he decided to set up on the floor by the door. He stripped the bed in the spare room of its bedding and wandered back into Louisa's room. She was still lying exactly where he'd left her.

Once the door was locked, he made up his bed. Most people would hate the idea of sleeping on the floor, but Six could quite literally fall asleep anywhere. He'd fallen asleep standing up during Hell Week and on missions when he'd sometimes had no choice other than to catch an hour of sleep with his body on the cold, wet ground. So a spongy carpet, some ridiculously soft bedding, and a couple of thick pillows would be a massive improvement.

He stripped off his hoodie and put his T-shirt back on. While he was 99.9 percent certain that the men wouldn't be back tonight, he wasn't going to risk sleeping without his clothes or boots. Hand-to-hand combat performed while naked was always a miserable experience.

Six turned off all the lights and looked over to the bed where he could see the comforter rise and fall with Louisa's breath. There was so much she was going to have to deal with, and he prayed she'd get a good night's sleep.

"Good night, Lou," he said softly, and closed his eyes.

CHAPTER SIX

Why had somebody turned the lights on? It was still the middle of the night, and Louisa had been sound asleep until the brightness on the other side of her eyelids had penetrated her slumber.

She rolled over and pulled the comforter over her head, reveling in the warmth and darkness. With a large yawn, she attempted to open her eyes, but the urge to stay asleep won the battle. Until she remembered that she lived alone, and that men had broken into her house the previous evening. She threw back the comforter and sat up straight. Her head spun at the sudden movement, and she struggled to open her eyes, finding the world to be a blurry mess.

As her heart pounded in her chest, she tried to make sense of what had happened. The men had broken in, but Six had saved her. If nothing else, she would find a way to thank him. Louisa shook her head one more time to clear the grogginess and looked around the bedroom. The curtains were wide open, letting in a blaze of sunlight. And a pile of neatly folded blankets sat on the floor next to the door, which was slightly ajar. Six must have stayed the night to look after her. The thought sent an excited shiver through her and cut through her panic. He'd protected her. Her own personal hero. It was all kinds of wrong to think of him that way because—she stopped the thought. Maybe his gentle touches were a little more than friendly, but he was a flirtatious kind of guy, and it struck her that he was simply a friend who had decided to help her out.

She tilted her head to see if she could hear any sounds of him still in the house. Quietly, she got out of bed and wandered to the landing. It sounded like water was running in the guest bathroom, and she wondered what excuse she could concoct to accidentally walk in there. The thought of Six, naked, likely covered in suds, forced her thoughts from fear to arousal.

Uncertain what to do with the mash-up of feelings coursing through her, she hurried into her own bathroom. She didn't know whether to be offended or relieved to find out that she hadn't slept in her bra. The idea that Six might have seen her breasts was as exciting as it was horrifying. Louisa placed her dirty clothes in the laundry basket and quickly ran through her own morning routine.

Once she'd showered and dried her hair, she threw on a little mascara and gloss, unusual for her in her day-to-day life. It was a foolish gesture on her part, she knew it, but for some reason it seemed important to convey the fact that she was back in control and not likely to fall apart again like she had the previous evening. Today was about making plans. She wondered if she could hire somebody from Six's company, Eagle Securities, to go with her for the day. If last night's break-in and the sample were connected, she wouldn't feel particularly safe otherwise.

Details, details, details. She'd have to go through everything in her head and document as much as she could. The lab had very specific security guidelines. Laptops were company property, and had to be left at the lab, which made all of this even more strange. Though Louisa hadn't given anyone her passwords, she was certain that any half-brained IT person would be able to quickly access the files and information. She'd never been able to bring information home, or even email files to herself. Always one to abide by the rules, she had never once tried to circumnavigate them. So all of her research notes were now property of VNP Laboratories. She needed to spend the day getting down every single thing she could remember. Thankfully, she made personal notes every day when she got home, so she had plenty of reference material. The problem, though, was that her handwritten notes didn't prove to anybody that the sample actually existed.

Crap. And church. She'd promised her mom she'd take her to the afternoon service, and get her some groceries.

She opened the door to her closet and pulled out a turquoise dress, which she cinched with the brown leather belt. She found her favorite brown ankle boots at the bottom of her closet, so she put those on too. Of all the things she was ready to face, Six wasn't one of them. Science in general had laws, equations that always added up. It was neat and orderly and could always be explained. But biology was a world unto itself. Sure, the anatomy of it all was well understood, but the heart of it, not the physical beating organ but the parts that allowed a human to dream, to experience complex emotions, and to cry at the stupid videos that went viral every second day were still a mystery. If they were fully understood, there would be no use for apps like Tinder. You'd just be able to load in your biological profile to meet somebody who would feel the same way about you as you did him or her, and the rest would be guaranteed. She had no biological explanation for her feelings about Six, but she knew she owed him a thank-you and couldn't hide away in her bedroom for the rest of the day.

Louisa cautiously stepped downstairs and braced herself by the kitchen door. There would be cleaning up to do, but for now, for her own mental health, she needed to ignore the bloodstain that she knew covered the tiles on the other side. She pushed the door open and was greeted by the smell of coffee and bacon. And as much as she loved both, neither were a match for the arresting sight of Six wearing nothing but a pair of shorts which rode low on his hips as he cooked. *Holy shoulders.* Learning the major muscle groups was biology 101, but she had no idea that the latissimus dorsi and rhomboid major could look so freaking—

"You okay there, Lou?" he asked without turning around.

There was humor in his voice, and she knew immediately that he'd caught her staring—though she wasn't sure how.

"Your footsteps stopped as you walked through the door," he answered, reading her thoughts. "I didn't hear the door swing closed, which means you're still holding it, and to top it off," he said, turning to look at her, "I could see your reflection in the window. Good morning, Louisa."

She immediately let go of the door, letting it swing shut behind her, and looked away, desperate to find something that could take her attention from him and the sexy-as-all-hell tattoo that crept up his back and over his shoulder.

Her eyes went straight to the shelves, which now hung straight.

"Hope I put everything back okay," Six said, waving his hand in the direction of the crockery and glasses that were randomly placed on them. She could fix them later.

"I appreciate that. Thank you," she mumbled as she headed over to the coffeepot, still embarrassed at being caught staring. "Can I fix you a cup?"

As she reached for it, a hand slid over the top of hers. He'd silently beaten her to it. "I was just teasing you, Lou. How did you sleep?" he asked, moving her hand. He pulled a mug out of the cupboard and poured it full of steaming-hot coffee. As he handed it to her, he did that thing, the one where he pushed her bangs from her face, but she couldn't bring herself to slap his hand away. Instead, she braced herself and looked up at him.

Louisa forced her shoulders to relax. "Better than I thought I was going to. Did you sleep on the floor?"

Spitting and hissing from the pan made her jump, and Six hurried back to the pan to scoop the bacon out and place it on paper towels to drain the fat.

"That's quite literally the second time you saved my

bacon," Louisa said, and sipped on her coffee to help fight back the grin.

Six laughed as he put the spatula down. "Did you just crack a joke, Louisa North? Because that felt a lot like a pun." He began to assemble what looked like BLTs.

"It's been known to happen," she said, grabbing the orange juice from the fridge. She collected two glasses from the open shelves and placed everything by the stools on the opposite side of the island.

Her mouth watered at the smell of breakfast. Bacon was the one reason she couldn't call herself vegan. She'd attempted to give up animal protein for health reasons, but the longer she'd deprived herself of bacon, the more she'd thought about eating it, until she'd conceded that a once-a-week treat was really not the end of the world. Six slid a plate in front of her, and they both sat down on the stools. Louisa bit into the sandwich and groaned. He'd used way more mayo substitute than she would have, but that was probably why it tasted so damn good.

"Thank you," she mumbled through a mouthful of food.

Politely, Six waited until he finished chewing. "You're welcome. Hope you don't mind me using your food. And to answer your question, yes, I did sleep on the floor, but it was no big deal. I've slept in places a lot worse."

Louisa managed to swallow. "You didn't need to do that. You could have slept in one of the spare bedrooms."

"Made it easier for me to keep you safe, having both of us in the same place. But you do need to think about what happens next. What are you going to do today?"

His question drew her eyes to the floor, but the blood

was gone, and as she looked around she realized that all the other signs of the break-in were gone too. "Did you clean up?" she asked.

Six looked at his plate and took another bite of food. He shrugged as he chewed, as if what he'd done was no big deal. "Had some of my guys drive some supplies over this morning. There are some things you should never had to deal with in life, and a huge pile of somebody else's blood, especially the blood of your enemy, is one of them."

Louisa placed her hand on his arm. It was soft and warm and covered in soft blond hair. "Thank you for everything you've done for me," she said.

When his eyes met hers, she felt a little kick in her stomach. "Anytime, Louisa."

There were few things that made Six crave the isolation of being perched on a hilltop with his rifle in a Middle Eastern country, but Home Depot on a Sunday was one of them.

Louisa had headed off to her mom's to take her to church. While she was showering, he'd inspected her car and his truck for any kind of tracking device, not that he'd told her. She'd clearly been shaken enough by the break-in, and the last thing he wanted to do was make her feel unsafe in her car as well as her home.

She'd looked pretty as a picture in that turquoise dress, and he'd wanted to tell her as he'd watched her get into her car, but the words had stuck in his throat. If he'd said them, she might have gotten ideas, and if she'd gotten ideas, then he would likely have gotten on board with them. Instead, he'd followed her to the highway, ensuring she had no tail, where she went north to Torrey Pines, and he'd hit Eagle Securities to provide backup to the extraction of the kid in Mexico. Once the plane was wheels up and on its way back to the US, he breathed a huge sigh of relief. Their first major job was over and it had been a success.

Yet his mind was still on Lou. He pulled another pack of window locks off the shelf. These were a whole heap more effective than the ones she currently had installed, and by all accounts never even used. There were a million other ways he'd rather spend his Sunday than trying to find products in narrow aisles with about ten thousand of his closest friends, but he'd felt unable to just leave her to her own devices. He'd needed to know she was secure. That her damn windows were locked. That she installed CCTV. So here he was, alone, in a hardware store.

Fuck.

A loud clattering noise, like semiautomatic gunfire, sounded to his left, and his heartbeat elevated at a dangerous rate. He forced himself to grip the metal shelf and look in the direction of the noise. A kid, messing around with a shelf full of fixtures and fittings, was being told off by his embarrassed father as loose plumbing supplies fell to the floor, the sound of metal hitting concrete resonating down the aisle. Six forced himself to breathe in through his nose and out through his mouth. *I'm fine.* He repeated it over and over. *I'm fine.*

If he said it enough, he might believe it. And unlike the plumbing parts, he'd not hit the floor, which was a good sign. Wasn't it?

His phone rang, and he grabbed it from his pocket.

The sight of Lou's face on his screen shouldn't be this reassuring, should it? "What's up, Lou?" he said, throwing six packets of the locks into his basket.

"This is going to sound really weird," she said, her voice shaken. "But you didn't ask one of your guys to stay near me today, did you?"

"Where are you?" he asked. He dropped the shopping basket to the floor and hurried out of the exit. Window locks were not going to be the answer to her prayers.

"I'm heading back from my mom's, but I saw this car outside the parking lot at church, and then it was behind me when . . . when I pulled into the grocery store. I think it's behind me now, about two cars back on the highway."

The highway. *Damn.* It would be impossible to get to her easily. He'd have to head north then turn around, attempt to come up behind her.

"Are you close to the Home Depot exit? Can you drive straight to me, Lou?"

"I'm a few minutes away." Relief washed through him. That made life easier.

"Okay, you're doing great. You don't need to do anything crazy, Lou. Just keep it steady but don't stop. Jump a red light if you need to. I'm gonna put the truck in the back left corner of the lot where there is a little more room. Just drive straight over to me."

"Do you think it's whoever tried to get me yesterday?" she asked, and he could hear the tears in her voice.

Six jumped into his truck and started the engine so he could move into position. "No idea, Lou. But just keep coming to me. Describe the car to me. What does it look like?" Once parked again, he pulled his SIG from his holster and stepped around the rear of the truck.

"It's silver, some kind of sedan. There were two men in it. It had a silver logo . . . Honda . . . Toyota . . . I don't know, on the front, but I don't know what make it was. I just pulled off the highway. Oh my God. It followed me, Six. They're only one car behind me." Her voice told him everything he needed to know. She was doing her best to stay calm, but it was an almost impossible task.

"Less than three minutes until you get to the store," he said, roughly. "I'm waiting for you. I'm behind the truck. Just stay focused." He witnessed the moment her Audi came into view. The silver car drove by the exit, but he had a feeling it wouldn't go far. "Rear left, Lou. You're headed toward me, drive straight in next to the truck then wait for me to come get you out."

She did as he asked, and he got a flash of her pale features and red eyes as she slid in alongside him.

He ran to her side of the car. There was no telling how long she had lost the silver car for. They were probably parked up by the exit, ready to pick her up again. Six yanked the door open, and she collapsed into his arms. Her body shook violently.

To keep her safe, he did the only thing he could think of—whisked her into his arms, spun her against the truck, protecting her with his own body, and pressed his lips to her neck. To get to her, they'd have to get through him, but it also had two other benefits. First, it would help snap her back into the moment, and second, there was the slightest chance it would hide her from those trying to find her. "You're safe, Lou, for now. But I need you to hold it together for just a little while longer."

She gasped in surprise, and he ran his hands up her ribs for effect. He knew the move distracted her. *Damn.* It was close to distracting him. Louisa froze as he tried to ignore the way she felt pressed up against him and focused on the task at hand. "Relax. Wrap your arms around me, sweetheart. I'm going to lift you into the truck. Okay?"

"Okay?" she whispered, her voice unsteady.

Six did as he'd promised and moved slightly, lessening his weight against her body but still using himself as a shield. It was unclear to him whether the people chasing her wanted her alive or dead, but he wasn't going to take a risk that they could get a shot off and hit her. He reached across her and opened the passenger door. In a move reminiscent of something a playful lover would do, he lifted her up onto the seat. "Buckle up, and when I pull out onto the road, duck forward and keep your head down. If they've been following you all day, I've got to believe they'll follow us now. I can't guarantee they haven't seen you switch cars, so we need to act like they did. They were armed last night, so we have to assume they will be today."

"What will we do if they get us?" He skin was pale and her brown eyes wide as she did what he asked.

"They won't. Trust me."

He slammed her door shut, ran around to his door, and jumped into the truck. It didn't matter who was behind the wheels of that vehicle; he'd pitch his emergency driving skills against anybody. They'd gotten him clear of trouble more times than he could remember in Fallujah. He fastened his seat belt and placed his gun on the seat between him and Louisa.

"You don't happen to know how to use that, do you?" he asked as they pulled off the driveway.

"I signed the gun control registry."

"Of course you did," he said with a wink as he pulled a hand-brake turn out of the hardware store.

Louisa grabbed the handle above the door and clung on for dear life as they sped up to the junction and then braked hard. The car was on his tail. Part of him wondered for a millisecond whether he shouldn't take her back to the Eagle Securities compound, but traffic heading into the city was always worse this time of day, so heading away made sense.

"Please tell me you have a plan," Louisa said as he took a hard left to double back on themselves.

Six looked in the rearview mirror and spotted the car. It was gaining on them while he tried to avoid the other vehicles around them. "I always have a plan. I'm like Hannibal."

"Lecter?" she asked.

"No, from *The A-Team*," he said as he beat the lights at a major intersection, trapping the car behind them. "I love it when a plan comes together. We're about to lose the car." He double-checked behind them. "Shit," he growled as the car followed them straight through. It had been gaining on them all along. "Grab the gun, Lou. If the car comes alongside and starts shooting, lean back behind the seat belt pillar, but feel free to shoot back. Aim for the tires. It will be enough to get them off the road."

Plus, he didn't want her to have to deal with the reality of killing a man.

He sped onto the highway, moving quickly across the

lanes to get around trucks and slow drivers. The car followed his path. An exit was coming up, and he checked the lanes. The car was trapped with a vehicle alongside it, so Six swerved the truck straight across the lanes, across the gravelly shoulder, and up the exit ramp.

Louisa cried out next to him. "Oh, shit."

He reached his hand out to pat her leg in comfort.

"Hands on the wheel, Rapp," she said, shoving his hand away.

Six hollered as he checked the rearview. "*Now* they're gone," he said, keeping his foot on the pedal.

"I think I'm going to be sick," Louisa said.

"For real?" he asked. "Because I'm not sure we'll be cool if you puke in my truck." Louisa gave him some serious side-eye, and he couldn't help but grin. Civilians never really understood the need for lighthearted banter in the direst situations, but many a time it had kept him sane.

"Well, in my quest for life or death, I'll do my best to not soil your precious vehicle. Are you sure they're gone?" she asked, turning in her seat to look out of the rear window.

There was no way the car could have followed him off the exit. "Definitely."

"So where are you taking me?" Louisa asked as they passed another exit.

"My house."

Louisa couldn't remember the last time she had made the drive to Encinitas, but she'd forgotten how lush and green it could appear compared to her own neighborhood. Though the grasses were dead, they drove past shrubby hedgerows vibrantly decorated with red flowers.

She attempted to quell the panic rising inside her. They'd called Officer Meeks from the car, and Louisa had been stunned by all the small details Six was able to recall, from the vehicle's license plates to descriptions of the men who had been sitting inside. All she could remember was the way she'd been tossed from side to side as Six had taken the corners and turns at high speeds. Oh, and her desperation to avoid being shot. And the way Six had held her, his lips brushing her neck, before he'd lifted her into the truck. He hadn't touched her since which told her it had all been a decoy to get her into the truck safely, which she deeply appreciated and yet . . .

She'd tried to pay attention as Six explained to her why what had happened was a good thing. Something about CCTV and road traffic cameras increasing the chances of the police getting a hit on something. Louisa understood the logic, but she was still processing the sheer terror of realizing somebody really was out to get her and she didn't know why for sure, although she'd have to be an idiot to not conclude it had to do with the lab.

"Would you mind if we turned the air conditioning off and opened the windows a little?" she asked, flexing her fingers for a moment to try to get the blood flowing through them. They felt like icicles, and she tucked her hands between her thighs for some warmth.

"Sorry, Lou," Six said as they turned off the road they'd been on for a little while onto a quieter side street. "I should've realized you might have been cold sooner, but we're right here. You okay?"

She pulled the phone charger out of its socket and started to straighten the knotted cord. "I'd be lying if I said yes. For the second time in twenty-four hours, someone attempted to, what . . . ? Kill me?"

Six looked over at her and sighed. "It's cold comfort, sweetheart, but if they'd wanted you dead, they would have killed you last night. They had time before I got there, plus you said they told you they wanted you to go with them. Whatever they want with you, they want you alive to do it."

Her stomach roiled at the thought. "I'm not sure that makes me feel much better."

He grabbed for one of her hands and squeezed it. "Trust me. Being alive is the best fucking thing in the world. If you're alive, you can fight, you can think, you can even wait for someone to come get you," he said passionately. "You'll come back from anything they can put you through. But there is no coming back from dead. That's as final as it gets."

Louisa squeezed his hand tightly. Because there was so much feeling in the words, she was confident he spoke from experience.

"Do you mind if I make a call?" Louisa asked. "I'm gonna lose my nerve if I don't do this now."

"Sure," Six said, letting go of her hand, and she regretted it the moment his fingers slipped out of hers.

She picked up her phone and called Vasilii.

"Louisa. How are you?" he said in his usually pleasant tone. "What are you up to today?"

"Why didn't you call the police about the missing sample, Vasilii?"

There was a long, pregnant pause on the other end

of the phone line, and finally Vasilii coughed gently. "Louisa. You know how important the lab's reputation is. We're still trying to—"

"Do you want to know what happened to me last night? Two men tried to break into my house and abduct me. And this morning, I was trailed by two men around my mom's neighborhood and back home."

"Dear Lord, Louisa. Are you okay?" The concern in his voice sounded genuine, leaving her confused.

"For now. Yes. But I told the police about the break-in at the lab. They were the ones who told me they had no record of it. Vasilii, I honestly think you put my life at risk, and Ivan's."

Six reached his hand across the seat and rubbed her thigh, his big hands gripping her gently. She placed her hand over his and interlocked their fingers.

"Wait. You think these things are connected," Vasilii said. "That seems like an awfully big conclusion. You are the only child of the extremely wealthy Isaiah North. There could be other motives. What did the police say?"

Rather than tell him, she decided to hold back. Since she was uncertain as to whether she could trust him or not, it didn't make sense to tell him more. "They're probably going to want to ask you some questions. About what happened. See any evidence you have collected in this *internal search* of yours."

"Louisa, I don't like the insinuation—"

"I need some time off," Louisa said quickly. She really didn't want to argue. She wanted some food, and a bed. Safety would be nice. "There are some things I need to take care of, and I just don't feel like I can—"

"I understand, Louisa. Take as much time as you

need, then we'll talk. Are you safe? Do you have somewhere to stay?"

Six turned the car onto a side road and let go of her hand. He pulled a little past a driveway, then reversed into it, avoiding a white mailbox and two fence posts with a speed and accuracy that told her he'd done this a thousand times before.

"Yes, I do," she said. "Good-bye, Vasilii."

She ended the call and looked over at Six.

"Mi casa es tu casa," he said.

My house is your house.

It wasn't her home, but it was safe, and she was incredibly grateful. "Thank you for bringing me here," she said.

Louisa hopped down from the truck and got her first real look at the pretty yellow split-level house. It wasn't what she'd been expecting at all. For Six, she'd imagined something sleek and glossy. Lots of glass and chrome. However, the lushly landscaped gardens and pretty terra-cotta-tiled roof wouldn't have looked out of place on the front of a greeting card.

She grabbed her purse from the floor of the truck and closed the door.

"Let me give you a tour of the place," Six said as he stepped up behind her. He placed his hand on the small of her back, and she reminded herself of his behavior in the truck. Friendly, caring, but not . . . more. No matter how good it had felt to have his hand on her, they were just friends, and he was just being polite ushering her up the steps. Instead, she tried to focus on the basket-weave pattern of red bricks that led up to the front door. "It's a bit of a mess," Six said apologetically. "I had tenants in here for several years, and I only moved back in last week. So my shit is everywhere, which I already know you're going to hate."

It was funny how well he was coming to know her, and while the idea that he was living out of boxes made her itch like a cheap wool sweater, she'd bite her tongue and deal with it. "I'm sure it's going to be fine," she said. "I appreciate you bringing me somewhere safe so that I can make new arrangements."

Six opened the door, and she stepped into a narrow hallway which led straight into the living room, a large space with dark floors and white walls that was sparsely furnished. Packing boxes lined the wall next to the door, and a well-worn sofa spanned the opposite one. "Living room," he said, leading her past two red armchairs tucked into an alcove and through an archway that led into a small dining room furnished with a small wooden table and four black chairs. A second archway led through into a kitchen with ugly yellow pine cabinets and a serviceable white countertop. "I hated these counters when Gran had them installed, and I still hate them now. It's going to be one of the first things to go when I get the money together," he said. "Help yourself to whatever you can find in the fridge. We're going to need to go shopping this afternoon anyway."

Two things struck her almost simultaneously. One, they hadn't discussed payment for his security services, and while it didn't appear that he needed the money, he obviously had plans that would require it. And second, he'd said the word "we're." *We're going shopping.* Did he think she was staying?

They wandered down a hallway, and he pointed out

an office and bathroom. "This is my bedroom," he said as they entered a beautiful bedroom with large windows and patio doors that led out onto a courtyard-style terrace.

"I'd buy this house just for this room," she said, taking in the shoji screen wardrobes and the whitewashed ceilings with wooden beams.

Six grinned. "I felt the same way every time I came to stay as a kid. Plus, I needed a room that could take a California king bed, because if I never sleep in a bed where my feet hang over the end again, it will be too soon."

Louisa looked at the bed, which was, as he pointed out, enormous. Suddenly she was very aware that she was standing in the room where he probably slept naked, and his eyes were on her. She'd never given much thought to the notion of predator and prey until today. Earlier on, during the car chase, she'd clearly been the prey, and it had been scary as all shit. But now, standing in his bedroom, the air between them positively crackling, she felt like prey of a different kind.

Feeling bold, she looked up at him. Gone was his smile. He looked like a brooding hero from the cover of one of the romance books her mother so adored.

"So," she said, enunciating way more letter "o"s than there were in the word. "I should make some calls, I guess, so I can get out of your hair."

Six smiled again, the three little lines that had furrowed his brow gone as quickly as they'd arrived. "Not going to happen, Lou." He walked by her, took her hand, and led her to another bedroom across the hall. "I've decided you're not to be trusted alone, so you aren't going anywhere until we've gotten to the bottom of what's going on. This is your room. Bathroom through there." He tipped his chin in the direction of a white door along the far wall.

Not going anywhere. But she couldn't stay here. With him. Even if it felt like the safest place in the world when he stood there, his biceps stretching the sleeves of his goddamn T-shirt and the faint outline of the gun at his waist. "You want me to stay . . . here . . . with you?"

"Where are you going to go? If you think someone can look after you better than I can, you can always leave. You're not my hostage," he said, stepping back and raising his hands in the universal sign of surrender. "I just don't want you to think you have to leave. Let me help you."

If she thought he was letting her go after everything they had been through in the last twenty-four hours, she had another think coming. When he'd said he wouldn't hold her hostage, he only kind of meant it. If it meant nudging her backward onto the bed that was a foot behind her and keeping her there for a while to persuade her, then he'd do just that. Because being leaned up against her by the truck, being so close to her that he could smell tart green apples that made his mouth water, was almost more than he could handle.

And it wasn't just the fact that she smelled so damn good. She was brave as shit in the face of what must have been a terrifying ordeal for her. Admiration didn't even begin to describe the way he felt about her right now, and the more time he spent with her, the more he wanted to learn about her. His body, unused to being denied, was in full agreement and had been since he'd checked out those sweet breasts of hers the night before.

All thoughts of his plans, his rules for himself, were evaporating fast.

Plus, even *she* couldn't deny what had just passed between them in his bedroom. Somewhere along the line, she'd found her way under his skin, and he was beyond intrigued, though determined not to rush things. She had enough to deal with without him dirtying the water. What she needed now was for him to behave like the trained operative that he was and help her figure out what the hell was going on in her life. Which required a plan. And action that wasn't even remotely sexual in nature. The rest could come in time, and for now, he was resolved that the only action his dick was going to get would come from a bottle of baby oil and his hand in the shower.

"You want me to stay here?" she repeated, and wandered over to a painting on the wall, which she straightened.

"Yes. I do. The house might be a mess, but the one thing I've done since I got home is install security." A buddy of his had hooked him up with everything from door and window alarms to security lights to CCTV that not only captured what was going on around the perimeter of his home but was also angled toward the stop sign at the end of the road so that anybody coming in and out of the street would be captured. It was all fed live to his laptop and recorded. "I also have a gun safe, fingerprint controlled, that has everything I need to protect us. I sleep with my loaded SIG in the bedside table. You can sleep with one in yours if you want, but only after I've taught you to shoot the damn thing."

Six shut up and waited for her to finish straightening the pillow she was currently fixated on.

"I'm sorry for imposing on you like this," she said, and finally looked at him again.

How could it be that the world seemed to fall into place when she did? He walked over to her and placed his hands on her shoulders. "You aren't imposing, although you might well get sick of my house before I get sick of you." He pulled her in for a hug and kissed the top of her head gently, but even though she felt perfect in his arms, he stepped away quickly, keeping it brief and friendly.

"First thing we need to do is call Meeks back and tell him where we are and that you are safe. I'm sure we are going to need to go in and see him, or at least have him come here and make an official statement. We'll keep the police informed from here."

"So what happens now?" she asked, and flicked her bangs to one side. Damn. It only made it harder to keep his distance when he knew how much the small act cost her.

"First, roomie, we need to get set up to hunker down. Like go get groceries. And as cute as that dress is on you, you are going to need more than that to stay here for a few days. I'd loan you some shorts and T-shirts but they'd be way too big for you." A small part of him lamented that he wasn't going to get to see her in his T-shirt anytime soon, but he knew his chances of keeping his hands off her would diminish if he did.

"Is there somewhere around here I can get some things, like pajamas and some toiletries?"

He was seconds away from telling her that she didn't need anything to sleep in, but he bit his tongue before answering. "Yeah. It may not be the fancy labels you're used to, but we'll get you set up. Then we come home, sit down with a pen and a pad of paper and go through all of this piece by piece. See if we can't make some sense of what happened by ourselves and get the ball rolling on some intel."

"Is it safe for us to go outside?" Louisa asked him.

"It is, because it will take them a while to figure out where you went. The truck is registered to the company, so it won't lead them back here. And let's say they are highly connected individuals—even then there's no way they can trace us using CCTV or anything like that because I took routes I know don't have them. So at best Eagle Securities will be their starting point, assuming they can even get that far. Then they'll have to narrow down which of us has the car and then figure out a home address. That'll keep them busy for a while, so we should go get what we need now and hunker down. Then I'll contact my guys and will see what we can figure out."

Louisa stood silently for a moment and then nodded assertively. "Okay. Is there any reason we shouldn't call them now? I think I'd feel safer if more people knew what was happening, but the only person I have really is my mom, and I don't want to scare her. Wait. Shit. You don't think they'll use my mom to get to me, do you?"

The truth was that it had crossed his mind. "Okay, let's talk as we go because we only have so much time." Unable to resist, Six took Louisa's hand and led her out of the house, grabbing his backpack off the hook in the hallway as they went by. It was only a couple of minutes' walk down the hill to the grocery store, but the fresh air would do them both good. Then they'd get in the truck, and he'd take her over to The Forum mall in Carlsbad for clothes.

"To answer your other questions," he said as they crossed the train tracks, "two of my team members know what's going on. They are the guys who brought over the cleaning stuff this morning. Unfortunately, everybody else is tied up on the job today, reuniting a kid with her mom, otherwise I'd have them involved already. With regards to your mom, you might want to give her a call. What you tell her is entirely up to you. You know her better than I do. Being honest is the best policy, for what it's worth."

"My aunt could go get her, say it's better while her ankle is still in a cast."

"That could work. If you tell her to just take a trip, she'll think you're crazy given her ankle, but if you tell her there is something going on, she'll take more precautions and move faster."

Ever vigilant, Six led them through the small lot. A loud noise came from behind them, and he turned quickly, hand on gun, only to realize it was the sound of the dumpster being emptied into a garbage truck. His heart raced, but the response wasn't as jarring as it had been the evening he'd met Louisa. Why the hell did it happen some of the time and not all?

A hand on his arm made him jump. Louisa. Shit. "Sorry," he said, trying to laugh it off with a grin he really didn't feel. "Occupational hazard."

"You don't have to pretend with me," she said quietly. "I've been faking normal for as long as I can remember."

"I can keep you safe. You don't need to worry about that." Where the hell had that come from? *Because you're a jumpy mess, you idiot.* He really didn't want to seem incapable in front of her.

She tilted her head to one side and smiled as she placed her hands on his biceps. "I have no doubt about that," she said confidently.

"Good," he said, ignoring the way his voice sounded like he'd smoked a pack a day for a decade.

It should have made him feel like a king that she trusted him. Relied on him.

But it didn't.

Because for once, he didn't trust himself.

CHAPTER SEVEN

"So you don't know the exact quantities of all the ingredients, but you know what the ingredients are?" Six asked as they ate her butternut-squash-and-black-bean burritos.

He'd challenged her about eating bacon for breakfast because he'd been surprised to see it in her fridge, and she'd confessed to the one thing she couldn't give up which was why she always said she was pretty much vegetarian. So they'd shopped side by side with two different carts containing two different sets of groceries. Uncertain as to how many days she would be staying with Six, she'd bought a week's worth of food. She could always take it with her when she left if her carnivorous friend didn't want it. But somehow between getting the groceries, picking up clothing from the mall, and Louisa starting to make dinner, Six had been curious about what was on the menu. And when she'd offered to make enough for the two of them, he'd agreed.

Louisa put some salsa, spinach, and the filling made

of rice, peppers, black beans, squash, and seasonings into her wrap and rolled it up. "That's right. We have so many different samples on the go, so many different tests, and sometimes I would do part of the preparation and Ivan would do the other. I honestly don't remember all the ratios."

"To play devil's advocate, though, why would they need you if they have all of the lab notes?"

It was something Louisa had been considering while shopping. "The sample has been gone for two weeks now. My only thought is that somebody has tried to remake it outside the lab and it hasn't worked for whatever reason. If that's the case, they have two options: reengineer it backward from the sample they know worked or find the person who made it to see if she can re-create it."

Six suddenly pinned her with his stare. "Didn't you say they *have* the sample, though? The one that was stolen? That's what started all this. Right?"

Damn. He didn't know what she'd done, and she couldn't decide whether *that* was the reason her mouth felt dry, or whether it was the way his eyes seemed to see her. *Really* see her. "They don't have the sample," she said. It was time to come clean, at least to him, and she knew it. She just hoped he'd understand when she explained. "On Friday, the day I saw you at the gala, I'd had a strange feeling that somebody had been in the lab. I couldn't quite put my finger on why. It's like the energy was off or something, which I know probably makes no sense to you."

But to her surprise, Six nodded in agreement. "I totally get that. I rely on gut instinct more than any intel, especially if I only have a split second to make a decision. So what did you do?"

"It bothered me, and I knew that the most . . . significant . . . thing we had in the lab was the sample and that the results of the trials we'd run were reasonably well known. I had to leave to get to the presentation, so I did the only thing I could think of. There was another thing I was working on, totally unrelated, so I switched the samples around. It seemed silly, but it was the only thing I could come up with."

"Ballsy move, Lou. So to the best of your knowledge, someone took the switched compound thinking it was the real thing and they've tried to re-create the test somewhere else but can't and now realize they don't have the real sample. And now they want you?"

Louisa chewed her food and nodded. "Or Ivan. But if Ivan or Vasilii *are* involved in some way, they could also be working their way through the lab trying to find it. Ivan and I cleared out the lab recently, but other experiments build up quickly. They may have figured out what I did and might try to identify which sample I switched it with, but that would lead them nowhere. I hate thinking of Ivan as the bad guy. He's been a good lab partner for a year even though he doesn't want to be on the lab side of things. Vasilii kind of insisted he had to spend time doing some of the research to learn about the business from the bottom up. I think it's a bone of contention between the two of them. But what I don't get is if they wanted me, it would have been easy for them to set up. They could have called me into a meeting anytime in the last week or so, and taken me from there."

They sat in silence for a few minutes as they ate their food.

"I know Ivan," Six said eventually, and Louisa's stomach dropped.

He said it so casually, like it was something she should have expected. Her gut told her Six was a good man, but it was hard to understand why he hadn't thought to mention that before. Confusion fought with trust at his revelation. She stood quickly, ready to leave if she had to. "What do you mean you know him? It's a little late to be telling me that, don't you think?"

Six grabbed her hand gently. "Sit down, Lou. I can't stand the sneaky asshole. He was a shit as a kid at school, and since his grandfather shared his money around, he's become an even bigger one. But we're growing our business, so we took the job at the fundraiser even though none of us like him."

Louisa's heart raced furiously, but she took a deep breath and attempted to not cave in to the panic. Nothing in her life had prepared her for what was going on right now. It had never been a life-or-death decision as to who she could trust. And truth was, she'd known Six such a short period of time, but his explanation made sense, and he'd saved her life twice already. Plus, even to her inexperienced eyes, there was something about the way he looked at her sometimes with a flicker of more than just friendship that gave her an unfamiliar squishy feeling of hope. "Do you think he could orchestrate something like this?" she asked.

"I honestly don't know, but I do know I've seen men do stranger things for weaker reasons."

Louisa pondered Six's comments. She might as well

tell him the full truth. "On Monday, I got into the lab early, and destroyed the real sample. Nobody can use it for anything."

"Wow, Lou. Just when I think you're the toughest woman I've met, I learn something new about you that impresses me even more. That takes guts."

After they'd cleaned up from dinner, Six went outside to work out in the garden. As much as she'd vowed she wouldn't, she'd spied on him, watching as he performed pull-ups, pushups, and burpees in a pair of shorts that hung low on his hips and no shirt. The sight of his abs flexing while he did jump-rope cardio meant there was every chance she'd be unable to sleep tonight due to a frustration she was unused to feeling. It felt like an itch she had no clue how to scratch. Eventually she gave in to the tiredness she felt and collapsed into bed, but the sound of the shower running followed by the low drone of sports news from the bedroom next door made her feel even more uncomfortable.

She'd never thought of herself as particularly sensitive. Cripplingly shy, yes. But years of conditioning had taught her how to make the best of any situation. Intellectually, she knew she was safe. Six had walked her through all the precautions he'd taken, and even though she had no intention of picking up the gun he'd left for her in the bedside cabinet, she appreciated that he was looking out for her.

Perhaps it was leftover emotion from the car chase. Adrenaline and lactic acid buildup could make her feel out of sorts. Plus, her stomach had felt as though someone was standing on it for most of the afternoon, although she wasn't sure whether that was nerves from being around another person for such a prolonged period of time. Or maybe it was simply Six, and the fact that the sheets she slept in smelled like him, or at least the scent she associated with him. She closed her eyes, willing herself to sleep.

As they'd shopped for groceries, it had felt so normal, like the start of a new relationship. Six was clearly well known in the neighborhood, and the cashier at the grocery store had called him by name.

She'd seen the admiring glances from women as they'd walked by, though, women who had plenty more to offer him physically than she could. It had taken every ounce of self-control for her not to compare herself to them or make internal bitchy comments about their IQs. She'd seen the confused looks as people tried to figure out exactly what she was to Six. Yeah, they were confused, and so was she.

Her thoughts wandered back to the man across the hall. Did he sleep in boxer briefs? Or naked? She shivered at the visual of the hot body she'd seen covered in sweat in the garden. Damn, she needed something else to focus on, like the logistics of their situation.

They needed to talk about contracts. If he was helping her out as Eagle Securities, then she was more than willing to sign a contract and pay. And it sounded like they needed the money. Perfect timing. But she couldn't figure out why Six was so *personally* invested. In her. Beyond the obvious business opportunity, it made no sense. Maybe she'd relied on logic for too long, but why the heck did he care enough to bring her to his home? He could have dropped her at her mom's and been on his way. She could have gone to stay with her friend

Julie in LA, even though she hated the damn place. Too many people. Too much everything.

Thoughts ricocheted around her brain, leaving her staring at the ceiling.

Eventually, Six turned the TV off, and the light spilling out into the hallway from his room went off. A garbage can clattered outside the window, and her whole body tensed. She listened carefully for the sounds of footsteps, windows opening, or even gunshots. Rationally, she knew it was more likely that it was just a new neighborhood with new sounds. But she was scared they were back. Scared they were trying to get into her room as she lay there.

Louisa pushed back the covers and crept to the window. With the tip of her finger, she pushed the curtains open a fraction just in time to see a cat jump off the neighbor's fence. A freaking cat. Wide awake, she gave up trying to sleep and wandered along the hallway past Six's bedroom. The door was open and Six lay on his front, his face hidden from view. For a second, she was tempted to crawl in with him, but she hurried past to the kitchen. The clock on the oven told her it was nearly midnight. She was going to be exhausted if she didn't find a way to go to sleep soon.

The plants in the bay window that had been left behind by Six's tenant bothered her. They were all over the place. Tall ones at the front, shorter ones at the back. Gray containers, blue containers, red containers. Normally she'd fix them, but with everything else going on around her, she didn't have the energy. She sat down on the sofa and debated turning on the television but was concerned it would wake Six.

With a sigh, she stood again. Bed was the best place to be, even if she could only rest instead of sleep. She padded back down the hallway and paused in front of Six's room. If she joined him, it wouldn't be that much worse than the night he'd slipped off her bra and slept on her floor. And being closer to him would definitely make her feel safer.

Mind made up, she crept over to his bed and peeled back the comforter and sheets. They rustled loudly, but Six didn't move. She sat down gently and lifted her legs slowly onto the mattress before sliding them under the covers.

Just as she was lowering her head to the pillow, Six turned suddenly and reached for her. His arms snaked around her and pulled her back to his chest. His body was hot, overwhelming, and unmoving. The soft snore over her shoulder and the warm breath ticking her neck, told her that he was asleep, that this was no deliberate move, but she relished it all the same.

She could feel every part of him pressed up against her as his hand drifted up to hold her breast. Everything inside her tightened. But she finally felt safe.

And no matter how good it felt to be next to him, she drifted off to sleep.

Six woke with a start. Death and loss were impossible to outrun in sleep, especially when dreams took him to that dark place he rarely revisited during his waking hours. Brock's death and his own gunshot wound had morphed into one impossibly connected and grotesque event that had left him lying and bleeding next to Brock's broken body.

In that place between being awake and asleep, he reached for the one thing that chased away the lingering chill of his nightmare. A woman. Nothing felt better than waking up slowly with a sweet woman in your arms, especially when your dreams had taken you to a hellish place. There was something about the fragility of a woman that helped him escape the dreams' clutches. Perhaps it was the comfort of another human being to be vulnerable with, the sense of connection that helped ground him back in reality. Lying on his back, he ran his hand down the curve of the woman tucked against his side and focused on her, on her skin. God, he loved the flare of a hip, just running his fingers softly along it and back. Sometimes touching a woman's skin was an innocuous move, like when watching a movie on a lazy Sunday afternoon, and others it was an invitation to the best kind of sex.

She turned in his arms and buried herself into his shoulder, the move making him smile. Her arm slid around his waist, her hand pressed flat against his skin, holding him close. While deployed, you could jerk off to relieve the sexual urges and tension, but nothing could re-create the intimacy in moments like this. The simple quietness, the honesty of it, even if it was just for one night.

Six rolled onto his side and forced his eyes open. *Louisa.* The minx had snuck into his bed, and he couldn't figure out how she'd pulled it off without waking him. Given she was obviously there by her own choice, he pulled her closer, savoring the way her breasts pushed up against his chest, and slid his hand down her back, reaching for her skin underneath the nightshirt she'd slept in. Their legs tangled under the covers. The subtle smell of fresh lavender tickled his nose. He kissed her temple and felt himself harden at the direction of his thoughts.

Gently, he moved his lips down the side of her face because he wasn't ready to fully wake up or for the moment of sleepy tenderness to be over. The tips of her fingers ran along his spine, and it made him shiver in the best kind of way. She tucked her hand in the back of his briefs and gripped his ass, pulling him closer to her. His cock, delighted by the game they were playing, jumped in readiness. But this wasn't about chasing release. It was about something utterly irreplaceable.

Six slid his thigh between hers, and she moved her knee over his thigh. He ran his hand along her hip, around the curve of her ass, and along her thigh before making the return journey, this time skirting under her nightshirt. God, she had the smoothest skin.

Unable to resist, he kissed down her temple and along her jaw until he reached her lips. She gasped when he brushed them with his, then moaned when he pressed his mouth to hers. Her lips were warm, and soft like the rest of her, and her hips began to move, a slow and steady rocking against his leg. Not needy. Not yet, at least. But a definite seeking of pressure he was more than ready to provide.

He ran his tongue along her lips, willing them to open, to let him inside so that he could savor her. As she did, she moaned, and when her tongue met his, he felt as though he'd died and gone to heaven. The movement of her hips sped up against him, and she gasped. Her fingers dug into him, holding him where she wanted him.

It was the sexiest thing when a woman took instead of waiting to receive, although he was more than willing to accommodate both. He rolled onto his back, taking her with him, pulling her higher up her chest so she could ride his cock. He didn't give a shit that underwear separated them. She obviously wanted pressure against her clit, and his dick wanted it too.

It felt so good, so right, and he groaned as she moved against him, loudly enough to rouse Louisa from her own sleepy sexual haze.

In a split second, so many thoughts collided. She looked so vulnerable, and delicious, and flushed and everything else he dreamed about, and so close to orgasm he needed to see it. Wanted it more than his next breath, the desire even greater than finding his own release. She was a millisecond from climbing off him in embarrassment, and it was all happening in slow motion. He could feel the moment her hands started to lift from his chest and the pressure between his cock and her clit started to ease.

"Don't go," he said, wrapping his arms around her. "Don't leave me." *Jesus Christ.* He shouldn't beg. He should tell her to go. To keep some distance. But instead he put his hands on either side of her face, using his fingers to move her bangs to one side so he could see her. "Finish this," he said, pulling her lips down to his before she had a chance to argue, to disappear back inside her own head. Six slipped his fingers into her hair, gently bunching it in his hands. It was thick and soft.

Louisa pulled her lips from his. They were swollen and deep pink from their kisses, and he wanted them on him, around him, just about everywhere. He was sure she was going to pull away from him, but then she sighed, pressed her lips back against his, and lowered her body to his until the two of them lined up perfectly. She began to rock against him with the same kind of urgency he was feeling. She felt hot and damp through her underwear, and he wanted to remove whatever she was wearing on top. He grabbed the hem and pulled it up over her back, and Louisa lifted as he tugged it over her head. When she returned to lying on him again, he groaned. Skin on skin was the best feeling in the world, and he allowed his hands to travel all over her, up and down her back and then over her ass, which fit perfectly in his hands as he gripped her butt and pressed his cock against her.

"Oh, God," Louisa cried out, and buried her head in the crook of his neck. Her breath was warm against his neck, and despite the fact it would make him look like he had no control at all, he could feel his balls start to tighten as she reached a pace and friction that was guaranteed to get him off.

"I want to feel you and hear you as you come, Louisa. Let go for me. Lose control in my arms, because I want to lose control in yours." He instinctively knew she needed permission, that letting go was something she rarely allowed herself, which made the moment even more special. Even more meaningful.

"Six, I . . ." It was a plea.

"I've got you. I promise." And he did. He couldn't explain the connection, but he felt her with every fiber of his being, and he was certain that it should be scaring the shit out of him, but it wasn't. It was only making him feel more . . . connected. "Look at me,

Louisa, please," he said, feeling his abs tighten as he got closer.

Louisa lifted up and looked at him. The trust, the honesty he saw in her eyes as she chased her own orgasm was enough to push him over the edge. About to come, he wanted to ensure she came with him, so he held her tightly to him, increasing the pressure between them. He felt the moment she began to let go, and the way her eyes fixed on his was his undoing.

"Louisa," he shouted as he came, and Louisa cried out and shook against him, finding her own release.

Fuck. If it felt this good without even being inside her, he could only imagine how it would feel to be buried deep.

His heart raced, and his hands shook at the power of his orgasm that was creating a sticky mess between them. He moved her off his chest and to his side, where he wrapped her in his embrace.

"Thank you, sweetheart," he said, all other words escaping him as he kissed the top of her head.

They lay in silence for a moment as he got his breathing back under control.

"Not that I mind in the slightest, but do you want to tell me why you're in here?" Six asked her, lifting her chin with his finger so she would look at him. Her eyes were heavy lidded, but there was tension back in her shoulders already. Whatever she was thinking, he wasn't sure he wanted to hear it.

"I couldn't sleep last night. It just felt safer here, but I should go. I don't think this was—"

"If you are about to tell me this wasn't a good idea, I'm going to have to strongly disagree."

"We just can't—"

A loud knock pounded on the door. "Wake the hell up, Viking." Cabe was outside, likely with Mac. Shit.

He kissed Louisa's lips one more time. "We've got company," he said, getting out of bed. "But you and I . . . we aren't done with this conversation."

"As jobs go, it couldn't have gone any cleaner," a voice she didn't recognize said from the direction of the living room. As best as she could tell from footsteps and voices, two men had entered the house.

"Straight ins and outs are the best kind. So happy airport reunion I'm guessing?" she heard Six say from the direction of the kitchen.

"Yeah, we recommended they see a psychologist as soon as possible for . . ." The voices drifted off as if they were moving toward the dining room.

Louisa pulled on her nightshirt and hurried from Six's room to the one she'd attempted to sleep in the night before. The idea of getting caught doing the walk of shame, even if it was just between bedrooms, made her feel queasy. Quickly, she grabbed her new toiletry bag and brought it into the bathroom. She caught sight of herself in the simple square mirror hanging on a wall of aqua subway tiles. If she hadn't been so stunned by her own reflection, she probably would have been envious of the beautiful bathroom. The reflection showed puffy lips and still-flushed skin that glowed as if she'd just bathed in some magical serum. Who knew the just-ravaged look would suit her? She emptied the contents of her toiletry bag onto the counter and placed the things she needed for the shower on a small shelf over the bathtub.

Desperate for hot water to soothe her, she turned on the spray, letting it warm as she pulled her nightshirt over her head and dropped it on the floor. Once under the spray, she allowed her mind to wander as she washed her hair and soaped herself. Between her legs was tender. No surprise given what she'd done earlier, and she was still totally at a loss to understand what had happened in Six's bed. When she'd wandered the hallway the previous night, unable to sleep, the only implication that had occurred to her was that he might not be okay with her slipping into his bed for some security. That he might ask her not to do it again. Never in a million years would she have crawled into his bed if she'd known she was going to make a total fool of herself. In her limited experience, she'd never woken up so damn aroused. So . . . needy. Embarrassment filled her at the idea that she'd taken advantage of a man who hadn't invited her to his bed. A man she'd woken up next to and then proceeded to ride as if she didn't know one end of a man's penis from another.

Six probably used the word "cock" . . . or "dick" . . . or some stupid nickname like "Kong." Meanwhile, she was being all prim and proper with her biological terms. He'd probably think she was prissy, or repressed, but she'd never had reason to think of that part of a man's anatomy fondly. It had all been perfunctory in the past. Nice. Biological.

But what had happened between her and Six was hands-down the best sexual experience of her life, and as much as she was currently mortified, the truth was she'd never forget the way he'd made her feel, the way she was certain he'd needed her just as much as she'd needed him, or the way that what they'd just done had silenced all the thoughts banging around in her head like firecrackers exploding in a small space.

Gah. Why had she done it?

It was unexpected.

She'd begun to think she just wasn't cut out for sex. Not asexual exactly, just too many other things going on in her life to focus on something that hovered toward the bottom of her to-do list. Nobody else had ever brought out that side of her, so the whole thing had been an exciting revelation. She had it in her to get truly turned on, so much so that she'd lost her inhibitions enough to orgasm in front of someone else. It had never happened before, and it had felt scary to let go of all the control she carried day to day, even if it was only for the briefest moment in time.

And it clearly wasn't a one-time thing for her, because what they'd done had left her yearning for so much more. Her body ached for him still, like an addict's response to drugs. She could only imagine what it would be like if he knocked on the bathroom door and offered to step in the shower to scrub her back, or some other euphemism for taking her up against the wall until she came in a quivering mess in his arms.

When she'd finished rinsing the soap away, she turned off the water, stepped out of the shower, and grabbed a towel off the shelf. It was incredibly soft and fluffy, which seemed at odds with her gun-toting SEAL.

Once dry, she wrapped the towel around her chest and walked back into the bedroom. After last night, she wondered if she should consider unpacking. For now, she'd leave everything in shopping bags until they'd talked. She pulled on underwear, a pair of denim cutoffs, and a loose navy-blue short-sleeve blouse. With wet hair, she looked way younger than her thirty years, but seeing as she hadn't been able to find a hair dryer in the bathroom, there was nothing she could do about it. She wasn't about to walk out there and ask Six if he had one. Although chances were he didn't. He was likely one of those people who just woke up in the morning looking perfect. Probably wide-awake too.

Unlike her. She needed coffee to function. Perhaps that could explain her behavior this morning. If there wasn't a rule that sex before coffee just didn't count, then there should be. But coffee was *out there.* Where they were. She couldn't face him. Or them. Whoever the voices were. *Crap.*

She flopped back down on the bed.

With a hand over her eyes, she attempted to separate her feelings. She tried a breathing trick she knew, slowing her breath to eight beats of her heart. The counting served as a distraction from the thoughts, and the breathing slowed her heart rate. The slower the heart rate, the slower she breathed. Virtuous circle. She knew that adrenaline, shock, and fear could make people do the craziest things, and she'd felt all three in the last twenty-four hours, so her behavior was understandable, right?

You liked it.

It was almost a whisper, but it was the truth.

She'd liked it. And for all her sins she wanted to do it again. To see what mind-blowing sex could feel like. Because mind-blowing would be the only way it could be with him. It was as if Six had magically removed every inhibition she had.

Louisa sat up on the bed. She was going to be mature about it. She was going to walk out there, get coffee, and act like jumping the bones of some poor man who'd taken pity on her happened every day.

In a minute.

No.

Now.

"No problems with moving the weapons then?" Six asked.

Mac shook his head. "None. I mean we have all the paperwork to move the guns from HQ to the airport."

Six thought about the tens of thousands they'd paid to get all the permits to store and move the guns in the tightly restricted state of California. "Ever wonder if it would have been cheaper to set up shop in Alaska, or Alabama?" He laughed.

Cabe laughed. "Yeah, but then we'd have to live in Alaska. Remember cold-weather training, how miserable that was."

Memories of fingers right on the periphery of frostbite made Six shiver. Footsteps in the hallway snagged his attention. Louisa. His thoughts went back to what they'd done that morning. How she'd managed to creep into his bed without waking him was beyond him. Years of programming had him waking at the slightest sound, but for some reason she'd been able to sneak in without creating any kind of audible alert.

She wandered into the kitchen, head down, wearing cutoffs that revealed the long legs he'd seen through her skirt at the fundraiser. His initial impression that they went on for days was completely true. And the cute blue blouse she was wearing was so her. A little prim, but it showed off the figure he was kicking himself for not really having paid attention to sooner.

A piece of screwed-up paper hit him in the face, and he grinned as Mac raised his eyebrow at Six.

"Hey, Lou," he called to her, holding his hand out in her direction. It would be interesting to see whether or not she took it because the look she'd given him when he'd gotten out of bed had the makings of regret. "Cabe's here. And I want you to meet Mac."

Gripping the cup with both hands as if her life depended on it, she walked over to the table. When her hair was wet, he noticed, it was harder for her to hide behind it, and he had a feeling she hated being this vulnerable in front of people. "I trust these guys with my life," he said. "We've been friends since school, signed up together, and set up a business together. There isn't much they don't know about me, and I know they have my back."

As he expected, she didn't take his hand, just kept her hold on her coffee cup. It made him grin.

"Guys, this is Louisa. Cabe, you remember Louisa came into the office."

He smiled at Louisa. "Yeah, I remember."

"Good to see you again," Louisa said, her voice falling flat. "And pleased to meet you, Mac."

"Lou has problems," Six said, more to Mac than Cabe. "She needs our help." The guys needed to know helping Lou was a priority. He couldn't explain why, even to himself. He just knew it was more than friendly concern.

"Yeah?" Mac said. "What's going on?"

"Someone broke into her house on Saturday night and tried to abduct her. I shot one of the assholes."

"You were there?" Cabe asked.

"Yeah," he said, knowing exactly what Cabe was getting at. "Saw a van, side door open, twitchy driver, engine running as I pulled up. And a window was wide open on the side of Lou's house. And then I heard . . . Well, Lou needed help."

"So you brought her here?" Mac asked.

"No, he didn't, not immediately at any rate" Louisa said. Six listened as she objectively and dispassionately explained what had happened the previous day and what had gone on in the lab in the time leading up to her problems. The way she explained it, it sounded like a lab report. Clinical, dispassionate. Not at all like the woman who'd shaken in his arms when it had happened or who had snuck into his bed to feel safe. When she was finished, she took a large gulp of coffee.

"Louisa, can I ask why you're so passionate about Huntington's? Like, why that disease?" Cabe asked.

"Huntington's is one hundred percent genetic. If one of your parents is a carrier, there is a one in two chance that you are going to contract it. My father died from it ten years ago. I never met my paternal grandmother because of it."

How did he not know that it was genetic? Six reached out and grabbed her hand, pulling her closer to the arm of his chair.

"Shit," Mac said. "That's rough, Louisa."

"Do you know if you have it?" Six asked, his voice rough as his concern for her grew.

"I don't know. There is a test for it. Genetic screening."

"And you haven't been tested?" he asked, pulling her closer.

"No, I don't see the point. I don't want to know."

"Why not? And please, tell us to shut up if this is personal," Cabe said.

"What's the point? If I don't find out but know it's a possibility, I live every day as if it was my last and do the things I am most passionate about. Like finding a treatment for it. Not knowing keeps the urgency going. Makes me want to do as much as I can now in case I do have it."

Silence settled around the table.

"I get that logic," Six said quietly. "We've done a job for years that we knew we might not come back from. But you have to go out and assume you'll come back, otherwise you die before you set foot in theater, sorry, out in the field. It's kind of reverse logic, but I get it."

"So now you understand why it's critical that I get all that research back. Sure, we went too far on the last trial, but it was closer than I'd ever gotten. The drug we were working on was to help with the shaking, the *chorea*. Most medications to manage it have the risk of triggering psychiatric conditions. Paranoia, anxiety, suicidal thoughts. I'm trying to fix that."

Jesus Christ. What did you say to someone who could be carrying a killer disease, just because they were born unlucky in the genetic lottery? His heart hurt for her and the mess she found herself in.

"What were you thinking, Six?" Mac asked.

"We need to try to confirm if it is Ivan or Vasilii who has it in for her, and why. I got the plates of the two vehicles that were used the night before last and yesterday. I suggest we start there. See who they belong to."

"I'm on it," Mac said.

"And I think we need eyes on Ivan, see who he is talking to, meeting with," Six added.

Mac nodded. "Great idea. Let's give that to Buddha and Gaz. Bailey and Ryder are coming in for interviews today so I need to be at the office for a little while."

Cabe tapped his fingers on the table. "This ties up a lot of our guys. What do we do about the work we have lined up?"

Shit. The woman had just told them that she could be carrying a deadly disease and was one of the leading researchers in the field. "It'll have to wait until we've taken care of Lou."

"That's all noble and shit, but we have bills to pay. You know that."

Louisa pulled out of his arms. "Don't worry," she said, looking up at him with those sweet brown eyes. "I can pay you." Six stiffened as she turned to look at the other men at the table. "I'm serious. I can afford to hire you. And it makes sense. You already said you needed money to build. It's not a big deal."

"Lou, sweetheart. Can you give me a sec with the guys, please?" Six asked.

She cast a glance toward Cabe and Mac and lowered

her voice to a whisper. "Please. Don't fall out with your business partners over me."

He placed his hands on her biceps. "We fall out over shit all the time, have done since we were five years old," he said, turning to glare at Cabe for a moment. "Just let us talk, and I'll come get you. Go sit in the garden with your coffee, okay?"

"Fine. But I'll be mad if you guys fight over this."

Six smiled at her and moved her bangs. "So noted."

Six watched her walk toward his room to reach the garden.

"Dude. What the hell?" Cabe said. "Thought we said she should go to the police."

"Yeah, well, for the record, we did. Things escalated pretty quickly. I want to help her, and I get we have to charge her, but I don't want to screw her over."

Mac laughed. "Are we talking financially or . . . ?"

"Fuck you." Six couldn't help but laugh.

"Joking aside, you know if she becomes a client, you can't be in a relationship with her, right?" Mac said.

He dropped the grin and ignored the way his chest tightened. They were only just getting started, and now he had to put the brakes on knowing just how good it felt when she came apart in his arms.

Cabe nudged him. "We can't be seen to be hooking up with clients. Does our rep no good whatsoever."

Six ran his hands through his fingers. "Yeah," he admitted reluctantly. "I do. Can we just . . . let's come up with a price that doesn't make me feel like an asshole."

Hours later, after they'd agreed on a fee and Louisa had wired them their retainer, Six watched Louisa as she puttered around in the kitchen. She'd eaten only a small amount of the pizza he'd ordered, even though he'd ordered a fully loaded veggie one just for her. He didn't know the first thing about Huntington's and wondered if he should be getting foods that kept her strength up or something instead of feeding her dough with cheap tomato sauce and pre-cut vegetables.

She wiped down the counter and then took the plates out of the cupboard, restacked them, and put them back inside. He wondered if she realized that she did stuff like that when she was stressed. From his spot in the dining room, he saw her gravitate to the bookshelves in the living room, which she promptly began rearranging. He wondered what her logic was. Grouping by type, so he'd find all his business books separate from his fiction? Or alphabetized, regardless of genre? Knowing Louisa as he was coming to, it would be a mix of both.

"You know she's a client now, right?" Cabe muttered under his breath, packing up his laptop.

Yeah. I fucking do. "I'm aware," he said calmly, trying not to give any more away to Cabe than he had to.

"Bro. I didn't do this to piss you off." Cabe stood and rubbed his chin, something he did when thinking. "I'm sorry we need to charge her but we can't afford to work for free because we feel bad for someone. And from the way you're looking at her, I'm sorry we have rules about dating clients. You get that, right?"

"Understood," he said gruffly, watching as Louisa paced over to the window and began to stroke the leaves of one of the plants as she stared out toward the water that was just visible above the rooftops and tree line.

"There's not more to it than you're telling us, is

there?" Cabe lowered his voice. "Did something already happen between you two?"

Six looked at Cabe, who was watching Louisa too. He had no intention of sharing what had happened between the two of them that morning. It was too important. Words to define it seemed just out of reach, but there'd been a hell of a lot more to it than purely physical. The way she'd looked at him, the way he'd drowned in those eyes of hers . . . it was everything, or it had been. Now he had to step away, be the good soldier, set the tone for the other guys.

"I got it, okay. Go home, Cabe," he said. Six really did get it. Nothing good ever came of mixing business with pleasure, but his feelings for Louisa had been developing way before she'd decided to hire them. Hell, they'd been developed before she had ridden his cock with an abandon he'd never experienced. And now he was anxious to see what they could be together.

"Left you a case of beer in the fridge. See you tomorrow, asshole."

"Yeah. 'Night," he said, not unkindly. It would all blow over before the morning. Grudges never worked out, no matter how pissed they were at one another. Plus, it wasn't as if he and Louisa could never get together. Putting their exploration of each other on hold would be a short-term thing. A postponement, not a cancellation.

He watched as Cabe said something to Louisa, who kept her head down but nodded before looking over toward Six. Cabe let himself out and Louisa walked over to him.

"You want a drink, Lou?" he said.

"I'd love one. I know it's wrong to use alcohol as a

crutch, but if I don't do something to take the edge off, I might never get to sleep."

"I'm pretty sure you're a long way from the alcohol-abuse side of the drinking spectrum." Six stood and placed his hand on her lower back. "Believe me, you deserve a little something." They walked to the kitchen and he opened the fridge. "I got beer or pinot grigio. Take your pick."

"Wine would be great," she said as she squared the stools against the counter. She was a conundrum. She wasn't consistent enough to be OCD as far as he could tell with his highly untrained eye—there was a pile of bills on the counter, for instance, that she hadn't straightened. It was as if she just needed something to do with her hands when she was stressed out. Or worried. Or both.

He opened the bottle, grabbed a glass, and poured her a larger measure than he usually would. It would help her sleep. Her fingers brushed his as he handed the wine to her. They were frigidly cold, and the urge to pull her into his arms, to warm her and reassure, was so strong that he had to force himself to act busy getting his own beer.

"You ever surf?" he asked her as she set her wine glass on the counter and folded her arms on the countertop. *Goddamn.* The position gave him a clear view straight down the V of her blouse, revealing the curves of two perfectly tanned breasts. It drove him crazy. He remembered what they'd felt like in his hand, pressed up against his chest. So did his cock, which was certainly starting to tent his shorts, though he didn't dare look down and draw her attention to it.

She shook her head. "Never took the time to learn."

"Then that's what we'll do. When this is over, I'm going to teach you how to surf."

"I'm not sure that's a good—"

Six laughed. "It's the best idea." He'd love to see her in a bikini on a board. She'd be focused. And hot. And damn. He was back where his thoughts had started. "Listen, Lou. Now you're a client . . . I'm not supposed to . . . Well, I can't set a bad example for the other guys."

"A bad example about what?" she asked, cocking her head so her bangs fell to the side. She had no idea how he'd do anything she asked if she looked straight at him.

"This." He gestured between the two of them. "Exploring *us*. It needs to wait until our work with you is over."

Disappointment saturated her features. "Oh . . . right. Okay."

"I'm sorry, Lou. It's just that—"

"No. No. I get it. It's fine," she said, pushing her half-drunk wine toward him. "I understand. I'm tired. Anyway . . . so . . . I'm going to go to bed. Good night, Six." He watched her hurry off toward her room, one that was less than ten feet away from his, and sighed.

There was nothing he wanted more than to slide in bed next to her.

But he had a job to do.

And right now, it sucked.

CHAPTER EIGHT

Never had a light cotton blanket been so utterly irritating. Louisa turned in bed again, hating the way the sheet brushed against her sensitized skin. Over the course of the day, she'd watched Six morph from the guy she'd woken up with into the soldier she guessed he'd been. All business. He'd stopped looking at her as though he wanted her, and he certainly hadn't returned to the conversation they'd started in bed that morning as he'd promised. Which frustrated the hell out of her because all she could think about was how good his body had felt pressed up against hers and how much she wanted his arms wrapped around her again.

Their conversation had ended awkwardly. *She'd* felt awkward. She'd watched for the light in his room to come on, but it never had. Instead, he'd spent the evening on the computer in the office, she guessed.

She understood and hated the idea that he didn't want to mix business and pleasure. But a small part of her, the part used to being rejected for her bookish behavior, worried he'd simply gotten cold feet in the harsh reality of day. Perhaps he was happy to help her scratch her itch, but maybe he hadn't found the whole thing quite as mind-blowing as she had. Or perhaps it was it finding out that she could be a carrier of Huntington's. That had happened to her before. He'd said it was because they now had a business contract between them. One that Mac had written and given to her. But then she could have sworn she'd heard Six mutter a curse word under his breath as she'd signed it.

Whatever the reason, she was now in bed, a place she wasn't really tired enough to be, and worst of all, she was alone.

Her phone vibrated on the bedside table, and she couldn't resist picking it up to see who it was.

I was too hasty. I am sorry about what happened at your home. The police came to see me. Please can we meet to talk some more? Vasilii.

It struck her as odd. Vasilii never texted. He always sent emails. Or called her. Or swung by the lab. Not once had she received a message from him in all the years she'd worked there. And for him to send a text message over something so serious was most definitely out of character. She'd mention it to Six in the morning and see what he made of it.

Part of her wanted to trust him, but equally she wondered if they could track her location through her phone? To be on the safe side, she quickly turned the power off.

Louisa lay back in bed and stared up at the white beams in the ceiling. Just like the previous evening, she couldn't sleep, but unlike the night before, she couldn't slip into Six's bed with him to make it all better. She was too hot, and, if she was honest, too horny with no clue what to do about it while sleeping across the hall from the man who was making her feel that way. *Pull yourself together, North.*

With exasperation taking her close to breaking point, she tossed the covers away with a huff and climbed out of bed. The house was warm, almost hot, but she couldn't decide if that was because of the air conditioning that Six had told her didn't work too well or because her thoughts were causing her to internally combust. She padded into the kitchen, got a cup and a tea bag, and set the kettle to boil on the stove. A cup of chamomile tea would help settle her nerves.

The house was silent, unlike the thoughts in her head.

"Couldn't sleep?" Six's rough voice washed over her, and she turned to face him. His eyes ran up and down her body, and she began to regret the decision to sleep in the little cami and shorts she'd purchased, so unlike her usual pajamas, especially when her nipples hardened in response.

Boxer briefs hugged his hips like a second skin and did little to hide the fact he was as well-endowed as she'd imagined, having not even gotten to the underwear-removal stage that morning. The kettle began to whistle, which made her jump, only adding to her embarrassment.

"No . . . I mean, yes. I couldn't sleep," she said, tripping over herself in an attempt to sound normal. With shaking hands, she poured the hot water into her mug and killed the gas. She yanked the drawer open to grab a spoon, but it clattered noisily out of her hand. She put her hand to her chest, fearing for her heart, the way it beat like there was a moth trapped inside her.

"Here," Six said, walking right up behind her. Not so close that they touched, but close enough that she could feel the heat from his body. He placed one hand to one side of her to hold the mug, took the spoon in his other hand, and scooped out the tea bag, flipping both into the sink, all the while keeping her hemmed against the counter.

Louisa could feel him as surely as if his fingers were on her. In the window, she could see his reflection as he lowered his nose to her neck and breathed her in. No part of him brushed against her, yet Louisa could barely draw in a breath. She looked down at his hands, which gripped the edge of the laminate countertop, his knuckles white. The feelings of embarrassment from earlier collided up against a burning desire for him to touch her. Why was she so confused and aroused? Again?

Anticipation raced through her as he lifted a hand and brushed her hair toward one shoulder, the action making her shiver and the hairs on the back of her neck stand to attention. She leaned her head to one side and closed her eyes.

"Tell me to stop, Lou," he whispered in the stillness. "Tell me this is a bad idea. That I need to stay away from you because you're my client."

The sensation of his breath on her skin made every part of her come alive. "I can't," she said, almost desperately. "Show me," she said.

He brushed his lips against the skin on the side of her neck so gently that she thought she was imagining it. "Show you what, sweet Louisa?"

"Show me how good sex can be. How good making love can be. How good it can be to . . ." *Damn. Just say it.* "How good it can be to just fuck and really mean it."

Six groaned and wrapped his hands around her gently, pulling her back against his chest, against the erection she could feel pressed up firmly against her butt. His hands trailed her curves and his thumbs brushed softly over her nipples, making her knees shake as he planted soft kisses along her jaw.

"I'm not supposed to do this, Lou," he whispered against her ear before he playfully nipped her earlobe. "But for some reason I can't stop myself." A hand slid down over her underwear and between her legs, and he pressed the heel of his hand against her clit. "I know you like pressure here, but what else do you like, Lou?"

She was sure she should be concerned by the fact they were standing in his kitchen with his hands between her legs, but she couldn't bring herself to care. She wanted whatever Six was willing to give her, and she'd stand there as long as it took.

"Would you laugh if I told you I don't know?" she said truthfully. Because she didn't. "I didn't know until this morning it could feel this good."

Six groaned into her hair. "Do you have any idea how hard that gets me? Knowing that I'm the first to turn you on like this?" He slid his hand into her shorts. "Hell, Lou. You're so wet already. I could tell this morning that you were turned on because I could feel how wet you were through your underwear. This feels even better."

Louisa bucked against him as he slowly slid a finger into her, pinning her to him. She pressed her palms down into the counter, needing to keep her balance. "Oh, God. Six," she cried out.

Sensations and feelings bombarded her as she rode his finger. When he added a second finger, it felt as though she was going to die, but not before she had an orgasm brought on by someone other than herself. She caught sight of herself in the window, her reflection revealing a woman she barely knew. One who looked . . . sexual. It was the only word she could think of.

"Fuck," Six gasped and removed his finger.

She cried out at the loss.

"It's okay, baby. I'm not going anywhere, except down." He tugged her shorts down her legs and his knees hit the floor as he encouraged her to step out of them. "Grip the counter, step those legs toward me and arch your back."

Louisa did as he said but stole a look over her shoulder just in time to see him grip her ass and bury his face between her thighs. "Oh, God," she cried out as he took her clit into his mouth to suck and lick it.

Without thinking, she rose onto her toes, widened her stance. Anything to give him more access.

"You taste so good, Lou," Six murmured as he slid a finger into her. "I can't wait to feel you come on my tongue."

She wanted to tell him he wouldn't have to wait long. Wanted to tell him to stand up and slide into her. To come with her. But she couldn't. Pressure started to build inside which burst forth like freaking fireworks, taking away her ability to do anything other than cry out as she came even more intensely than she had that morning.

Over and over as Six's tongue stroked deep inside her, making it impossible to stand or do anything else except slump forward until her head rested on her hands.

Feeling Louisa let go with such abandon had to be the hottest thing to happen to him since his return. The shock in her voice as she came told him she found the experience to be just as much of a surprise to her as it was to him. Being able to deliver the goods for her made his heart soar and his cock throb.

He should just end it there. Remember the rules and help her step back into those ass-hugging shorts that had driven him wild in the first place. Be the good operative he was meant to be. But breaking rules was what he did best, and there was no way he wasn't sliding deep into Louisa tonight, no matter how much it would piss off his friends.

Her legs shook, and he gripped her hips to help her stay upright as he continued to stroke her with his tongue. No, he couldn't stop, not when she'd already let him taste the most private part of her. He loved going down on a woman, loved the intimacy it created. With one more kiss, he stood and turned her to face him. Beautiful brown eyes, wide with shock, looked up at him without the security of her bangs, and he wanted her to always look at him this way. Unable to resist, he pressed his lips to hers and groaned as she melted against him.

Louisa threw her arms around his neck and he lifted her into his arms. She wrapped her legs around his waist, bringing her in line with his cock, which was desperate for release. Part of him wanted to just hitch her onto the counter and drive straight into her, but instead, he carried her back to his bedroom and laid her on the bed.

"Lou, baby. I can walk away right now. My cock might never forgive me, but I can. Give this another five and I am going to be so in you, there'll be no stopping until we both come. It's a bad idea, but tell me you want this. Make the decision for us, Lou, because I want you so much it hurts."

It was true. Every word. It was no secret that he'd slept with his fair share of women, but holy hell, did he want Louisa.

She sat up on the bed and lifted her cami up over her head, revealing those perfectly pert breasts. "I want you, Six. I don't know how much clearer I can make it. I'm not a virgin, I just . . ."

"Just what?" he asked as he dropped his boxer briefs to the floor and then grabbed a condom from the bedside table. Her eyes went straight to his cock, and it did his ego good to see the way they widened as she took him in. He slipped the condom on and used her silence to crawl over her, resting his weight on his arms on either side of her head.

"I just never saw stars like I do with you."

He pushed her bangs to the side and stared deeply into her eyes. Cautiously, Louisa placed her hand on his cheek in a move that was both sweet and teasing. He wanted her to see the whole universe.

"This makes things complicated, Lou."

"Weren't they already complicated?" she asked.

He kissed the tip of her nose, a move that made her smile and his heart trip in his chest. Then he made his way along her ribs and sucked her nipples on the way for good measure. They were so responsive as they hardened to his tongue's demands. Six crawled between her legs, where he could see the wetness from her first orgasm, and groaned as he crawled back up her body. "I've thought about this a thousand times today," he said, gripping his cock and sliding the first scalding inch into her. "You feel so good, Lou."

Louisa gasped beneath him, and he pressed his lips to hers, stealing her breath away. Her hands traced down his back and cupped his ass, and he loved the way she encouraged him deeper. Usually, he'd just dive in. Literally. But he wanted to know that Lou was with him every step of the mind-blowing way.

He eased out and slid in deeper. *Fuck*. Tight and wet. Could she be any more perfect? He gripped her leg behind the knee and slid her thigh along his as he pressed in deeper.

"Oh, God. Please, Six." Her voice was breathy and low, her eyes closed as she arched her back and let her head fall farther into the pillow.

He'd move heaven and holy hell to give her what she needed as he slid out of her and pushed back deep inside her welcoming warmth. Once safely tucked back inside, he rolled them so he was on his back and his girl was astraddle him. *His girl*. It sounded good. And he was done pretending that he wasn't developing feelings for her as she giggled at his maneuver.

"I love it when you laugh," he said as Louisa rose up on her knees and lowered back down on him.

"Touch me, Six. Devour me. Show me everything."

He put his thumb to her lips. "Suck me," he said, and

she opened her mouth, giving him access. Her tongue teased him, flicked around him, getting him good and wet. God, it felt good. Made all the better that from down here, she couldn't hide behind her bangs and he could see how hooded her eyes got as she continued to ride him. He usually liked to dominate. Unleash all his sexual frustrations and desires for a woman's body. But Louisa deserved something more giving, more . . . loving. He banked the thought and withdrew his thumb from the hot confines of her mouth. One day he'd ask her to suck his cock with that mouth of hers.

Lou pressed her hands onto his chest like she had that morning, but she looked to the point where they were joined and gasped. Yeah, it was hot to watch the way he disappeared inside her, and he loved that she enjoyed it too.

The view of her riding him was something else. He placed his thumb to her clit and rubbed as she raised herself to her knees and sat down hard on him. He could tell when the movements began to change from sexual enjoyment to pure desperation. Louisa's rhythm became jerky. Her hips rolled forward as she lowered on him, making sure her clit was getting the pressure she needed, and his abs tightened in response. There was nothing hotter than a woman getting off on his cock, but somehow, knowing it was Louisa had him harder than granite.

Telltale shivers began down his spine. She was going to ride him until he came deep inside her, but he needed to take control. He flipped them again so that she ended up beneath him.

"Wrap your legs around me, Lou," he instructed and

groaned as she did, sending him deeper and deeper into her. His pace increased, slamming into her. He wanted to ask if it was too hard. He wanted to ask if she felt the honesty of it. But his breath was stuck in his lungs and showed no sign of being released anytime soon.

"Six," she gasped. "I'm so close. I can't . . . I don't . . ."

He pressed his lips to hers in a soft wet kiss that attempted to tell her just where his feelings were and just how close to coming inside her he was. But all he could do was take. Take everything she was offering as she grabbed his ass, digging her fingertips in hard. As she gasped against his lips. As he breathed in her air. As she began to shake against him and tighten around his cock.

"Oh my God. Yes, Six. Please," she cried as she threw her head back against the pillow.

The sight and feel of her coming was his undoing. His own orgasm began to rip through him as she pressed against him, burying her head into his shoulder. Unable to help himself, he pulled her close as he braced his knees and pounded into her, finally giving in to his own release.

For the second morning running, Six woke up with Louisa wrapped up in his arms, and for the second morning in a row, he savored the way she felt there. Only this time, the immediate awareness of who it was made it feel even better. Perhaps it was the fact that she wasn't some temporary distraction. He mentally shook his head. She most *definitely* wasn't that.

There had been no nightmares. Just a wonderful night of sex and sleep.

Her skin was soft and warm under his fingertips, but he remembered how goose bumps had formed as he'd kissed his way along her ribs. Those curves currently pressed up against him tighter than his neoprene diving suit, snug in all the right places, had moved *poetically* against him. He ran his hand up and down her spine and wondered how she'd react if he grabbed an ice cube and ran it down the arch of her back. Gently, Six trailed his hand over the curve of her ass.

Reluctantly, Six opened his eyes and looked toward the window. The sight of all the crap on his bedside table made him smile. Louisa was a post-sex munchies kind of girl, and for a woman who ate all clean and healthy, she'd devoured brownies after their first round and a large bag of barbecue-flavored chips after their second. It was a blessing that she'd fallen asleep before a third round because he was all out of snacks.

God, the look on her face when she'd come apart was something else. His cock tightened at the memory, eager for a repeat performance. Sex had always been the go-to way to relieve stress, but something about sex with Louisa had relaxed muscles he hadn't even realized were tight. He felt loose and limber and ready to take on the world.

The sound of a vehicle pulling onto the driveway crushed the idea of taking his thoughts and hard-on any further, reminding him that she was in trouble and needed a lot more than just his cock to be okay. She needed his protection and his company. She needed his control and for him to take his responsibility seriously. His partners were going to be pissed. Part of him wanted the chance to talk to Lou before they got here to decide how they were going to play it. For a moment he considered asking her to lie, to hide who they were together and what they were getting into. But lies and secrets didn't seem like the best way to start a new relationship. She wasn't something he was ashamed of. Yet confessing his feelings about something so new and demonstrating his abject lack of control flew in the face of everything he was trying to build. He shouldn't even be having this conversation with himself because he shouldn't have touched her. He should've honored the promise he'd made to Cabe—or more important, the one he had made to himself.

Delicately, he untangled his arms from around her and moved out of bed. He slipped on some shorts, ran his hand through his hair, grabbed his SIG from the bedside table, and walked barefoot to the front window, relieved to see Cabe's truck, before going to the front door.

"Come on, Viking. I ain't got all day. Get your pretty ass over here."

Six pulled the door open.

"Louisa's payment cleared, so all systems are go," Cabe said, walking into the house with a weapons case.

Mac followed close behind. "Figured you might want to double down on protection." He jerked his chin toward the gray metal box.

More reinforcements were a great idea, although he had a collection of his own in his gun safe. Job one was to teach Louisa how to fire one of them and get her a permit so she could have a gun in her home. A friend of his had some hard-core acreage about forty minutes east. The middle of nowhere would be safe enough to teach her the art of firing a weapon. But that would take time they didn't have right now, so they'd have to manage with a quick primer on how to load, aim, and fire safely enough in the event of another break-in. "Thanks, bro. You guys had coffee yet?"

"Nah. Would love some. Louisa around?" Cabe asked as he followed Six to the kitchen.

Six tilted his head in the direction of the bedrooms, careful not to indicate one room or the other. "Still sleeping," he said, pulling the coffee out of the cupboard.

"Look, man," Mac said, grabbing three mugs. "About yesterday. I know it seemed harsh, but we can't run this place like a charity. We aren't the Equalizer."

It pissed Six off that Mac was right. "What if Delaney were in trouble?" Six asked anyway, referring to Brock's younger sister and the only woman Mac had ever loved as far as Six could tell. "Would we charge her?"

"Fuck you. That's a low blow and you know it. Delaney would be different. We'd look out for her because of Brock. She's family. You've known Louisa what? A week."

Six shook his head. It was impossible to explain his feelings to Mac when he couldn't even explain them to himself. "Never mind. How is Delaney? Do you know?"

Brock's death while they were in college had left them all with scars, the emotional kind. And Mac carried the brunt of them. Even though the findings had cleared Mac of any wrongdoing, he still blamed himself. Mac had attempted to stay close to Brock's family, the only way for him to absolve himself of the guilt he carried from Brock's death, but neither Delaney nor her mom had spoken to him in years.

"Still doing some crazy-ass investigative journalism. I find out like the rest of you do when her stories hit the headlines."

"That's so Delaney, though," Cabe said. "Heck, we all know Brock intended to enlist after graduation. Maybe in her own way she's continuing Brock's need to serve his country or something."

Six nodded. While she hadn't enlisted, her form of journalism—tracking down the world's most wanted and feared—helped keep the country safe.

The coffeepot began to splutter, and Six poured them all a cup. "I had some feelers out overnight and was just going to check on them," he said, grabbing his laptop. They walked to the dining room and sat down.

"You still make god-awful coffee," Cabe said with a shudder.

"And you've nuked your taste buds with all those extra-hot wings you eat, man." The team joked that Cabe had an asbestos mouth. The guy would eat anything claiming to be hotter than Hades. That said, it *was* unusual coffee, a Moroccan blend that he'd gotten a taste for while doing work-up exercises off the coast of Morocco and which he now ordered online. It was strong as shit. Funny, Lou had drunk it without so much as a comment.

"Ivan seems to have gone to ground. No sign of him at the lab or his home," Mac said. "Buddha went in last night and placed a camera that covers his driveway and door so we can watch it without being there. We do much more, though, and we're gonna need to be more transparent with the police. You know that, right?"

"I know. But we have resources they don't. They've

got the plates of the car, our statements . . . They have everything we have so far, so let's see how fast they work. We find anything, and we hand it over. We should have an eye on his finances today," Six said, opening his laptop. "Do you think we should be watching the old man?" His gut wasn't giving him clear direction on Vasilii yet.

"Was wondering about that myself," Cabe replied. "He might lead us to Ivan. Let's see what today turns up."

Six scanned his email. His friend at vehicle licensing had come through. "We got an address for the van from the first attempt. Let's check it out this morning."

Louisa walked into the kitchen wearing the shorts and cami she'd bought, no bra, which of course Cabe noticed with a swift double take. Asshole. She looked over to them but quickly looked away and grabbed Six's hoodie that was on the table, yanking it over her head. Her cheeks were pink with embarrassment and Six felt shitty for not warning her they had company. On the other hand, she probably had no clue how utterly delicious she looked in his clothes. Quickly, she made her way over to the fridge. "Did you guys eat?" she asked.

Perhaps he was imagining it, but her voice sounded sexier than ever. Like every word was an invitation to sex, not breakfast. Six shook his head. "No. But I can make you something if you give me another ten."

"It's okay. I got it. This is something I can do."

"Go easy on me, Lou," he said, teasing her. "I can't do spelt or cold oats crap this early in the morning."

Lou rolled her eyes. "Just because I prefer not to eat animal products for health reasons, I don't mind cooking them," she said.

He watched the way she efficiently grabbed eggs and vegetables from the fridge before setting them on the counter. He wondered if she realized she was standing in the exact spot where he'd fallen to his knees and introduced his tongue to her insatiably hot pussy. His cock twitched, and suddenly he wanted Mac and Cabe out of his house so he could drop those shorts just enough to slide his ever-hardening cock inside her.

"Tell me you didn't," Cabe whispered across the table.

Six shook his head. "None of your business, man," he warned. Louisa was busy chopping, too far away from them to hear their hushed words.

"Yes, it is. You can't think with your dick," Mac said. "We talked about this."

"No," Six warned. "*You* talked about it. I didn't agree."

Cabe rolled his eyes. "Yes. You sure as shit did."

"Okay," Six admitted with a shrug. "I did. Turns out I didn't mean it." What he didn't add was that he had meant it, right up until the moment he'd seen her. It had proven impossible to stay away from Louisa, even though he knew better.

"You aren't going to think clearly. You're too close. It's a weakness of yours. Women."

His stomach tightened at the thought of what Cabe was suggesting. His judgment wasn't clouded by Louisa, was it? Unable to formulate a response that would make any sense to Cabe, he flipped him the bird.

"Wow, real mature, Six."

"Don't make me spell it out, asshole. She's different. Okay?"

Shock pinched Cabe's features. "What the hell? For real?"

Six nodded. "Don't ask me to explain it because I can't. And we've got shit to do." He looked down at his laptop. "We got an address for the van. Which one of the guys is outside?"

"Gaz is out there, but Mac came to relieve him. What are you thinking?" Cabe asked.

"Lou needs to go give her formal statement. So, Mac, maybe you could take her, and Cabe, I'm thinking we should go see if we can't persuade the van's owner to share what he knows."

Cabe grinned. "I'm in."

Over the omelets that Louisa made, they finalized their plans, but something nagged at the back of Six's brain. The idea of leaving Lou in Mac's care was driving him crazy. And not because he didn't trust his best friend's intentions, which he did implicitly, but because it wasn't *him*. He should be looking out for her. But he also didn't want anybody else going out to follow their lead in case they screwed it up.

"Give me two minutes to get ready," Six said, pushing his plate toward Mac, who'd already begun to clear the table.

His head was filled with their conversation about Lou and his own confused thoughts as he walked toward the bathroom. The SEAL and the man in him had never been in conflict before. It was crazy that his feelings for her were clouding his judgment. As much as he hated the idea of putting some distance between himself and Louisa, as much as he wanted to rally against what Cabe and Mac said, a small voice told him it was for the best.

At least until this was over. Louisa deserved the best protection he could provide, which meant she needed him to be Six the SEAL right now. Because he needed her to be alive for him to see what they could be together. Their timing sucked. So he'd give them space, even if Six the man knew doing that would hurt like hell.

Louisa wrapped the towel around her chest and fastened it tightly. Using the back of her hand, she wiped the mirror in the bathroom of Six's bedroom and studied her reflection. Hooded eyes and lips swollen from a night filled with kisses stared right back at her. And best of all, she felt . . . energized. Now that she knew what amazing sex felt like, she made a pact with herself that she'd never accept anything else. Hopeful that Six would continue to scratch that itch for her, she parked the thought of finding someone after him because all it did was cause her heart rate to spike and a pit to develop in the center of her stomach. Instead, she focused on the way he'd felt beneath her.

Though most of her ached to have Six's hands back on her because, dear God, they were huge, and strong, and had manhandled her in a way that had sent delicious feelings congregating between her thighs, she felt more than just sexual excitement. It was clear that he was grappling with a combination of his sense of duty, the contract she had signed with them, and the same kind of pent-up frustration she was feeling. She thought about the words he'd whispered in her ear. *Tell me to stop, Lou . . . You're my client.*

What if he regretted it? He'd been out of bed before

she'd woken. At first she'd wondered if that was just a military habit, but thinking about it now, perhaps he hadn't meant for things to get so carried away between them. Louisa shook her head to clear all the high-school-esque thoughts. He was a grown man. She hadn't forced him. Far from it. He'd approached her in the kitchen. He'd laid his hands on her. All she'd done was be honest and tell him that she wasn't strong enough to stop him from touching her. That she wanted his hands sweeping her skin. No. There was nothing for him to regret. And she was just being foolish. It was sex. And it had been sublime.

Somehow, she needed to find the words to tell him just how badly she wanted to learn from him, how she wanted to learn more about herself . . . what she liked and what worked for her. And his tongue. Oh, Lord, his tongue. When he'd knelt behind her, she'd wondered what on earth he was going to do, but then he'd licked her like she was a freaking popsicle, and she'd shivered from top to bottom. Her thighs tightened at the thought of it now.

She dried her hair with a hand towel, and then, as she began to comb it, Six pushed the door open. His eyes immediately dropped to her breasts, which were still covered by the small towel, and then lower to where water droplets ran down her thighs.

"Shit," he muttered under his breath as his eyes finally met hers. "Sorry, I didn't realize you were in here. Just wanted to brush my teeth before I head out." It was hard to discern from his tone whether he was grumpy that she was using his bathroom instead of the guest one or frustrated because he was in a hurry. Or if he was actually mad at her for what they'd done.

"I'm almost finished," she said, refusing to apologize for something she wasn't even sure she should be apologizing for. "Where are you going?" Her voice sounded exponentially calmer than she felt inside.

Six leaned back against the wall and crossed his arms. "Got a lead on the van, so Cabe and I are going to go check things out. Just some recon—see if we can't pick up a trail to figure out what is happening."

"Should I come with you?" she asked quietly.

He shook his head. "No. It's way safer if you stay here. You're their target, and I don't want you in any crosshairs. You would just be a distraction."

"You should know that Vasilii texted me last night. I don't know if it has anything to do with the van, but he wanted to talk to me."

Nothing about his features or tone suggested any kind of happiness to see her, and it sucked. Really sucked. He was obviously in SEAL mode. And he looked fierce. "What exactly did he say?"

"Just that he'd been too hasty. That he was sorry someone broke into my home, and that the police had been to see him. And that he wanted to talk some more."

Lines formed on Six's brow. "Well, for now, just ignore it. And definitely don't try to go meet him, at least not without talking it through with one of us."

"Okay," she replied. It was ridiculous that underneath the talk of texts, and tracking down van drivers, she was desperate to ask him about the two of them. But she wasn't going to be that girl. The one who asked, "*What are you thinking?"* No. She was just going to get on with finishing up so she could be crushed in private. "Just give me two more minutes."

When she was done, she turned around and saw that Six hadn't moved. His eyes still fixed on her, he ran his tongue along his lower lip.

Deliberately, she adjusted the towel, fully aware that Six's eyes followed her every move. Intellectually, she knew it was wrong for his gaze to turn her on so much when he seemed suddenly so distanced from her.

Pathological shyness had taught Louisa one important thing. Never poke someone into conversation. Louisa hated it when people tried to engage her, like at the drive-through when they tried to ask her about her day. She just wanted her food and to be on her way. Or when people who knew her a little better forgot to work with the fact that she felt uncomfortable around anyone other than her mother and proceeded to act like untrained psychiatrists to get to the bottom of *her problems.* She often wished people would just leave her alone. So she got the fact that Six was sticking to strictly business and would never be the one to break the terms of their professional agreement, even though it broke her heart that she really wanted to feel his arms tighten around her and a good-morning kiss on her lips.

"All done," she said, hanging her hair towel on the hook next to the shower. With her head down, she hurried to the door and was reaching for the handle when Six's hand grabbed her hand.

"I'm sorry, Lou," he said. "I couldn't stop myself last night, but I should have known better."

Hurt gathered in her belly, making it tighten. As always, logic was her go-to strategy. She looked up at him, though she rarely felt comfortable enough to look someone straight in the eye. Especially when he was dressed and she was wrapped in a towel.

"Don't look at me like that, Lou. I know what it costs you to look straight at me, and I am so not worth it, believe me."

Six looked tortured. Common sense was telling her that it was best to just go back to her room and let him work through it, which totally lined up with her usual MO of avoiding, well, life. But for once she held her ground. "Okay, first please quit the martyr act. We are grown-ups who had consensual sex. I'm sure you've done that before, so don't start getting weird just because it was me. Second, I'll look at you any way I damn well please. You didn't care how I looked at you when I was riding . . . well . . . you know," she said, gesturing toward his shorts. "Third. If the only difference between you tugging at the corner of this towel to do something . . . *urgh* . . . hot, or sexual, or something, and you walking out of the bathroom without kissing me good morning is the fact that I gave your company a check, I'll cancel it. I'd rather pay you to help me, but I'm sure I can find somebody else if it's the difference between us doing this or not." Her knees were shaking and her voice was loud enough that she suddenly realized if any of Six's team were still in the house, they'd likely heard her stumbled words. She felt pink spread to her cheeks.

She stepped toward the bathroom door, feeling like she was going to pass out before she made it to her own room. Her heart was pounding, and her head was spinning.

"Lou," Six said quietly, his hand looping her wrist. "You like your lists? Fine. I'll give you mine. First, I'm not being a martyr. We can't build a reputation as a professional firm if I hook up with one of our first clients. Professionally, you must see how weird that looks, no matter how badly I want to. And what kind of message does it send to the guys who work for me? And yes. I have had sex before, lots of it, but what we did was much more than that. So please, for both our sakes, don't minimize it. Just because I shouldn't have done it doesn't mean it wasn't perfect. And for the record, how you looked riding my cock—and yes, you can say that word because, as you mentioned, we're both grown-ups—was burned into my memory. And third, if it was as simple as just giving into this, you'd have been out of that towel and up on the counter with my face between your legs before you could cry out my name. It's just . . . Shit, Lou. I'm trying to figure out what the right thing to do here is, and my duty wins out every time."

Six ran his finger along her jaw and applied just the tiniest amount of pressure to encourage her to look up at him.

"I don't have expansive experience at this, Six," she said, honestly. "But I am not prepared to go through everything it takes to open myself up to you if you aren't sure."

He released her chin and sighed, and she knew they were done with the conversation. From the way his eyes held her, she knew their relationship was, at best, on temporary hold. For a moment, she considered whether she was brave enough to stand up on her tiptoes and initiate a kiss. Or whether she had what it took to simply drop her towel and stand in front of him, naked. She was certain she could convince him. But she'd never know for sure if he'd really wanted her or not.

And who wanted a guy who needed convincing to be in a relationship with you?

CHAPTER NINE

Six was glad they'd decided to take Cabe's black truck. It blended into the night better than his would have, and being invisible was just what they needed right now. Plus, the darkness totally matched his mood. Agitation crawled through him, and the absolute silence he could usually find when he needed to focus was creeping further and further out of reach.

After lunch, a quick call into Officer Meeks had confirmed that the van used in the attempted abduction of Louisa had been found, burnt out, in an abandoned lot. None of the police's efforts to find the owner, Demyan Kovalenko, had been successful.

Which was why Six was currently parked down the street from Kovalenko's home, doing something the police didn't have the manpower to do. Waiting and watching. Yet for some reason, the patience he'd had in spades as a sniper had gone AWOL. Sitting in Cabe's truck, waiting, was driving him crazy and he didn't know why.

Well, maybe he did, but admitting it meant admitting Cabe and Mac were right. What they were doing felt too urgent, too important, too . . . everything . . . to get wrong. Because if they didn't get it right, then Louisa was at risk. And that made him a liability.

He hated the idea that she was in his home right now and he wasn't there to protect her. He'd hated the look in her eyes when she'd left the bathroom, and when he got home he was going to make sure she understood this was only a delay in getting to know each other better. Except he hated the idea that he might have to go back to her and tell her that they had no new information, that he hadn't achieved anything that might reassure her that she was safe.

"You flip my glove box open again and I'm gonna kill you," Cabe said. He was sitting upright, arms folded across his chest like he had since they'd come to a stop, eyes forward. "How long do you want to give this before we call it a dead end?"

Six shook his head. "Let's do another couple of hours. Then I think we tell the cops we are putting cameras outside his home."

"You know, if we truly believe there is potential for this drug to be a weapon, I bet we could get some kind of authorization from Aitken to investigate this further."

Andrew Aitken, Six's CIA contact within the Ops Directorate, was a great call. Six looked at his watch. It was close to midnight, too late to call him now.

"I'll hit him up in the morning. The Russian angle alone will probably be enough to pique his interest. I don't really love the idea of getting caught up in a CIA versus FBI battle over jurisdiction but doing nothing appeals to me even less."

The two of them fell into silence again, and time crept by painfully slowly, the neon green numbers of the dashboard's clock taunting Six. He fiddled with the earpiece he was wearing, a protocol when they were out on a job to ensure they were never out of contact.

A runner jogged passed the truck, completely ignoring Six and Cabe, both of whom were dressed in black, fading into the background their specialty. He was bulky, the kind of gym rat who only worked out his chest, which was covered in a dark hoodie, an odd choice given the August weather. Something didn't fit and it wasn't just the slouchy gray track pants that he had to periodically stop to pull up.

"You seeing this?" Cabe whispered to Six.

"That's not Kovalenko, but I'll take anything we can get."

They watched as the man ran toward Kovalenko's home. He looked left, then right, as if checking out the neighborhood.

Six reached to check his weapon. "Shit." The man ran straight past the house. Disappointment flooded him. He'd been so certain—

"Bingo!" Cabe said as the man doubled back and abruptly ran down the narrow path alongside Kovalenko's home.

After a few moments of darkness, a flicker of light as if from a flashlight appeared in the upstairs window. Six ran through the scenarios. Kovalenko was still alive and on the run, but needed something from his house to flee. Or Kovalenko was dead and something needed cleaning up . . . evidence needed destroying . . . something.

"We going to pick him up as he leaves, or you want to follow him."

"Follow him," Six said. "He might tell us something if we stop him now, might not. But if we follow him, we'll learn more. I'm going to follow him on foot, I'll keep you posted on location. Stay close."

Six slipped out of the truck and closed the door quietly, disappearing into the shadows behind the truck.

Several minutes later, the guy left the house and headed straight past them again on the opposite side of the street. Now he carried a small black sports bag.

Confident that the dash cam would have captured the man's entrance and exit from the house, Six began to jog, careful to place his feet deliberately on the ground to avoid the usual slap of boots on the sidewalk. This he could do. This felt like taking action. And there was no way on God's green earth that the guy could outrun him.

Less than two blocks away, the runner dropped from a run to a walk, then headed for a car on the other side of the stoplight. He fumbled in his pocket, then the lights on the car flashed and he squeezed his large frame inside.

"Cabe, get up here. He's getting into a car and will be mobile in less than a minute."

As the driver pulled away, Cabe's truck pulled up alongside and Six jumped in. Instead of calling the detective on Louisa's case, they called Noah, feeding him all the information they had. Keeping a steady distance behind, they trailed the truck for twenty minutes until it came to a stop outside a nondescript two-story condo unit in San Ysidro. The dirty cream-colored stucco was chipped and faded. Four pitiful plastic loungers were placed around an empty pool.

The man stepped out of the car and entered one of the lower-level buildings, leaving the bag behind.

"I got the address, local units will be out there shortly," Noah said. "I've explained who you are, what you are doing."

"Thanks. Will keep you posted if he moves," Six said and hung up the phone. "I want to know what's in that bag." Six unfastened his seat belt and silently opened the door, slipping out into the darkness. Cabe followed.

Six breathed a sigh of relief when he tried the rear door of the car and found it unlocked. Quickly, he unzipped the bag and found a passport and a phone on top of clothing that had hastily been shoved in.

He looked over to where Cabe was taking a photograph of whatever documentation he'd found in the glove box.

Thankfully the phone was charged, and Six quickly found the number. He took a photograph of it and made a mental note to get a trace on it as quickly as possible.

A bright light illuminated the concrete, disappearing quickly as though someone had opened and closed a door. Six held his breath, listening acutely for sounds of footsteps heading in their direction. They sounded as if they were coming from around the side of the building. He tapped Cabe's shoulder, giving him the signal to withdraw.

Silently, both he and Cabe quickly stepped away from the vehicle, closing the doors with the gentlest click, before jogging back to the truck, settling back inside as two unknown men walked to the vehicle and retrieved the black bag.

Six pulled out his phone and called Lite, another of their new hires.

"S'up?" Lite mumbled, clearly half-asleep.

"I need full access to a phone. Now."

"Text me the number."

Six hung up and messaged Lite the number. With any luck, they could flip the phone into a recording device and capture whatever was going on inside that apartment.

Neither Cabe nor Six spoke again until blue flashing lights, several of them, appeared in their rearview mirror. Six wanted in on the takedown. Cops were good, but SEALs were better.

He stepped down out of the truck.

One of the cops glared at him. "Stay out of the way," he said gruffly. "You don't have any authority here."

"What the—"

"He's right," Cabe said, placing his hand on Six's shoulder.

They were going to screw it up, he knew it. There were going to be exits left uncovered, evidence left behind. And damn, he knew he was being unfair to the hardworking cops, but it was Louisa who was at risk if any stone was left unturned.

Six began to pace as he heard the loud hammering on the door, the shouting, the yells for everybody to get down. In the recess of his mind were images of all the times he'd burst into a room and yelled the very same things.

Goddamn.

The sound of feet hitting the pavement drew his attention to the left, and he saw the man who had broken into Kovalenko's house running away from the building. Six began to run, powering his legs as his heart pumped furiously, to catch up with the man fleeing the scene. There was no way in hell he was getting away.

As Six pulled closer, the man began to look over his shoulder, then sprinted faster. The loose gray track pants began to slip, and the man grabbed hold of the waistband, which slowed him down just enough for Six to leap across the distance between them and take the guy to the floor.

"Fuck you," the guy said, attempting to buck Six off him.

"Stay down," Six yelled as the man squirmed beneath him. A rogue fist caught Six on the side of the head, not with enough power to hurt. In an attempt to get the man onto his front, Six's knuckles hit the hard concrete, sending pain shooting up his arm.

Cabe's boots appeared in Six's peripheral vision.

"I got about two minutes," Six growled as he finally subdued the man, "before those cops come out and take you away. And I got a handful of bullets in this gun, that I am more than happy to use to get you to tell me who the hell you all work for."

With his knee on the guy's back, Six pulled a cable tie from his pocket and secured his arms behind his back. He had no intention of killing the guy, but he sure as shit was cool with using the threat to get what he wanted.

Six pulled his gun and placed it next to the guy's head. "Anytime you're ready."

"Don't, please. Don't shoot. It's Lemtov. Victor Lemtov," the guy cried out.

It wasn't a name that had come up in conversation with Lou, but Six fully intended to figure out who the hell he was. Quickly, Six reholstered his gun and stood. Cabe dragged the guy to his feet.

It took another painful twenty minutes of waiting to learn that Kovalenko was not in the building, and a further twenty to give their statements and hand over all the information they'd collected.

It was nearly three in the morning by the time he crept back into his own home and grabbed a bottle of water from the fridge. He looked over to Lou's room, where she was still sleeping. As tempting as it was to lose his clothes and crawl in bed next to that warm body of hers, he didn't. He didn't trust his feelings around her. When she'd looked at him in the bathroom like he was a giant ice cream sundae and she was the five-year-old allowed to eat it before breakfast, it had made his week. But by the time she'd left the bathroom, she'd looked like she felt as bad as he did. For a moment, he could've sworn that she wasn't going to take his no for an answer, and he wondered how he would have reacted if she'd acted on that flicker of confidence. Yet she hadn't.

Footsteps on the wooden floor behind him made his heart race a little with excitement, something he hadn't felt about a woman in a really long time. He closed the fridge door and turned to look at Louisa. Dark circles ringed her eyes, and her lips were pursed.

"Are you okay?" she said, quietly, as she looked down at the floor.

Back to hiding again. Look at me, Lou.

Damn. She'd put her wall back up while he was gone, and while it was the best thing for the two of them, he hated it.

"I'm fine. You?" he said, placing his hand on her shoulder. He did so to comfort her, but he was the one who suddenly felt better. At least he did until she shrugged slightly and moved out of his reach and walked over to the window.

"I'm fine," she said in a voice that told him she was many things but fine certainly wasn't one of them. "What happened last night?"

"We found a guy, followed him to what we think was some kind of safe house, and got some leads on who might be involved," he answered honestly. Technically, she was his client, so he owed her answers, but, shit . . . What if she couldn't deal with the reality about how he came by them? He couldn't bear it if she hated him for what he'd had to do to get them.

Louisa gripped the back of the stool, finally looking at him. "Just like that? You knocked on the door and said, 'Hey, who hired you?' and he told you?" She raised one eyebrow suspiciously.

"Well, it wasn't quite that straightforward," he said. He followed her gaze to the bruised knuckles that he flexed subconsciously. There was no keeping anything from her. "No," he answered because he could tell from the look on her face, all squinting eyes and pursed highly kissable lips, that she was going to demand answers even if his natural instinct wanted to protect her from them. "It wasn't that easy. It took some very physical persuasion. But we found out that he'd been hired by a Russian who lives in LA. A Victor Lemtov."

"Ivan and Vasilii are Russian. Are they connected? I mean, it's kind of obvious, really."

"We'd be foolish not to assume so. And if they are, they're probably smart enough to realize that you will come to that conclusion. Somebody wants the drug you created, which means *someone* had to tell them it existed."

"That's reassuring," she said before shuffling around the take-out menus he kept on the counter until they were in size order.

Though the confidence with which she spoke was undermined by the nervous actions, he was impressed by how she was keeping everything together.

"You didn't kill the man you spoke to yesterday, did you?"

It had been difficult not to, but he shook his head. "He was still alive and in the back of a police car when we left," Six said, deliberately being light on details. "We got the information that we needed and we now have the means to keep an eye on him too."

"So, what happens now?" she asked.

"Mac and Lite are working the LA angle, just grabbing some intel about the guy before we go up there and see what we can find out. Lite is covering feeds from Ivan's house and the phone belonging to Kovalenko, the guy who attempted to abduct you. Buddha, Gaz, and I are technically off rotation today. Sherlock is tracking the other vehicles to see if we can find out more from them."

"I thought the whole call-sign thing was a myth," Louisa said, tucking the menus back behind the phone.

"They're just nicknames. Mac is actually short for his real name, Malachi, which he hates. Buddha's real name is Joel Budd. Gaz is Gareth. Lite's first name is actually Miller. Miller Lite, right? Sherlock's real name is Jensen Holmes. I get Six from Sixton, but I get Viking too, sometimes. My dad's family descended from them."

"Hmm," she said. "I want a nickname too. Can I pick one?"

Six laughed. "It doesn't work that way. The team kind of picks it for you."

"Will you pick one for me?" she asked, her voice lighter, breathier. God, he wanted to get her back in bed, to hear her whispered words float over his lips before he kissed her. But he couldn't. Not again. He'd let her down once already by giving in to the thing he wanted most. She needed his focus, and he needed to get them out of his house before he forgot everything he'd been telling himself for the last twenty-four hours.

Without answering her, he changed the subject. "I need some sleep, Lou, and so do you." He took her hand and led her to her bedroom door, noticing her pout when he didn't follow her inside. The thought that she wanted him as much as he wanted her was going to make sleep hard to come by. "But tomorrow, do you want to take a walk, Louisa?" She'd been cooped up at his house for three days. He'd take her down to the narrow beach, get onto the long strip of sand that would take them down to the meditation gardens.

"Yes. Yes, I do," she said quickly.

In that case, he'd better rest up, and then get armed.

Being outside had never felt so liberating, yet so terrifying.

Three days of hiding away at Six's house had made her crave the simple freedom of movement, about which she'd never been overly concerned. It was an odd feeling, but she wanted to be outside, even if she was scared for completely different reasons than normal. Now, she craved being in a crowd. Safety in numbers was a very real thing, and the idea of being isolated freaked her out. Plus, three solid days in Six's presence had also made her crave sex—something else that hadn't been high on her list of things to do, but which now seemed just as vital as breathing. Six's idea to head outside had stopped her from doing something foolish to thank him for hurting himself for her sake. Those knuckles were swollen and blue, and though it was primitive thinking, she loved the idea that he had stood up for her. Things were stirring inside her, and for the first time, Louisa began to question the way she'd been choosing to live her life. Crippling shyness had led her to live with as little human interaction as possible, but something was changing. Well, she couldn't exactly say a wall had broken down inside her, but there was definitely a small crack in the mortar, and she wondered how hard she'd have to push for the crack to grow.

She'd had to wait for Six to make a call before they'd left to a CIA contact of his, someone who had the power to give Eagle Securities the authority to legally dig more deeply into the affairs of Vasilii, Ivan, Kovalenko, and a name she hadn't heard before, Victor Lemtov, under the guise of national security. When he'd hung up, Six had assured her that while his contact needed to do some follow-up of his own before agreeing, Six was confident they'd have the authorization he needed before end of day.

The hot Encinitas sun warmed her face, and Louisa focused on the natural vitamin D she was getting. Anything to take her mind off the tall man next to her who was wearing a light jacket, despite the heat, so he could wear not one but two guns and a couple of knives strapped in his boots to protect her. His eyes were constantly on the move. He looked down the hill, and then turned to look back up it. And she hadn't missed the way he'd switched sides to stand between the platform and her as they'd approached the train station. He'd explained his rationale before they'd even left the house. They'd be most exposed on the short trek down E Street to the wooden staircase that would lead them down to the sand.

"It kind of freaks me out that you are carrying," she said as they walked. "But then I'm relieved that you are. You don't think they'll shoot me, do you?" Her hand brushed against Six's, and for a moment she wondered what it would be like to walk alongside him, holding it, like a real couple.

For the briefest moment, he took his eyes off their surroundings and looked at her. "No, I don't. They've shown repeatedly that they intend to take you alive. If anybody is going to get shot, it's me. I'm standing between you and them."

"Well, that's reassuring," she said, her mouth going dry at the mental image of him down on the pavement with a gunshot wound to the chest. Her heart squeezed at the thought.

Six laughed. "Reassuring that you'd be okay, or that I'd get shot?"

She eyed him teasingly. "Both."

"Nice, Lou," he said as they reached the staircase to the sand. He placed his hand on her back, leading her in front of him. "Ladies first," he said. "If anyone was watching for us, they'll be behind us. So I want you in front of me. You know, so I can get shot instead of you."

Louisa stopped and turned to look at him. "This isn't really funny, you know. I don't want you shot on my behalf."

"I know, but it's my job. One I do willingly. One I am good at. I don't want to get shot any more than you don't want me to. But I'll always put you first." He ran his finger along her jaw and then snatched it away quickly. Even after his flesh left hers, the line he'd traced burned. "Anyway," he said, circling his finger to encourage her to turn and start moving again, "irreverent humor is the best way to get through shit like this. Plus, if you go first, I get to look at your ass."

Despite her nervousness, Louisa laughed. Perhaps he was right. There was only so much she could control. Another item to add to her list of things she'd learned since spending time with Six. Control wasn't everything. The design of every experiment she'd ever done depended on her having control of the inputs, all variables accounted for, excluded, or measured. But there was no way she could control what was going on in her life right now.

She made a move to kick off her sneakers on the last step, but Six put his hand on her arm. "No," he said quietly. "Always keep your shoes on. You need to be able to run, should you have to. And if you do, head for the harder sand. It's easier to sprint on. Running on soft sand takes more effort."

"I'm not sure I'd have been so eager to come out if I'd thought it all through," she said, looking at the water wistfully. The gentle shushing of the waves hitting the beach and the faint tang of saltwater in the air teased her. It was the perfect day to walk along the water's edge, feeling the surf bubble over her feet, cool and refreshing.

Though the local kids had gone back to school the previous week, the beach was busy. Families played in the warm sand and paddled in the shallow water. Three young men were lazily throwing a football between them. And a group of older ladies in wide-brimmed hats walked in their direction. Tourists. There were too many of them, and her heart rate quickened further. Six began to move, but she stayed rooted to the spot. Realizing that fear was no way to live her life and doing something about it were two different things. Recognizing she was guilty of one didn't directly mean that she could fix the other.

"What's up, Lou?" Six said, moving close to her side.

He was so close that she could see the beads of sweat on his brow and could feel the heat radiating from his body. She closed her eyes, allowing herself to focus on him and his presence, not all the other people on the beach outside of their circle. "I just need a moment."

Six put his arm around her shoulder and pulled her close. She could feel the hard line of the gun under his jacket, but more importantly could bury her head in his chest for just a moment while she shored her defenses. His hand was between them, and she knew it was on the holster in his shorts, just in case. Louisa let his strength and absolute lack of fear seep into her. His hand crept to the back of her neck and massaged it slowly as he kissed the top of her head. "You're cool, chickpea. Just take a deep breath."

She let her breaths line up with his, slow and sure. "I'm not having a panic attack," she said, quietly.

"I know," he said, his words reverberating through his chest. "You're too in control for that, right?"

Was she? Her insides felt like unset Jell-O, and her skin was the plastic mold holding it all together. She just needed to put one foot in front of the other, take one breath after the next.

Reluctantly, she pulled out of his arms and squinted as she looked up at him. His hair looked even whiter in the sunshine, but she couldn't see his eyes through his sunglasses.

"I hate being around people, Six. I know this will make no sense to you, and I guess the fear of being kidnapped is awful for anyone, but couple that with the fear of being around *any* person is almost . . . I'm worried that it's more than I can bear. There are obviously a number of people involved. If they need my help to re-create the sample, it will need to be in a lab, a cleanroom. And I can't imagine I'll be alone."

"You're going to hate me for saying this because it sounds so trite, but I think you'll find it's pretty amazing what you can deal with when you really need to. Have you ever heard of BUD/S?" he asked, starting to walk down the beach. He placed his hand on her lower back and she shivered at the contact. With gentle pressure, he escorted her around the groups spread out on the sand and those headed toward them.

Without thinking, she reached for his hand, wanting to continue the reassurance she felt in his arms, but he squeezed her fingers gently and then pulled away. Heat flooded her cheeks, and she took a step away from him.

"Don't read anything into that, Lou," he said quietly, running his fingers through his hair. "I need my hands in case anything happens."

Of course he did. His comment made her feel even more stupid, and she shook her head. "It's SEAL physical training, right?"

"Yeah, although it's much more than that. During the first phase is what's called Hell Week. Crazy as all shit. They quite literally put you through hell. I remember being so exhausted that I fell asleep getting hosed by one instructor while another screamed in my ear." He turned at her and grinned. "It's physically grueling and pushes you to the very brink in an attempt to get you to ring out, to quit. But the truth is, it's all mental. As soon as you get your head around the fact that it's impossibly rare for someone to die during SEAL training and that your body is pretty much capable of whatever you can imagine, you realize the only thing forcing you to quit is your own head."

Louisa thought about his words, let them sink in rather than respond to them immediately. Would she rather be alive and surrounded by people than dead? Of course. Would it cripple her with fear? Possibly. Would she survive it?

"Where'd you go, Lou?" he asked.

"Just thinking about what you said. Even as I say my concerns aloud, I know how stupid they sound. I'd like to say that of course I'll get through whatever happens. But you saw me that night before the presentation."

It was high tide, and the water forced them closer to the cliffs so they could scramble over the low rocks to stay out of the water. A man stood in the shallows doing what looked like yoga, his skin the color and texture of dark leather. Six nodded in his direction. "He's here every day. I last lived in Encinitas eight years ago, but he was a fixture in that spot long before then. You ever try yoga?"

"Once. Actually twice," she said, watching her step as Six reached for her hand to help her down onto a wider stretch of sand. "Turns out I have the grace of a newborn giraffe."

Six laughed and led them to another wooden staircase. "I don't buy that."

Louisa turned in the sand and looked at him. "And what does that mean?" she challenged.

"With practice, I believe you can get good at anything."

"I call bullshit," she said, lifting her bangs off her face. "See that?" she said, pointing to the jagged scar that ran from her hairline toward her crown. "Six stitches from hitting the coffee table says you are so wrong."

Six looked closely then raised his hands in surrender. "I stand corrected. But for the record, I'd be more than happy to help you learn how to do it properly without taking down inanimate furniture."

Louisa laughed. "Fine. Maybe I'll give it another go." The idea of a seminaked Six working on her flexibility provided all kinds of visual inspiration.

"So, Ms. Biologist. What other alternative remedies have you ever tried? Hypnotherapy? Aromatherapy? Acupuncture? Meditation?"

"A couple of them," she said. "No real noticeable difference, except for breathing exercises."

They started the walk up the steep wooden stairs.

"What, no argument about Eastern medicine being hocus-pocus?" he teased.

They reached the top of the stairs, and Louisa would have answered if she hadn't been completely out of breath. Six's breathing hadn't changed, probably because of all that working out he did on that frame in the garden. Perhaps she should get him to help her get into the kind of shape he was in. "None," she said. "I'll give anything a try if it will keep my mind off things."

"In that case," he said, turning up a side street, "the meditation gardens are right here." He took a left through a metal gate and pulled her to one side, carefully searching the road they'd turned up. "We're not being followed," he said. "Let's go find a spot to sit."

The garden was beautiful and lushly planted, interspersed with stone benches and little alcoves for quiet contemplation. Everybody walked through in a way she could only describe as deliberate, taking a moment here and there to touch the plants. Or take in the view. A sense of tranquility washed over her as Six took her hand and led her to a nook with a small bench that overlooked the ocean.

"Sit, Lou. And take a breath."

So much for being outside!

He'd thought, incorrectly, that being in a wide-open and public space with her would lessen the need to be with her, but it had heightened it. It started with a need to hold her hand, and he really didn't care if it was politically incorrect, but he'd wanted all the assholes on the beach who'd looked at her more than once to know she was with him.

Which she wasn't. At his request. Which was noble . . . and fucked up.

And now she sat primly an arm's length away from him on the bench in one of his favorite places on earth, so stiff that it looked like she had a pole up her spine.

"Relax," he said, putting his arm along the back of the bench. Her hair tickled his skin, but he resisted the urge to grip her shoulder and pull her close to him. Instead, he focused on the blue of the ocean, and the green of the plants, and the pinkish red of the flowers. Colors he'd missed when deployed to dust bowls in Satan's kitchen, where the landscape came in varying shades of beige and brown.

"Am I supposed to have a mantra or something?" she asked. "Or say om?"

"Funny, Lou. You ever hear about box breathing?"

She tilted her head to look at him, and it took every ounce of his control not to lean forward and kiss her.

"Is it like breathing in for eight and out for eight?"

"Not quite. You breathe in for four, hold for four, breathe out for four, and hold for four. Just focus on your breathing. Don't think about anything else. If you find your thoughts drifting, just stop as soon as you realize it and go back to your breath."

"This is very New Age of you, Six," she said quietly, eyes closed and a serene smile on her face despite her teasing.

He watched as she followed his instructions and he found himself breathing in sync with her. "Yeah, well. You'd be surprised at the shit I know."

They sat in silence, but he couldn't focus. Couldn't help sneaking sideways glances in her direction. At the way her long eyelashes fluttered against her cheeks, or the way she ran her tongue over her lips. Periodically, her chest would lift, highlighting the way her thin T-shirt hugged her breasts, and she'd release her breath in a long sigh that reminded him of the moment he'd slid inside her for the first time.

You need to get laid. Of course he did. When he'd been back in Virginia, there'd been no shortage of women willing to spend time with him. And he'd had an ongoing understanding with a couple of women happy to receive the occasional booty call. So once in two weeks was almost as bad as being deployed. Going out and finding someone would be no problem, except the idea that it wouldn't be Louisa made his chest hurt. It would be empty, a word he'd never associated with women before.

He felt it, the moment Louisa finally relaxed. She had an anxious, frenetic energy usually. Her shoulders slumped, rounded. And her head dropped forward. At first he thought she'd fallen asleep, but then she opened her eyes.

"It's hard to keep thoughts at bay, isn't it?" she asked, linking her fingers.

It sounded more like a statement than a question, and if he didn't know better, he could have sworn she read his mind. "Yeah, it can be. But it gets easier over time." He was clearly out of practice, even though it had been his nightly routine when he was deployed to clear shit he couldn't unsee from his brain just long enough to grab a couple of hours of sleep.

"How do you do it, Six?" She turned on the bench to face him and lifted her sunglasses, popping them onto the top of her head.

For some reason it felt important that he do the same. To look her in the eye. "My mom teaches meditation, and my sister teaches yoga. I've been doing both since I was a kid."

Louisa smiled. "That's a really sweet story," she said. "And I want to hear more about little Sixton, the yogi. But I meant gear yourself up to put yourself in danger. You never seem bothered by it."

"If I thought for a second that it would help, I'd panic along with those I'm to defend." He offered her his hand and marveled, when she accepted it, at how small hers seemed in his. "But, unfortunately, it doesn't. Fear affects your ability to think straight, to make good decisions. In the toughest moments I've ever experienced, I've dug hard for the quietest place I can find inside myself. Try to get rid of all the noise, and crap, and panic, and focus on the little voice inside you that knows the answers."

"You do realize that sounds a little like *Use the force, Luke*?" She looked down at their joined hands, and he noticed she had a dimple in her left cheek that showed when she smiled broadly.

"It takes a certain kind of person to be a SEAL. It's hard to explain. Ask any of us and we'll tell you there is a moment of absolute clarity as things play out in slow motion in front of you."

"I can't imagine it. I mean, I've watched movies about SEALs, and you see images on TV, but it must be something else to be there in person. You're a bona fide hero."

Six shrugged. "I don't know about that. I think you're way braver than I am. I can't imagine what it must be like living in the shadow of such a debilitating disease."

Louisa let go of his hand and stood. She wandered to the railing that overlooked the water and turned back to face him. "It's not debilitating. It's deadly. Usually within fifteen to twenty years of the onset. But my dad didn't die directly from the disease." She pulled an elastic band from her wrist and pulled her hair up into a ponytail.

He stood. "What happened?" he asked, and followed to lean on the railing next to her.

"The most characteristic symptom of Huntington's is the *chorea*, the jerky movements. My dad had already started to show some neuropsychiatric manifestations, but the medication he took for the chorea exacerbated it." Her nose twitched and she looked upward, blinking tears away. "He went from anxiety and depression to suicide in a matter of months. I was the one who found him hanging in the garage."

"Oh, Lou," he said as he stood. He scooped her into his arms and pulled her close to his chest. He kissed the top of her head.

Once more she took a step back as she swallowed deeply, but thankfully she didn't pull away from his arms, where, of course she shouldn't be in the first place. But he didn't give a damn.

"He'd killed himself shortly after I left for school and my mom had gone to LA to visit a friend. By the time I found him, he'd been dead in our baking hot garage for nine hours."

Six thought about the way bodies decomposed in hot temperatures. The smell alone would have been enough to make her ill. And hanging. Christ. People occasionally lost their shit. Literally. Violent death was not something anyone should have to witness.

"I'm sorry. That's a horrible thing."

"Yeah. Well. Now you understand why it means so much to me. The meds that were supposed to help with his symptoms pushed him over the edge. That's why I need to find something to help with this while others race for a cure for the disease as a whole. That might take a really long time because it doesn't get the kind of funding that cancer does. So this feels like something I can do."

Unable to resist, he pulled her close again, and she went willingly. "We're going to figure this out, Lou. I promise you. I don't know how long it is going to take, but I promise you we will. And hopefully the CIA route will come through today so I don't need to circumvent the police. They have due process, and warrants, and fewer means of making people talk. This contract will give us a different kind of latitude to get things done quickly. We'll keep the police and the feebs, the FBI, posted every step, but we'll do it our way."

"What happens now that some of the dust has settled?"

He brushed the wisps of her bangs away from her face with his thumb. "We go back home and see what we've got. Line up all the pieces. And I'm going to put a tracker on your phone and one in your shoe. If for whatever reason they are able to get past us all—if they do get to you—I'll be able to find you. They might take your phone, but they aren't going to take your shoes."

Louisa nodded. "Agreed. Put as many as you want on me. It'll make me feel safer. What about . . . never mind."

"No, go ahead. What about what?"

"Nothing. Honestly," she said. She slipped out of his arms, and he hated the loss of her. "I'm anxious to get home and get started."

She set off down the path they'd walked up without so much as a look backward.

He had a feeling she had been about to ask about his own demons.

And if she had, he might have told her.

CHAPTER TEN

Victor Lemtov wasn't a part of the Russian Mafia, which according to Six was a brilliant thing because organized crime had arms and legs and relationships with other families. So the threat's reach wasn't as far as it could have been, but this, too, was a double-edged sword. Lemtov was flying below the radar. Minor transgressions, usually involving shoddily organized henchmen, had set him back, but the localized dealing and death of minor dealers couldn't be pinned on him, no matter how hard law enforcement tried. Kidnapping and abduction of non-drug-related targets seemed to be a bigger playing field than he was used to, and the FBI were interested in his ramped-up operations which was apparently causing a little pushy-shovey between Six's CIA and feeb contacts over Eagle Securities' involvement. But as Six had promised, his contact had come through, and now Eagle was officially acting with their consent.

After their walk, they'd returned to Six's house and he'd shown her how to load and fire one of his guns.

He'd told her what make it was, but she couldn't remember, only that it had felt cold and heavy in her hand. Then he'd resumed the protective-bodyguard thing, putting the distance back between them. It was driving her crazy because she could totally tell he'd checked her out occasionally during their time on the beach. And when he'd pulled her into his arms, she could have sworn his breath caught a little. Or maybe that was because she'd hugged him a touch too aggressively.

Her itch for him was getting worse. How hard could it be to get him on board with going back to where they'd been when they'd fallen into bed together? For the first time in forever, she contemplated masturbating—something she'd never really needed before, but God, a woman could only cross her legs so many times before she internally imploded.

In need of something cool, she picked up the green juice he'd bought for her at the store from the table on the covered patio and took a sip. A fan turned monotonously above her as she drank and tried not to stare at the way Six was reclined in a rattan chair, feet up on the low coffee table, a laptop perched on his lap. He'd also convinced her to get a four-ounce juice shot with ginger and cayenne in it, which had tasted foul and burned her throat as she swallowed it, but he'd just chugged it back and laughed at her expression. Now, he was shirtless, obviously reading something through. He was as focused as she was distracted.

She checked her phone. There were a number of messages from Aiden asking if everything was okay. It was rare for her to ever miss a day at the lab, so her absence was likely conspicuous. She tapped a quick reply that there had been some issues but she was safe.

"So," she said, knowing she was interrupting Six's concentration. "What else do you have?"

"Just reading through some stuff from Sherlock."

She waited for a moment for him to expand, but he didn't. Perhaps he needed a moment to finish it. Not everybody was a speed reader like her. A few more minutes ticked by as the fan whirred above them. If this were her home, she'd replace the fan as quickly as she could. The whirring and creaking were driving her mad.

Unable to wait any longer, she interrupted again. "What does it say?"

Six shook his head and shrugged with looking at her. "Nothing much. More confirmation of what we still don't know."

It was impossible to explain how, but deep down in her gut she knew Six was keeping something from her. "There's more to it than that, isn't there?"

"Lou," he warned, but she continued.

"You said Mac and Lite were following up on Lemtov. So either they suck in intelligence gathering or you know more than you are telling. You've given me zero from the cameras at Ivan's house. Has he been to the lab? Has he seen his grandfather? Is the lab just carrying on as normal? And you said you have ones set up for Kovalenko *and* the guy you pulverized." Six winced at this, but she bulldozed on. "Were they charged? Who did he phone? Are they out?"

Six looked across at her, his mouth set in a grim line. "There's nothing solid. Nothing that leads us to any kind of conclusion yet. Anything I told you would be pure speculation."

Leaning forward, she tapped her pen on the paper. "What are you trying to keep from me?" she asked.

Six closed his laptop and studied her. "I promise I'll tell you when there is something important. You have enough to worry about already."

"And you get to decide that?" she asked, hearing her voice go up an octave.

It was clear he noticed the angry hitch too. "Wait, Lou. It's not like that at all."

"No. Because it sounded a lot like you were deciding what I get to hear about a case I am actually paying you for."

"You have to trust us to do our job," he said, frustration lacing his words. "*That's* what you are paying us for. To keep you safe and figure out what's going on. To make it stop. To deal with the perpetrators."

"Well, it doesn't sound like you are doing such a great job of it, seeing as you have zero to update me on." She threw her notepad down onto the table in anger.

"For fuck's sake," Six mumbled. "There's no need for you to *hear* all this."

"I'll decide that," she railed. "And I'll do it based on you telling me *everything* until such time as I decide I don't need to hear it."

"Some things can't be unheard, Lou, or unseen. And some of it's classified."

For a moment, she wondered if he was talking about her or his own experiences. "This involves me. You have no idea what little detail you might have that might trigger something in my head about conversations I've had in the past, or people I've met, or companies I know. You gather intel, so don't you realize how stupid not following up with me would be? And finding patterns is my freaking job. A job I am *really* good at. I could help."

Tears pricked the corners of eyes, but they weren't sad ones. They were tears of frustration that she'd always felt when she was marginalized by the male researchers she'd worked with in the past. Louisa stood, and Six jumped to his feet too. The look on his face could only be described as predatory, just like the time when they'd been in his bedroom together.

"I don't want you to have nightmares about everything after it's all over. I'm trying to protect you from this, not hide shit from you."

"I don't need protecting, Six."

"Yes, you do. I see you, Louisa. I see the brave face you're trying to put on this. But then I see the books on my shelves are now alphabetized and that the plants in the window are now in size order. You make your bed and leave the pillows perfectly in line, and everything in the fridge faces forward. And don't tell me it's OCD because if it were, you'd be compelled to do that kind of thing all the time. But you don't. You do it when you are scared. As soon as we sat down at the coffee table, you began to pile the rocks. Look."

She looked at the pebbles in the center of the wooden table that had formed a centerpiece with a large piece of driftwood. Without thinking, she'd separated them in such a way that they now ran from the palest gray to black, like a monochrome rainbow.

He marched over to her and pressed her back up against the wall, his hands on either side of her head. "So don't tell me you don't need protecting, Lou," he said, thunderously. "I see it even when you don't. And I want to be that guy for you."

His lips seared hers as anger and frustration gave way to the one thing that had been building between them. Of all the things he could have said or done, this was the only thing that could disarm her, leave her forgetting what exactly they had been fighting over. It wasn't resolved, but she was willing to table it until whatever this was was over.

His hands slipped around her waist, pulling her to him, and she slid her hands into his hair, holding on for dear life as his erection pressed against her hip. Dear God, she wanted him to take her. Right here. On the back porch, with the stupid creaking fan cooling them from above.

"Lou," he gasped just before his tongue entered her, and she groaned in response. He tasted of the mango smoothie he'd bought, and she shivered as his hand slid up inside her T-shirt and along her ribs until his thumb brushed across the lace of her bra.

"Please, Six," she groaned as he pressed more firmly against her. His phone, which he'd left on, began to ring, but thankfully he ignored it.

He lifted her T-shirt above her head and threw it onto the chair before returning his attention to her breasts. He reached around her back, nuzzling her neck as he did so, and popped the clasp of her bra. The straps fell down her arms, and he lowered his mouth along her clavicle and down her breastbone before sucking her nipple into his mouth. She threaded her hands back into his hair and gripped him to her, silently encouraging him to lick and suck harder, which he did, making her knees weak.

Heat gathered between her legs, and she desperately wanted to relieve the pressure. The phone began to ring again and he looked toward it. She reached between them, slid both her hands into his underwear, and gripped his erection firmly.

"God, Lou. Yes. Don't stop," he said, lifting his head to look at her, his blue eyes cooler than an arctic glacier. Heat was building between them, but one that was different from their first time together. This was flammable. She was going to combust if he didn't take her soon.

Excitement shivered through her as he thrust into her hand. He wanted her as badly as she wanted him. "Not here," he said. "My bed." They started to move toward the bedroom, her hand tucked into his, but the phone rang again. "Goddamn," he shouted, but picked it up anyway. With a cursory glance at the screen he answered it. "What?" he snapped. He ran his thumb over her nipple and winked. Perhaps it was because he was on the phone with someone else, but she suddenly felt exposed and raised her arm to cover her breasts. His hand dropped away, his face losing the desire that had been obvious in his hooded lids and slack jaw. The soldier was back as he bent down to pick up her bra and handed it to her.

"See you there in an hour," he said, and hung up the phone.

Sniper school had taught Six the most important lesson of all: how to simultaneously block out everything else around him and focus on the target, yet take in all the changes in the environment. And how to ignore the dull ache in his cock. Pulling away from Louisa had been an impossible task, but he had a mission. Never had it been so difficult to fall back into his role as a SEAL. Boyfriend was starting to have a nicer ring to it, and hopefully he'd make it back to her bed before she fell asleep.

For now, all he needed to do was focus on the job at hand. Their plan was simple: surround, surprise, and drive them to surrender.

Demyan Kovalenko was about to be haunted by ghosts. Thanks to the wireless phone tap that Six had put on the guy's cell phone, they knew that Kovalenko was pissed that he hadn't been paid, even though the attempted snatch on Lou had been a bust. In a train wreck that Mac, who'd been listening in on saw coming a mile off, Kovalenko had called someone named *Mitty* demanding payment and protection.

One way or another, things were unlikely to end well for him.

Six watched from his spot behind the derelict brick wall behind the abandoned building. Bailey and Ryder, who'd decided to accept the offers to join Eagle Securities, weren't happy to be assigned protection duty for Louisa, but the meeting time and place had been arranged, and Mac, Cabe, Six, Buddha, Lite, and Gaz had spent the afternoon casing the location to ensure that no matter where the action went down, they had eyes on it. They'd also done some serious heavy lifting. The collapsed portions of the wall had stuck together in clumps of seven or eight bricks, and they had carried piles of them into the road to prevent vehicles from passing through in a move designed to limit car use on the cracked concrete road.

"So, I hear you and Louisa are getting tight," Mac whispered from his hiding spot seven feet away, muting with one hand his mic that kept them all connected through their earpieces.

Six looked toward the main entryway, curious as to whether the two parties were going to arrive by car or on foot. He muted his mic too. "It's unlike you to be chatty on a job, Mac. You've been hanging with Cabe too long."

"She's easy on the eyes, I'll give you that. Reminds me of Delaney that way."

Despite Mac's needling him, Six hoped that Mac and Delaney would figure their shit out one day, as highly unlikely as it seemed. She hadn't spoken to Mac since the day she'd slapped him in front of her brother's coffin. "If you spend more time looking around for our targets than gossiping about Lou, this night will be so much more productive."

"Headlights." Positioned on the third floor of the building where he could see the road leading up to the warehouse, Lite was sparse as ever with his commentary.

"Do we have eyes on how many? Visible weapons?" Six asked.

"Working on it."

Moments like this always seemed to drag on forever, seconds feeling like minutes, but Six knew the value of taking their time, especially on the shot, until they had all the intel.

"Three. None visible."

The car pulled around to the back of the warehouse and to the side of the road, just before the bricks. If shit went down, Buddha was going to take out the front tires from his position. Their vehicles were over on the shoulder of a road not easily accessible from the warehouse unless on foot, with a pissed-off Gaz behind the wheel of one of them. He wasn't happy to be left out of the key action after being left behind from the gig in Mexico, but he hadn't said a word. Instead, he'd let his driving speak for him. They'd been lucky to have not been pulled over by the police.

"Second vehicle, one driver, no passengers."

"Wow," Buddha whispered from his hiding spot. "That was almost a sentence, Lite."

"Fuck you. How's that for a sentence? Verb and pronoun included."

Mac looked over toward Six and grinned.

The second car parked behind the first. Rookie mistake, Six thought. The driver should have turned the car around, left it facing in the direction he needed to exit. Now if he had to run quickly, he'd be faced with the prospect of having to do a three-point turn under pressure, and possibly in a hail of bullets.

A battered and bruised Kovalenko jumped out of his car without killing the engine and recklessly marched toward the other vehicle, a small gun tucked in the back of his jeans. "Where's my money?"

Six rolled his eyes. It was playing out like a bad scene in a B-list movie. All stilted dialogue and bad acting. The driver of the first vehicle stepped out. Typical meathead. Thick neck and sausages for fingers. Looked the size of a small tank, but would run slower than a turtle. He'd be an easy target to take down.

The driver opened the door to the back of the car, and two men got out, both in jeans and T-shirts and one of them wearing a leather jacket despite the heat, which told Six that he was likely heavily armed.

"Mitkin," Kovalenko said loudly. "You need to pay me."

Mitty. The abbreviation made sense.

"And tell me why you think I should do that," Mitkin said. "Because I most definitely don't have the girl."

The driver of the vehicle was slowly sliding his hand behind his back, which was all the confirmation Six needed that at least two of the people they were watching were armed.

Six's mic clicked in his ear. "Buddha, driver. Cabe, leather jacket. I got the gray T-shirt," Mac whispered. "Six, Kovalenko."

"I need to get away. Someone was watching my home," Kovalenko said. "They came for me. They know who I am and where I live. I need money to get away."

Mitkin looked between his two henchmen and smiled. "I still don't understand why you think this has anything to do with me. You screwed up. And there are always consequences."

"You made it sound like a simple in and out."

Laughter cracked through the silence. "I offered you a job, you took the job, and you failed on the job. There is nothing to be gained by crying to me about your own inept failings. But you can be of use to me."

Kovalenko wiped his brow as he looked between the three men nervously. "What do you need?"

Mitkin walked toward Kovalenko, and Six shook his head.

"Bye bye, Kovalenko," Lite sang quietly through the earpiece.

Six sucked in a breath and waited for the inevitable.

"I want you to be a lesson to those who think they can fail and expect payment." Mitkin stopped a few steps away from him.

Suddenly sensing what he'd gotten himself into, Kovalenko reached around his back to pull his gun from its holster, but it was too late. Six shook his head as the driver of the vehicle stepped forward and pointed his gun, ready to pull the trigger until the gun was shot out of his hand by Lite. They needed Kovalenko alive. They needed *all* of them alive.

Mitkin dove for cover, and Kovalenko crumbled to the ground in fear.

"Go!" Mac shouted.

"Put your weapons down," Six yelled as he tore up the distance between them, gun pointed directly at Mitkin, even though Mac already had him covered. With Kovalenko already down, the focus should be on the boss. Cries instructing the three men to get down on the ground echoed around him.

Capitalizing on the element of surprise and seeing the shock etched on the faces of Mitkin's men, *his* men hurried from their hiding places with Lite providing cover from above, hitting the driver squarely in the shoulder as a bullet went whizzing by to the left of Six's head. Already doubled over from the gunshot wound, the driver was the easiest target. Six saw Buddha charge him, sending him sprawling onto the floor, face-first. With a loud yell, Buddha landed squarely on top of him, placing a knee directly in the small of his back. Roughly, he tugged the driver's arms behind his back and secured them tightly.

"Cover me," Mitkin shouted, but there was no one left to do that. The driver was out, and Cabe was in the process of disarming the guy in the leather jacket.

Six focused on Mitkin, who took in the confusion going on around them. Shock was etched across his face. Six held his gun directly at him. "On the ground," he yelled, but being the ill-informed, weak asshole he was, Mitkin instead made a dash for Kovalenko's car. Six groaned. "Down on the floor," he yelled and fired a warning shot that deliberately landed just inches away from Mitkin's foot. There was no way Six was going to let him get away. He charged over the uneven concrete as if hell was at his heels. He'd shoot the guy before he'd let him get away. With a grunt, he threw himself bodily onto Mitkin and forced him to the ground. Even with Mitkin's slight frame absorbing the majority of the impact, Six's knees made contact with the concrete and pain rushed up his legs.

"You have no idea who you are messing with," Mitkin yelled. "You'll be dead before morning."

"Unlikely," Six said, jamming Mitkin's head to the floor for good measure.

"Clear," Cabe shouted.

"Clear," Buddha echoed.

Six restrained Mitkin's hands and checked him for weapons. "Clear," he added finally.

Mac turned off Kovalenko's car engine. "Let's take them inside," he instructed.

Their captives fought for a moment longer, but quickly became subdued when they realized they were outmanned and outarmed.

Six hauled Mitkin to his feet and dragged him bodily to their waiting vehicles. Mac and the others followed suit, and once everyone was in the vehicle, transported them to the San Diego FBI field office as agreed. Unlike in the movies, they made no move to Mirandize them. They *wanted* the men to talk. "Loose lips sink ships" was a saying for a reason, and he'd take any information he could to help Lou.

In spite of Six's hopes that they might fight with each other, revealing something crucial to Louisa's case, Mitkin had done little more than glare at Kovalenko as they'd driven. As soon as they got into the federal building they were separated. The driver and henchman were put into holding until they could be interviewed. Six and Cabe took Mitkin to an interview room, Mac and Lite took Kovalenko.

There was a fine line between interview, interrogation, and intimidation. The two feebs on the other side of the two-way mirror probably had just as blurred a view of the subtleties as he did. And given what was at stake, he was in no mood to mince his words. So he got the reading of Miranda rights out of the way.

"You're going to prison, and probably at the end of the sentence, you are going back to Russia," he said before Mitkin had even had a chance to sit down. "The only thing that will affect your sentence is what you say next."

Six pulled the chair out, turned it around. "So, what's it going to be?"

Once the sun had gone down, Louisa had realized there were too many windows without curtains in Six's house. Every room had at least two, and suddenly she felt exposed.

Perhaps it was because of the time she'd spent giving her official statement, but she suddenly felt very alone.

She shouldn't, of course, because Six had left her covered by two of Eagle Securities' guys who he knew and trusted. She knew she should take his word for it that they were as good as he was, but from her spot on the bed, she pulled the drawer open and checked for the thousandth time that the gun was still there. Earlier, she'd even taken it out and held it in her hand. It was cool to the touch and smoother than she'd imagined it being. Her hand had been shaking as she'd placed a finger on the trigger, but thoughts of pulling it had her quickly placing it back in the drawer and slamming it shut.

Even now, even with everything that was going on in her life, she still couldn't imagine a scenario when she might actually need a weapon enough to fire it.

Meanwhile, though, Six was out hunting the men who'd attempted to hurt her, and the idea of him doing that unarmed was unthinkable.

Louisa picked up her laptop and scrolled through the agenda of a neurology conference at which she'd been asked to speak the following January. In the past, she'd tended to defer these talks to others because she hated presenting . . . and people—two elements that were usually a given at large conferences. But she was beginning to think it was possible to push all that to one side and do it anyway for the good of what she was trying to do. She wondered how many potential donors, or, candidly, how much more research, she might have been able to achieve had she spoken more.

How much further might her reach have extended?

Perhaps the organizers could work with her to keep the impact and volume of interactions to a minimum.

She looked at the clock in the corner of the screen to find that only ten minutes had passed since she'd last looked. Where was Six? Her heart raced a little, and she wondered how military spouses coped when loved ones went on deployment, facing threats on a daily basis. Louisa could only imagine how hard it was to bury the fear and anxiety to get on with life. Saying good-bye to Six for the afternoon had been hard enough, even though she'd been as angry as she was aroused. Jealousy squeezed her lungs as she wondered whether there had been a time when Six had had to leave a girlfriend behind before.

The shift in him earlier had been instantaneous. One moment, he'd been about to devour her on the porch; the next, he'd chastely kissed her on the cheek, albeit with a look of longing and a very stiff erection, and had handed her her clothes before disappearing inside. She'd waited for him to come out before asking him what was going on, and her frustration had bubbled over into anger when he'd explained little more than that they'd had a lead. Finally, he'd given in and told her that the lead was the person they suspected of paying

Kovalenko to abduct her, but then he'd kissed her on her forehead and headed for the door, telling her that Bailey and Ryder would be outside.

The ring tone on her phone startled her, and she quickly grabbed it off the nightstand. "Hello," she said.

"Ah, Louisa." One of Vasilii's quirks was the way he drew her name out across the three long syllables. *Looo-eeee-zaaa.* Blood pumped through her heart so quickly that she could hear the rushing in her ears.

Should she play it cool? Or should she just come clean and tell Vasilii that she knew what Ivan was up to and that she had nothing left to say to him? No, she'd keep quiet, her shyness having inadvertently taught her that people often said more than they meant to when the other party stayed silent.

"Vasilii. What can I do for you?" she asked.

"I am calling to apologize. I'm sorry I didn't handle the break-in at the lab . . . differently." He sounded uncertain. Which was strange, because if there was one thing that Vasilii wasn't, it was uncertain.

"Thank you, Vasilii," she said, surprised by his admission. "I'm glad to hear that."

"I need to see you in person to discuss . . . things. I know you asked for some time off, and I am more than willing to honor that, but I believe we should talk. Clear the air. Can you by chance come by the house?"

Despite being scared, she felt a tiny tremor of anger surge through her. "You delayed talking to the police, putting me at risk. Have you corrected that? Do the police now have all the details?"

Vasilii exhaled noisily. "I have spoken to them. Yes. If the sample has truly been stolen, which I now believe it has because a thorough clear-out of all laboratories in the building has failed to find it, I am nervous about the fallout. I don't want the publicity of losing a dangerous sample to reflect badly on the lab . . . or you," he added in a way that unless she was sorely mistaken was an implied threat.

Louisa stood and began to pace. She reached for the pens she'd left on the small desk earlier and began to line them up, then dropped them as she remembered Six's words about her habit. "Why would it reflect badly on me when it is a lapse in lab security? I came to you about it as soon as I realized they were gone. If there is any delay in an investigation to understand what happened, that's on you. If there is no security camera footage, that's on you too. But people have attempted to kidnap me twice, and I am certain the two things are connected. Your refusal to handle this properly for the sake of *reputation* left me hanging in the wind." The conversation had taken a sudden turn south, leaving her confused.

"This is my reason for wanting to talk. Away from Ivan. Away from the lab. To see if we can't come to some kind of agreement. At a minimum, we should talk about your future. I want you to continue working for me. I would hate for this . . . misunderstanding . . . to jeopardize this. "

The shock at his words made her shake. "It's much more than a misunderstanding."

"We need to move on, Louisa. I made a mistake, I have said I am sorry. And now we need to figure out how we go forward."

Fury replaced every other thought in her head. Its

heat streamed through her. "*Go forward.* I'm still trying to figure out who is trying to kidnap me. I can't believe I am saying this, but put the research on hold. Schedule the lab for its detailed clean or something. Ivan is good, but he does not have what it takes to forge a breakthrough, and you know it. He was my arms and legs, but he was never the brains. You are a businessman. You should have looked at this objectively. You should have taken action. You should have told the police when the sample was stolen."

"I understand, but please try to see things from my perspective. Where is the objectivity you have always prided yourself on? I have explained my reasons. They were wrong. You were wrong to divulge company information to the police. Please. Come to meet with me. It is most urgent that I speak with you. Right now, you are overwrought. You should—"

"No, Vasilii. I shouldn't do anything." Her head throbbed with the idea that he thought she was in the wrong. "*We* should be working together to find out who took it because whoever they are, I have a feeling they are struggling to re-create the test sample and they are after me to help them do it. It is either a competitor of the lab, in which case we definitely don't want them to get ahead of us. Or it has been stolen for a much more dangerous reason. Yet you call me and tell me nothing I don't already know. And seriously, if you suggest I was wrong to give the police information that I thought was imperative to my personal safety, information *you* should have already provided to them, again, I will sue your ass for any and every reason I can think of and I'll use that money and my own to set up my own lab."

The idea hit her hard, and suddenly she became excited. For the first time in nearly a week, she realized she could form a plan of her own. A lab would be a pricy proposition. But perhaps her mom would help her. For insurance purposes, though, she wondered if she would need to disclose that her father had carried a hereditary disease. Perhaps it was time to know one way or another.

"You are behaving irrationally, Louisa. Your paranoia is taking over. Maybe it is time for you to get tested because I worry—"

Louisa rolled her eyes at the mention of the symptom of her illness he knew she was sensitive to. "We're done, Vasilii."

She hung up and flopped back down on the bed. She knew she wasn't paranoid. Was confident that this wasn't the onset of her illness. She wasn't her father.

The collision of mad, excited, and sexually frustrated was an energizing combination. She leapt off the bed and grabbed a sheet of paper. With a black Sharpie, she wrote a title at the top of the page. *True North Pharmaceuticals.* Then she screwed it up and threw it in the garbage. She grabbed a second sheet. *True North Laboratories. Better.* But it still lacked . . . ambition. Size. *Shit.* How the hell was someone who hated being around people going to run a company? She folded the paper into an airplane and aimed it for the trash can. It drifted past and crashed into the glass doors to the garden.

At the top of the third sheet, she wrote *True North Industries.* Go big or go home, right?

She drew a tick box and added *Hire a CEO.*

Just because she owned it didn't mean she had to run it.

For the first time in days, the tightness around her chest released.

Six turned the key in the lock and gingerly stepped into the house. No amount of adrenaline was able to prevent his body from realizing that two hundred and thirty pounds of bone and muscle hitting concrete hurt like a bitch. Despite the energy coursing through his body, he walked like an old man and needed the ice packs from the freezer in the garage, which felt too far away down way too many steps for his messed-up knees.

It had been the driver who'd cracked first, and Buddha owed him ten bucks because of it. Meatheads were all mouth and no balls. And Mitkin had learned an important lesson about holding phone conversations in the back of a car. Turned out that Mitkin was Lemtov's son-in-law, and the one responsible for hiring Kovalenko. Even more interesting, they now knew that Lemtov was Ivan's godfather. And that at Ivan's request, Lemtov had sold the formula to an underground criminal organization in Russia. It didn't look good for anybody involved that they couldn't create it, and now they needed Louisa to solve it.

The lights were off in the living room and the kitchen, but he could see the light shining from underneath Louisa's door. Deciding that a shower would be the best bet before ice, he made his way to his bedroom, pulling his long-sleeved shirt over his head as he walked.

Louisa's door opened suddenly, and a gust of air hit the hallway. "You're home," she said, her eyes wide with . . . something. Excitement. He couldn't quite tell.

"Are you okay?" she asked, running her hands all over him, in his hair, and then working their way down his biceps as if checking for injuries.

It tickled. And it mattered that she cared. "I'm fine, Lou," he said, grabbing both of her wrists in his hands between the two of them.

"Thank God," she said with a sigh. Using the hold he had on her as leverage, she pushed herself up onto her toes and crashed her lips into his. "I was worried about you," she mumbled against them, and then kissed him in the way he craved right now. Dangerous, and hot.

When he opened his mouth to hers, he couldn't hold back a grin as her sweet-as-anything tongue met his. Jesus Christ. She was like a spider monkey, practically climbing up him. Their moment on the porch had destroyed the last remnant of his self-control, so if that's how she wanted it, he was more than ready to comply. As was his dick, which was already rock hard and ready for action. Scratch that. *Desperate* for action.

He placed his arms around her waist and stood up straight as she wrapped her legs around him.

"Shit," he gasped as his knees took the weight of both of them. Gently, he lowered her back to the ground.

Louisa took one look at his face. "Where are you hurt? You should have told me."

"The only thing hurting Lou, is my dick," he said, taking her hand and leading her back into her room. Papers covered the floor and table, and as much as he was intrigued by what she'd been doing, the only thing he could focus on was getting her naked faster than the speed of a bullet. Horny as hell, he felt like he'd spent the last forty-eight hours in a permanent state of arousal.

"You're limping," she said, tugging him to a stop. "Let me see."

"I'm serious, Lou. That thing about balls turning blue and dropping off, it's no lie."

"You're forgetting I'm a biology major, sailor. This is my territory," she said, placing her palm on his chest. "Let me be your nurse, Six."

Well, when she put it like that. "Yes, ma'am," he said, and saluted her.

"Very good. Now where does it hurt?" she said, running a fingertip down his chest and over his nipple. "I promise to kiss it better." Her voice was low and husky.

It was clear she wasn't going to continue until she knew what was going on. "My knees hit the concrete, but it's no big deal, honestly."

This time she took his hand and pulled him in the direction of the bathroom. "Let me be the judge of that. A good nurse always triages her patient. I need to assess what parts of you hurt most, and treat them in order," she said, running her hand down the length of his cock in a move that made it jerk and him jump. The first time they'd made love had been incredible, even though she'd been uncertain. Now, as she fisted his cock tightly in one hand while looking him square in the eyes with a look that said she wanted to devour him, she had confidence in spades. And he loved both sides of her equally.

"So, *sailor.* Where do you hurt?" she asked, tilting her head to one side.

He stole a quick kiss. Couldn't resist the playfulness. "Everywhere."

"Everywhere?" she repeated.

"*Every*where."

Louisa took his belt in her hands, unbuckled it, and then released the button and zipper of his pants. "Well, I am going to need to check out *everywhere* to confirm that."

He placed his hands on either side of her head and kissed her hair gently, then released her and put his hands in the air in an act of surrender. "Be my guest."

She dropped to her knees, and the sight of her down there, especially when she looked up at him and winked, had blood rushing from one head to the other. He leaned back against the sink and grabbed the counter. Studiously, she untied his boots, and he toed them off. Then, slowly, she slid his pants and boxer briefs down his legs, easing them over his knees, which were a bloody, raw mess.

"Six," she said, sympathy lacing every word. "I need to clean these for you, honey."

Honey. It was the first time she'd called him anything other than Six. And he liked it more than he probably should.

"I was going to shower before I came to see you, but then you jumped me in the hallway."

"I didn't jump—okay, maybe I did. As your nurse, I insist on a shower . . . as long as you let me join you. Just to clean you up, of course."

"Purely medicinal. Got it," he said and reached into the shower to turn on the water.

Louisa wiggled out of her pajamas. "Do you need my assistance walking in, or can you make it on your own?"

"Funny, Lou," he said, tapping her ass to nudge her into the shower. Shit, she had a great ass.

She leaned her head back and he watched, slack-jawed, as water ran down her face, over her breasts, and between her legs. "Stand there," she said once she was deliciously wet.

"Yes, ma'am," he said and stepped under the spray, letting the hot water do its thing. She dropped to her knees again, this time with a cloth in her hands. He stood stoically as she washed his cuts. He'd had worse, much worse, and he ran his hand down the scar on his stomach.

Once she was done, she looked up at him, in no rush to get to her feet. "What else did you say hurts?" she asked. Her eyes drifted up to his cock, so he gripped it, pointing it in her direction.

"I'm pretty sure this does."

Her hands gripped his thighs, and her mouth opened. Those pretty pink lips of hers parted wide enough to let him inside. He resisted the urge to rock into her, clenching his ass and tightening his abs in a bid to let her take the lead on pace and depth. But damn, it was hard not to sink into the hot wetness. At first, she sucked the tip, leaving a trail of saliva and pre-cum on his cock, causing him to gasp at the visual.

"Goddamn, Lou," he breathed.

With both hands, he pulled her to her feet and kissed her soundly, passionately, savoring the way her wet, naked body felt against his. Then he lifted her into his arms.

"Your knees," she said, quickly.

"I'm fine, Lou," he said, turning the shower off and

leading them to his room without stopping to dry off. He placed her on his bed, and she got onto all fours to crawl into the center.

Fuck.

"Stay right there," he said gruffly as he reached for the condom and put it on.

The air felt cool to his heated body, water dripped from her wet hair onto the bed, yet he shivered as he gripped her hips and pulled her back to the edge of the bed. *Holy shit.* She was going to let him take her while he stood. "Mmm. You look seriously hot, Lou," he said, trailing a finger between the cheeks of her ass, going lower until he found her wetness. "Ready, too. I love that."

Six slid his finger into her and then another, scissoring them gently.

"Oh, Six," she cried out, lowering her forehead to the bed.

"Yeah. I feel it," Six said, his voice low. Tension suspended between them, like an elastic band ready to snap. He lined up his erection and pressed slowly into her. A groan escaped her lips, and his, as he pushed his way deeper until he was in as far as he could go and stopped.

"I wish you could see what I can, Lou. See the way you open for me, see how wet you are, how drenched my cock is."

Louisa shivered at his words. He gripped her hips tightly as he slid out and back in, the sensation leaving him dizzy and desperate. Unable to control herself, Louisa ground against him. "Yeah, push back against me. Do whatever feels good, Lou."

She bucked when his fingertips pressed against her

clit in firm circles and her knuckles went white as she gripped the comforter with all of her might. He brushed his lips along her shoulder and pushed the hair off her face. "You feel so good, Lou," he growled in her ear. "Watching you as you are now, uninhibited, taking what you need from me, is so incredibly hot. Do you feel what you do to me?" He drove into her harder. "I want you, every part of you, so badly. I want your breath, your skin, your sweat, your orgasm. Give it all to me, Lou."

His thoughts scattered away as he focused on her. The way she was pinned to the bed as she took everything he wanted to give her, the way his breath came in short bursts against the side of her neck, the way their sweat drenched them both, and the way the need to come overtook him.

"I'm close," she whispered, and closed her eyes.

"You're squeezing me so tight right now, I can barely keep my shit together. So do it, Lou. Come. Show me how much you love us like this."

God, he was so close, and he needed the release more than a junkie needed a high. He chased it, craved it. And when the telltale tightening began, he groaned in desperation. Rougher than he had before, he pressed his fingers against her clit, giving her the extra pressure she needed to get off.

"Six, oh God, I . . ." The oxygen was sucked out of the room as she exploded, crying out in relief and release.

Six continued to pound into her, milking every last moment of her orgasm until she was left breathless and panting. Stars fluttered in his peripheral vision as he sucked in air. Lou opened her eyes and looked over her shoulder at him. She was right there with him. Really with him. Etched on his soul.

"Please, Six," she begged. "Make me come again."

Six looked at her, pinned her with his eyes as he thrust in and out, every muscle in his body defined. "Lou," he shouted, and through the sheer strength of his orgasm, he could feel the moment she went over the edge again too.

"Goddamn," he moaned into the comforter beside her as he continued to slide inside her. Slower now. Pressing hard up against her, holding it, before pulling out. "Every single time with you, Lou."

Silently, after removing the condom and crawling onto the bed, they lay there quietly for some time, just holding each other.

"Do you feel like telling me what happened tonight?" Lou asked, eventually.

"I thought about that after I left earlier. I have memories from things I've been involved with. Memories that I can't shake. I don't regret any of the things I've done, but I can recall every one of them. I was just trying to save you from having to deal with having memories like that yourself. I wasn't trying to patronize you."

She ran her hand down his stubbled jaw. "I appreciate you trying to do that. But I need to know what's happening. It's my problem. Not yours."

"I get that. I really do," he said, brushing her hair from her cheek. "And if you were a regular client, I wouldn't feel so conflicted. But the idea of you getting hurt freaks me out like nothing else . . . but I get it. Just . . . can we do it in the morning? Over coffee."

"As long as that's a deal, yes."

Six exhaled. "It is. I just want to enjoy this. Us, right now. Listen, I don't want you to think this was just another slip of control on my part. I'm done trying to pretend this isn't happening."

Louisa paused for a moment, then said, "Good."

"Good?" Six asked, unable to hide his grin.

"Well, it's not like I haven't made my position perfectly clear," she said, her eyes wide and bright.

"Oh, that's right, you wanted me to *show* you . . . What did you say? Oh, that's right . . . *Show me how good it can be to just fuck and really mean it.* So how did I do?" He reached for the light switch and plunged the bedroom into darkness.

"It was fine," she said, but he could hear the laughter in her voice.

He wrapped his arms around her and pulled her back up against his chest. "Just fine, Lou?" he growled in her ear, and she giggled.

"Okay, perhaps a little better than fine."

"I fucked you senseless, and you know it."

"Good night, Six."

"Good night, Lou."

CHAPTER ELEVEN

Every single time with you, Lou.

Lying next to a sleeping Six, she thought back to the way he'd taken her the night before. Embarrassment had battled with need at first. She'd felt exposed on her knees and had been convinced her ass must have looked huge from that angle. But it had been something she hadn't realized she was longing for. For someone to want her so badly that he'd come to her despite injuries and despite "rules" saying they shouldn't. Someone willing to overcome the odds and still want her.

She wasn't exactly sure what he'd meant by the words he'd said, but there had been so much reverence in his tone that she hadn't felt the need to ask him. *Not all questions needed answering.* Then she grinned. Answering questions had been her life, but for the first time she realized that it wasn't everything. Sometimes you didn't need to *know* the answers. Sometimes you just had to feel them.

Louisa had always poo-poo'd *butterflies in your*

stomach as an idea, because, well, it was stupid, and her nervous stomach felt horrible when it flared up. But suddenly she felt them, and even though they were a biological misnomer, they were beautiful.

Daylight filtered in through the dark curtains as she turned in his arms, and he sleepily opened his eyes.

"Mmm. I could get used to waking up to your sweet face, Lou," he mumbled gruffly.

"How did you get this?" she asked, and trailed her finger along the purple line on his stomach.

Six grabbed her hand and kissed her fingertips. The playful touches made her heart swell. "Gunshot wound, doing something I can't talk about, in a place we likely should never have been."

"Oh my God, that's awful. I'm so sorry. You're a regular hero. I hope they gave you a medal for that." She linked her fingers with his.

"They gave me two." Six shrugged as if it was no big deal. "A Purple Heart and a Silver Star."

Louisa ran her fingers through his hair. "Do you have other medals?" she asked, her stomach tightening at the thought of him being in so much danger, or worse, hurt.

"A Bronze Star," he said, putting his arm over her waist and pulling her closer.

"What's the difference between a Bronze Star and a Silver Star?"

"My level of awesomeness," he said, tugging her to his lips for a sweet kiss.

She couldn't help but laugh. "Your level of *awesomeness*?"

"Yup. *Awesomeness*."

"Well, Mr. Awesomeness. Do you feel like telling me what you know? You promised you would last night."

Six shrugged out of her arms, kissed her forehead, and sat up. "Not here. Not in our room," he said, and her heart spiked at the use of "our." He pulled on some shorts. "Come on, I'll cook while we talk. I know you're a sucker for bacon."

An hour later, Louisa sipped the last of her coffee, her stomach full of their compromise. Tofu scramble and bacon. Six had told her about everything he'd learned, and she'd told him about Vasilii's phone call and text.

"It's highly probable he wants you to go see him so they can take you from there. So rule one-oh-one . . . no matter what happens, no matter what he says, you don't go to Ivan or Vasilii for any reason at all."

Lou looked up at him. "Yes, sir," she said, and saluted.

"I'm not joking, Lou. He contacts you again, tell me right away. And that was the worst freaking salute I've ever seen," he said, and took her plate. There was a loud clatter as he dropped it into the sink.

Lou pondered what they could do to try to find out what Vasilii might be up to. "I have a friend," she said, immediately thinking of Aiden. "He runs the lab opposite mine. He's a good man. I think we should go see him and see what he might know. He might have seen something and doesn't realize it. Or maybe he already heard something from the lab search."

"You sure he won't reveal anything to the Popovs?"

Six said, and came around the counter to stand in front of her.

"Positive," she said, and placed her arms around his waist. It was a wonder that she got to enjoy this man.

"In that case, why don't we get cleaned up? I can give the guys a call on the way over and update them."

Two hours later, after a shower which had picked up where they'd left off the previous evening and a forty-minute drive to Aiden's Chula Vista home, Louisa stood on the porch and rang the bell.

"Louisa," he said with surprise. "Please come in. Are you okay? I've been worried about you."

Louisa watched the way he looked Six over, trying to size him up. "Aiden, this is Six, a . . . friend of mine. He's helping me right now."

Six offered his hand. "Pleased to meet you, Aiden."

Aiden shook it tentatively. It wouldn't have served any purpose to tell Six that she was aware of Aiden's crush. Nor would it have been fair to Aiden. Except in the moment, it was obvious to everybody, and she wished she could have prevented that.

"Vasilii said you were taking some time off for personal reasons," Aiden said, casting his eye toward Six. "And your lab is closed. Is it because of the theft?"

Louisa nodded as she followed him into the living room. She sat down on the sofa, and Six sat down next to her. "Can you tell us what's been happening in the lab this week?"

Aiden filled them in on the details. The thorough check for the samples, the lab scrutiny, and over the last couple of days, there had been a number of detectives passing in and out of the building. "There have even been some FBI agents. Liz is frustrated," he said, referring to Vasilii's assistant. "Vasilii is in the middle of this big land deal that she wishes he'd just put on hold while all this is going on, but he's scared the seller will back out if he does."

"Has Ivan been around?" Six asked, and Aiden shook his head.

"No. I guess with Louisa's lab being shut, there isn't much in the way of research for him to do. I assumed he was involved in this land deal. But the lab has been one hundred percent lights off. What happened to you, Louisa?" he asked.

Louisa explained what she could, and the fear in Aiden's eyes made her feel a little guilty for what she was about to do next. "Aiden. I hate to ask this, but, could you . . . It would be great if you could see what you can find out from the inside. I don't want you to get into trouble, but trust me, I have good reason to believe that Ivan, and possibly Vasilii, are involved in what happened to me. Any information you might be able to find would be so helpful. Especially anything out of the ordinary. Unplanned trips, reservations, etc."

Aiden stood from his chair and wandered to the window that looked over his street. "I will," he said. "As long as my research isn't compromised. Alzheimer's means as much to me as Huntington's does to you. I can't just abandon my research."

Louise stood and hurried over to him. She reached for his hand, needing to beg. "I completely understand, but please . . . try your best." She looked in his eyes.

They were sweet, but they weren't Six's and never would be.

"For you, Louisa. I will."

Everything about Louisa felt right. And it wasn't just the sex, which had been a revelation every time. It was so much more. Like the way she was currently asleep draped across him, finally relaxed enough in sleep to forget about her internal walls and turn off all her alarms. Like the way he'd looked at the papers on her desk while she'd showered and found the makings of a business plan for a company called True North Industries with a financial plan that made his eyes water. The woman was smarter than he'd ever be, and clearly wealthier than he'd imagined, given the amount she was planning to invest.

And she was funny, and made him laugh, and didn't let him get away with shit.

Which had all the makings of being in love. He waited for his stomach to turn at the idea, to clutch at thoughts related to settling down. But nothing happened. Except a feeling of inner peace at the mental declaration that his mom would be proud of. He'd texted both his mom and sister and told them to stay away. Of course, he'd played it off as a client staying with him, which was completely true. His mom had always been able to tell if he was lying, even if it was electronically. But he was actually looking forward to introducing her to his family.

Watching her today with Aiden had been odd. For the first time, he'd been jealous of their friendship. It was clear to him that Aiden had wanted a relationship with Lou, but the look in her eyes had told him all he needed to know. The only person *she* was interested in was him.

He'd been unable to sleep. Cabe was right. It was harder to think clearly about what the right thing to do was because it was Louisa. They were convening at Eagle in the morning, and he'd already agreed to take Lou with him because there was no way she'd accept being left behind, and Louisa was right. She was smart and might be able to help. But part of him wished he could lock her in the house and surround her with a hundred ex-military guys instead. Love and duty made for uneasy bedfellows.

Lou rolled onto her side and buried her head into her own pillow. The sound of metal scratching against metal caught his attention, and he sat up quickly, craning his head in the direction of the sound. If he didn't know better, he'd swear it was the garage door. Quickly, he rolled out of bed, pulled on his shorts, and slipped into his shoes, which were exactly where he'd lined them up.

He pulled his SIG out of the drawer and placed his hand over Louisa's mouth. She woke with a start, but he placed his lips next to her ear. "Shh. Someone's here." Quietly, he slid her drawer open and pulled out the gun he'd left there for her. He handed it, and his phone, to her. "Get in the bathroom and lock the door. Don't open it for anyone but me. Anyone kicks the door in, you fire this straight at the chest like I showed you. You hear bullets, call the police."

Like the smart woman he knew she was, she took both and grabbed her pajamas and sneakers on the way.

Once he heard the lock click, he held his gun out and moved into the hallway. His first job was to keep whoever was attempting to enter the property away from Lou. Which meant they couldn't get to the back of the house. He reached the doorway into the kitchen in time to see the handle at the top of the stairs that led down to the garage turn ominously. He dropped to the ground to the left of the archway, which offered concealment, not cover. Depending on what type of weapons they might have, they could possibly rip drywall to pieces, so his location was less than ideal, but he didn't have the time to run to the other side of the kitchen.

Everything around him went silent and into slow motion. The door opened and three men ran in. He had the advantage of surprise on the first intruder and shot him straight in the chest. The impact caused him to stumble backward, and he crashed into the second intruder, who moved so quickly that the bullet Six fired at him went through his shoulder instead of his heart. The latter would have killed him, like his buddy, instantly, but it was enough of a strike to have him dropping down for cover. Before he could take aim at the third intruder, pain ripped through his side, the force of which jerked him sideways. The bullet didn't knock Six off his feet—gunshots rarely did—but he managed to keep hold of his gun as he pressed his hand to his wound. A second bullet hit the floor next to him, and Six scrambled around the corner. Footsteps told him that the guy he'd hit in the shoulder was on the move, likely going around the living space to come at him from the other side. There was no way he could help Lou if he was dead, so he pulled himself to his feet. He stared at a painting on his hallway wall. The streetlights outside of his home had caused it to be reflective, and in the glass he could see the third assailant, who was as yet uninjured, moving closer. Anticipating his next move, Six aimed his gun around the corner and fired four bullets in quick succession, feeling nothing but relief as he heard a body fall to the floor with a thud.

His side throbbed like an absolute bitch, and he could feel blood running down his leg, but he ignored both. Pain was fleeting, which he'd learned at BUD/S, and what he was fighting for, Lou's safety, was far more important.

Six turned to listen for the second assailant but was too late. He turned face-first into the barrel of a gun. His training fired to life and he pushed the barrel upward, gripping the assailant's hand and hearing the satisfying crack as he broke the guy's trigger finger. It was damn near impossible for a guy to make a kill shot when he couldn't fire his gun.

A gunshot rang out down the hallway, and he looked around for a fourth assailant. Shit, he'd screwed up. There must be someone else in the house. Another point of entry maybe. All he had to do was keep them alive long enough for the police to arrive. The man he'd been fighting slumped against the hallway wall and released his gun into Six's control as he slid to the ground. A red bloodstain smeared the old wallpaper.

"Did I kill him?" Louisa said, her voice shaking. She stood there in aqua pajamas and bright pink sneakers, gun in one hand, his phone in the other, a detail he took in as she looked right and screamed. A bullet missed her by inches, sending glass flying as it hit the mirror on the wall. "There are more of them," she yelled as she hurried toward him.

"Let's go," he yelled, quickly formulating a plan that involved getting out of the house. They were most certainly outnumbered, and he had no idea how many of them there actually were. If they left via the front door, they'd be exposed to anybody keeping watch outside. The garage might be safer if the three men they'd already dealt with were the only assailants, especially if they could get into the truck.

Gripping his gun, he reached for her hand as she crossed the distance between them. He hurried them through the kitchen, where he picked up his keys and wallet and she grabbed her purse and phone off the counter. They moved quickly over the two bodies in the kitchen and down the steps to the garage. Shot or not, he needed to get them out of there, and for the first time in his life, he felt fear. Not for him, but for Louisa. He pulled the truck door open and hurried her inside before racing to his side of the vehicle. Once inside, he raised the garage door and gunned the engine. In the rearview mirror, he saw two more men run out of the house and begin to fire at them.

"Duck," he ordered Louisa, relieved she did as he instructed immediately. She stood a better chance of not getting shot if she was protected by metal rather than glass. He could feel her fear and hear the way her breath was coming in nervous pants as the metallic ping of bullets hitting the truck reverberated around them. Panic wasn't going to help either of them.

He charged the truck out of the driveway, noticing the dark van parked on the opposite side of the street, and immediately took the first left he could. "Do you still have my phone?" he asked calmly as he looked behind them. A couple of men ran across the street and jumped into the other vehicle.

"Yes," she said.

"Okay, call Cabe. Tell him what happened, and tell him we are going to Eagle Securities. Tell him I'm shot."

Louisa sat up immediately. "You're shot? Where?" she cried.

"Doesn't matter, sweetheart. Just do what I said." He did his best to ignore the tears on her face. There would be time to hold her later, to reassure her. But now he needed to focus. "Then find Eric Lestap in my contacts, and tell him the exact same thing. He's captain of the North Coastal Station, and we served together. Tell him what happened and that I'll call him when we get somewhere safe. Tell him to contact Officer Meeks at SDPD."

He took a hard right onto the South Coast Highway, past La Paloma Theatre with its ornate ticket booth, where he'd take her one day. He weaved back and forth through side streets and then looped back to connect with the I-5. With one eye on the rearview mirror, he listened as Louisa pulled herself together enough to make the calls.

"I need to apply pressure to your gunshot wound," she said.

It throbbed like a bitch, which made him think the bullet was still in there. "Gym bag in the back of the cab. There's a towel in there."

Louisa slipped off her seat belt before he could warn her not to. He was driving right now with full-on evasive maneuvers, and he sure as shit didn't want to brake hard while she was wedged between the two seats. He wouldn't stop now, not even for the police. The kind of men who were following him were ruthless in their pursuit and would think nothing of killing cops to get what they wanted.

"Got it," she said, breathlessly as she flopped back into her seat.

"Fasten your seat belt," he said.

"When I've taken care of you," she said, leaning toward him, but he batted her hand away.

"Lou, please. Fasten your seat belt so I don't have to worry about driving like a maniac."

"For fuck's sake," she huffed, pulling the strap over her shoulder.

"Did you just swear at me, Louisa North?" Expletives coming out of those lips just seemed wrong. He looked behind them. Still no sign. He must have lost them back in Encinitas.

"I'll do more than swear if you don't let me look at your side," she said, leaning over him. She pressed the towel so hard against him that he gasped. "I have a gun sitting right here, and I've already shown I can use it," she said, her laughter sounding like it was half genuine, half nerves.

He placed his hand on top of hers.

"We're fine, Lou. Remember what I said about being alive. It's the only thing that matters."

Except you. Because she was beginning to mean more.

Mac flung open the door to Eagle Securities as Six pulled the truck into the parking lot. For somebody who usually hated people, Louisa had never been more relieved to see anybody in her life. Especially when that person was clearly armed to the teeth. She'd protested that Six should pull over and let her drive, but he'd given her a look, one that said it was never going to happen. Then she'd campaigned hard for having Six drive straight to a hospital for treatment, but Six had explained that Mac had trained as a medic and was more than capable of dealing with a gunshot wound, except, as he put it, "without the six-figure price tag."

A black car screeched up alongside his truck, and Louisa screamed. She grabbed the gun she'd placed on the floor and held it toward the window, ready to shoot again if she had to.

"No," Six shouted, snatching the gun from her hand. "It's okay, sweetheart. It's Cabe."

Tears threatened to fall as shock and relief and panic all unfurled within her. Six did something to the gun. What, she wasn't sure—probably released all the bullets or chamber or whatever the hell it was called.

"Don't fall apart yet," Six said quietly. "We're going to get inside, get safe, and get cleaned up. Three steps. I know you can hold it together to do that."

Cabe jumped quickly out of his car, hurried to Six's door, and yanked it open. "What the hell happened?"

Six killed the engine and removed her hand from the towel. "It's time to go, Lou. Step one. Remember? Get inside. But wait for Mac to come get you and give you some cover. I'm pretty sure we lost them, but we can't be too careful."

He turned to drop out of the cab, and she could tell by the way he let all of his weight hang in his shoulders and arms that he was trying to limit his movement as much as possible.

"Jesus Christ, get him inside," she heard Mac say, gun in hand, as he made his way over to her.

She pushed the door open and lowered herself to the ground. Mac shielded her with his body as he pushed her forward toward the building.

"Keys," Cabe said, holding out his hand toward Six.

Six pulled them from his pocket and dropped them into Cabe's palm.

"I opened the side door," Mac said, nodding his head toward the side of the building. "He's going to pull your truck inside, just in case you did gain a tail."

Action was going on all around her. Cabe ran outside, slamming the main door behind him. Mac locked everything down and then offered his shoulder to Six, who was leaning on the front desk, leaving a bloody smear with one hand while the other pressed the towel to his waist.

"Let's get you into those medical rooms," Mac said. "Nice of you to have given the paint the chance to dry before you got yourself shot up."

"Funny, asshole," Six replied. When he turned and winked at her, she could see the sweat on his brow and the way his skin had taken on a pallor. It was taking a lot for him to remain standing, she could tell, and she wondered how much of that was for her benefit. She should feel safe in a secure compound with three men trained to kill. Without Six's intervention, she would certainly be in the hands of the people who wanted her. Her entire body shook at the thought. But they'd nearly killed him. She'd seen the bullet wound with her own eyes. Ten inches higher, and his heart would have been in a whole world of trouble. Part of her wanted to tell them that the contract was canceled, that she didn't want their help in protecting her if it put Six's life at risk. But she was too much of a coward to go it alone, and too smart to truly consider it.

She shuffled after them, still wearing her pajamas, through another key-coded door, down the hallway, and then through a wide-open space. It had the proportions of a small airplane hangar, but that couldn't be possible given its location so close to the university. Six's truck roared into the building through the wide-open door, and no sooner had Cabe brought it to a stop than he was out of the cab and lowering the heavy roller shutter into place.

They passed through a small gym into a series of rooms at the back that looked, and smelled, like a locker room. Six pushed the door open to a room that looked part medical, part dorm. At Mac's instruction he hopped up on the bed.

"Here." Cabe dropped a large fleece around her shoulders. "We don't have any women's clothes, but it will help you get warm."

Louisa struggled to get her brain to function. It was hot outside, yet she was frozen. She watched, almost impartially, as Mac cut away Six's shorts and then stuck a needle into his side. Over the years, she'd dissected animals and even humans, but somehow the sight of Mac fixing Six made her feel ill. Despite how cold she felt, she needed air. She turned and ran into the gym before throwing up in a garbage can.

"Lou?" she heard Six shout. But she needed a moment before she went back to see him. *You're fine. He's alive. He'll be fine. It will all be fine.* Except it wasn't fine. She threw up again.

Once she'd finished heaving, she wiped her mouth with the sleeve of the fleece and sat back on her knees.

"Here. Drink this." Cabe offered her a bottle of ice-cold water, and she placed it against her forehead. "You're doing great, Louisa. Stressful night for everybody."

"Lou?" Six yelled again.

"She's fine, Viking. Stay where you are," Cabe shouted back.

"They shot him," she blurted. "So I shot one of them. He's on the floor. I think I killed him."

Cabe sat down on the floor next to her, resting his forearms on his knees. "Yeah. That happens sometimes. And it's really rough that you experienced it. But if you hadn't, what do you think the outcome would have been?"

"They would have killed Six and taken me."

Cabe fiddled with the watch on his wrist. "You're a scientist, right?"

Louisa nodded.

"So you know all about how to design experiments, alter variables, and trade off options, right?"

She took a sip of water. "I'd like to think so," she said quietly.

"Well, here's the thing. In the moment you stepped up to fire that gun, your brain had already made the decision that Six's life and your safety were more important than the other guy's life. And from what you told me, there were more of them than there were of you. All those shots did was even the scales. You didn't do anything wrong, Louisa. In fact, for someone who hates guns—and yeah, Six told us how much you don't like 'em—I'd say you did everything right."

In the past, Louisa had never had any difficulties putting emotion to one side to look at things clinically. Despite her deeply personal connection to Huntington's disease, she'd never felt panic in her attempts to find medication to help people living with it. Certainly she'd spent a number of years feeling a burden of responsibility to find a treatment quickly, but never had she felt the torrential river of feelings that currently coursed through her body.

She finally understood what Six had been trying to keep from her. It was this. This feeling, the images she would never get out of her head, the way her stomach flipped at the memory of Six and the assailant fighting. She looked down at her hands and saw Six's blood all over them.

"You did what you had to do to stay alive, and there is no crime or shame in that," Cabe added. "Why don't you go into the locker room and get cleaned up? There are towels on the counter, and I left some shorts and a T-shirt in there. I'll tell Six what you're up to. He'll cope a lot better if he knows you aren't losing your shit."

The sound of a groan came from inside the medical room.

Louisa stood. "I should be with him," she said, and headed toward the door, but Cabe stopped her.

"No, you shouldn't. First, you hurled when you saw what was going on. Doctor or no. Second, that isn't a fully equipped med room. We don't have morphine or those kinds of painkillers. Six is probably only just holding his shit together. Third, let Mac do what he needs to."

Cabe moved between her and the door and folded his arms. Like the guardian at the gate, he wasn't going to let her through.

"Fine," she snapped and turned for the locker room. The shower would give her time to pull her own shit together. There were police to talk to, and new plans to make.

But once she came out, she was going to see Six.

And there was no way Cabe was going to stop her.

CHAPTER TWELVE

Six looked down at the gauze that covered his side. The bullet had skimmed through his waist, leaving a wound that hurt like a bitch while Mac stitched it, yet the whole time he'd been worried about Lou. He might possibly have the luckiest freaking torso on the planet, surviving two gunshot wounds, and now he'd have matching scars on either side of his body. Only this time, nobody was going to be lining up to give him a medal. But the way Lou had paled as she'd watched Mac poke him broke his heart. He'd seen the color drain from her face. And it was impossible to miss the way she'd started to sway on her feet. He'd almost been relieved when she'd run out of the room. When he'd told her there where things she'd never be able to unsee, he hadn't imagined she'd be faced with the sight of him banged up on a table. Now, every time she looked at the scar, she'd be reminded of this time in her life.

Cabe had jogged out after her, and Six had wanted

to know how she was. But nobody had passed him word. At least not immediately.

He looked across the room now to where Louisa was curled up on the bottom bunk in a pair of shorts that were so long on her that they looked like capris and a T-shirt so large that the neckhole kept slipping off her shoulder. As always, she let go in sleep, and he wondered if she realized just how different her energy was when she was like this.

When Cabe had eventually told him that she'd been sick in the gym, he'd felt like shit that they'd left her that exposed. Their team was still small, with other jobs on the go, and there hadn't been enough men to put an extra patrol on their house that night. Overly confident that there was no way of tracing Lou back to his house and that the key players were locked up, they'd made a bad call. Now all that mattered was figuring out just how the assailants had found her, and later, as a company, they'd have to talk about how to expand or they'd never be able to manage multiple jobs at any one time.

In the meantime, he was going to have to deal with the guilt he felt at letting her down. Had he not been naked with her in her bed, but in his own room across the hall, closer to the garage, maybe he would have heard them sooner. Every time Cabe had said she was a distraction, he'd been right. He should have kept her at arm's distance and waited until it was all over, but his dick, which had nearly been blown off by his own shortcomings, had been doing the thinking for him.

Not that he could go back at this point. His heart hurt at even the thought of it. The thought of leaving her in somebody else's care stung worse than the bullet hole in his side. But in the morning, he was going to find somewhere safe for them to stay while they figured out what to do. If he had to fly her somewhere, he'd do it. Call in a favor with one of his buddies who had their own planes and get her somewhere without any kind of paper trail.

He was embarrassed that he'd let it come to this. He was better than this. More capable. And yet he'd messed up. The sensation didn't sit well.

"She doing okay?" Cabe asked quietly as he walked into the room.

Six drew his eyes from her sleeping form. "Yeah. She's strong," he said, attempting to keep the admiration out of his tone. They'd spent hours dealing with the police, the FBI, and updating their CIA contact. He'd been completely truthful with Officer Meeks and with Detective Pitt who'd been assigned to the case about what had gone down at his house. He'd told Pitt how Louisa had hired his company to figure out what the hell was going on.

Kovalenko wasn't talking, knowing he'd be killed by the end of his first day in prison if he revealed any secrets. And they only had the testimony from the driver, which was unsubstantiated; they still didn't have any real proof of Vasilii and Ivan's involvement. As for Mitkin, he'd lawyered up tight, leaving them with a whole bunch of nothing.

Lou had done what was needed. She'd gone inside, gotten safe, and gotten cleaned up. Then she'd answered questions like it was lunchtime rather than three thirty in the morning. The first freaking day in September.

Two more days and all their jobs were meant to kick off. Hell, two more days and Cabe would be on his way to Sierra Leone with half the team.

"I think we need a change of plan," Six whispered, boosting himself up on the bed.

"Yeah, well, we weren't anticipating this kind of job in our first week of operation. Slow start, we said, remember?" Cabe raised an eyebrow at him, and he knew they were going to fight.

"Louisa is paying a shit ton of cash to do this," he hissed, looking over to where she still slept peacefully. The last thing he needed was for her to be privy to Cabe's thoughts. "And what, she nearly gets taken? Again. On our watch."

"Okay. One. It was your watch. And two. If you weren't so wrapped up in her, you'd have recognized this deal for the cash cow it is and kept your dick in your pants."

Six's legs were swinging off the bed before he knew it, gunshot or no gunshot. "Fuck. You," he spat. He and Cabe had had their fallings out in the past, but he had a feeling there'd be no coming back from the one they were about to have. "One. It was *our* watch. And two. *We* let her down."

"Well, maybe if you two weren't knocking boots, you would have had any eye on the job instead of her pussy."

At that, Six ripped the drip of antibiotics from his arm, and despite the pain that ripped through his side, he stood. "You want to say that again, asshole?"

Mac marched into the room, his first look over at Louisa and his second between the two of them. "She's our client," he hissed. "Outside, now."

Six marched out the door, not giving a shit if Cabe was behind him or not. In fact, better for him if he wasn't. Because Six was likely to go off any second, and Cabe was going to feel the brunt of it.

"Okay," Mac said once they were in the gym area. "You two are both idiots. Should we ream off the litany of stupid shit you just pulled? Arguing in front of a client, asleep or not? That's got to be the most stupid business decision." He turned to face Cabe. "You—if you can't see that this is different, then you need to go get those eyes of yours tested, because anybody with half a brain can see Six is halfway in love with the girl, even if he doesn't have the balls to admit it yet." Mac then looked straight at Six. "And you. She isn't the kind of client we want. She isn't even the kind of work we really want to do, but we're doing it because you asked us to. And we needed the money. So pull your neck in. It wasn't like the Norths of San Diego couldn't afford it. So why don't we talk about what we are going to do."

"We could always ask Lou for more." Cabe stubbed his toe into the ground. "Think about it. She floats us more cash, we can hire some more guys. Screw starting small and quibbling over which of us gets the day off."

"What if she already has plans for her money?" he said, thinking of the business plan he'd seen scattered all over the desk. True North Industries.

"Then convince her to back us," Cabe said. "You can be persuasive if you tried."

"You know what," Six said, walking a little away from the guys to sit down on the leg raises station. His stitches were at risk of coming open, and he had a mild case of the spins, not that he'd ever admit that to anyone. Losing that much blood had obviously taken its toll, leaving him adrift. "I don't need to be persuasive. I'm sure she'd give me money if I asked her—"

"Perfect," Cabe said, clapping his hands.

The guys walked over to where he was seated.

"Just let me finish, jackass. But I'm not going to ask. She came to me for help, Cabe, and we've found a weakness in our plans. There aren't enough of us to do any kind of meaningful rotation on a full-time basis *and* do the intel work to figure out who is behind this. So we're going to have to address our growth plans to figure out how we afford that. And by the way . . ." He looked over to Mac, confident enough to say the words out loud to his friends that he wasn't quite ready to say to Lou. "Yeah. So what if I love her? I get why that seems odd. I met her for the first time three weeks ago. It makes no fucking sense to me either. So can we stop talking about her like she's an item on our to-do list? Because I'm going to lose my shit if you don't."

He shuffled back to the medical room, desperately needing to lie down.

"I can help, you know," Louisa said as he was about to get onto his bed. Instead he wandered over to her bunk and sat down gingerly.

"What do you mean?" he asked, surprised to find her awake. He placed his hand on her leg, but she shuffled up the bed and sat up, leaning against the headboard.

"I overheard. If your funds are running low, I can help. It feels like the least I can do for keeping me alive."

Six shook his head and reached for her hand. "Thank you, Lou. But we'll figure it out."

Lou took a deep breath and pulled her hand from his. "Will you be able to keep protecting me?"

"What the hell, Lou. Of course. And please. Stop trying to pull away from me. It's bugging the crap out of me, and to be honest, my side hurts like a bitch. So please. Go easy on me."

Immediately, she stopped tugging. "Fine. Go ahead," she said in a tone that told him that his balls were at risk if he made a misstep.

He caressed the inside of her wrist with his thumb, feeling the way her pulse raced in the vein beneath her skin. "I told the guys that this was not a job anymore. Because somewhere between learning that you know what a *Dieffenbachia fortunensis* is and watching you shoot a bullet into the guy who would have willingly killed me, I fell in love with you, Lou."

Her whole body snapped to attention at that, and she stood. "You can't possibly mean that, Six. I mean, you don't even—"

"Whatever argument you are about to give me, stop. You asked me whether I intend to keep protecting you. The answer is yes, for the foreseeable future and beyond that." He slid his hands around her waist and drew her close.

She placed her hands tentatively on his shoulders and shook her head gently. "You and me . . . we . . . Oh, lord."

Six laughed and pressed his forehead to her chest, relieved when her fingers wound their way into his hair. As always, she needed time to think. She might read faster than anyone he'd ever known, but her decisions took forever, and for a guy who really needed reassurance that he hadn't just puked his feelings onto her feet for nothing, waiting for her to figure out what she wanted to say was torturous.

"You really meant all of that?" she whispered into his hair before placing a kiss on the top of his head.

"Yeah, Lou," he said, pulling away to look up at her. "I love you."

She stared at him, those dark brown eyes of hers shimmering with tears. "Even though I might have Huntington's?" she asked. "It could affect everything. Life span. Having kids."

He'd considered that too. "There are no guarantees in anything. You might, you might not. And while you might have just scared the crap out of me by mentioning kids, Lou, there are lots of ways to have them that might avoid passing the disease on."

"Preimplantation genetic diagnosis and those kinds of things are one way. But it feels like a lot to take on."

Six sighed and shifted his hands to her hips. "You went straight to the biology of it. The disease, the way to have kids. There is more to life and love than just biology, Lou," he said, grateful they could have this conversation in private. "What about the chemistry of it? What do you feel?"

Louisa took a deep breath, her eyes fluttering shut on her exhalation. For the first time since he'd walked into the room, she smiled, the permanent look of worry on her face fading. Her eyes flashed open. "I think that—"

"No. Don't think." Six took her hand and placed it over his heart, pressing it flat to his skin. "Thinking is what comes easy to you. I want to know what you feel, Lou. Not how you can rationalize this, or how some biological reaction makes your heart speed up the way it does. I want to know how you feel when I look you in your eyes and tell you I love you. Does your heart feel it like mine does?"

She covered his hand with her own. "Yes, I feel it, Six. I feel it down to my toes." Her cheeks flushed with pink as she said those simple words. She leaned forward and buried her face in his hair. Six waited as her brain likely thought through every facet of the words she'd just said to him. Just being with her was enough. It was slow, and real, and the opposite of his life, which up until now had been fast, and impromptu, and sometimes shallow.

Eventually she stood straight and looked at him. "Did you know that penguins undergo what is called a catastrophic molt?"

Six laughed—he couldn't help it—and it pulled on his stitches, making him groan.

"What's so funny?" she asked. "It was a genuine question."

"Oh, I know it was, sweetheart. But I just laid it all out for you that I love you, and your response is to ask me about penguins."

The corner of her mouth twitched in the making of a smile. "Anyway, do you know what the catastrophic molt is?"

"My guess is something to do with losing baby fur or something, but go ahead. Tell me, because I can't wait to see you turn this into a relevant analogy." He grinned at her but managed to grip her wrist when she playfully went to hit him.

"It's called a catastrophic molt because it's when the baby loses all of its baby feathers at once. The old feathers won't fall out until the new ones have fully grown in. It lasts about two or three weeks, and during that time, they look weird and awkward and uncomfortable. It's not painful, just strange."

Suddenly he got it. She was the penguin. He wrapped his arms tightly around her. "Lou," he said carefully.

"Two or three weeks ago, I didn't even know you. I honestly never thought I would meet someone like you. The lab and my research have been my everything for so long, and now they're gone. My safety was a privilege I took for granted, and now it isn't," she said, and ran her fingertips across the gauze taped to his side. "So it feels weird, like new things are growing while old things are still lingering. Like my life is changing radically in a very short space of time." Louisa pressed her lips to his just long enough to stir him up before pulling away. "I love you, Six, and it feels strange, and wonderful, and a little bit terrifying amid this huge change happening in my life. I don't know where I am going to end up when this is all over, but I hope it's with you."

She loved him, and the warmth he hadn't known was missing from his life filled him as if someone were heating his blood. It settled in him. Grounded him. Made him forget about everything else except the sheer perfection of having Louisa in his arms, knowing that her feelings for him were as strong as his for her.

Standing in her clean jeans and a T-shirt, Louisa helped herself to another croissant. It was her third, and she piled more than her fair share of the juicy tropical fruit platter onto her plate. Six looked across the large table at her and winked. Her heart stuttered. She was officially in a relationship. With him. The way he looked at her, like he did now, like he wished he could eat her instead of the pastry in his hand, made her knees weak.

The coffee Mac placed next to her was steaming hot and very strong. She added a little cream and sugar to help keep her awake through the next hour. Thanks to Buddha and Bailey who'd made a drive to Encinitas to grab bags for both her and Six, she was thankful for the return of her belongings, and her dead phone was now charging. Plus, she'd showered with products that didn't smell like they'd double as disinfectant. Transience usually left her agitated, so she doubly appreciated her own things around her.

"Okay," Mac said, dimming the lights. A projector shot images of people and buildings onto the white wall. The full team was sitting around the table with her, men she'd seen around Six's home before. Men who were willing to help her. Each one was as intimidating as Six had been at first, but every time she felt herself flutter around the edge of panic, Six would tap her foot under the table. "So here is the timeline. On Friday the twelfth, Louisa noticed that someone had been messing with her files and switched the samples as a precaution. Let's call the dangerous sample A and the innocuous sample B. On Thursday the eighteenth, she noticed that sample B had been taken, and she assumed that whoever took it thought it was sample A. Unable to find it in the lab, she went to talk to the owner of the lab, Vasilii Popov, and his grandson, also Louisa's lab partner, Ivan Popov."

Louisa listened attentively as he ran through the details with the team. She looked at the floor as the details poured out, but felt marginally better when Cabe leaned his shoulder against hers, giving her a nudge of support.

As she listened to Mac recap the relationship between Kovalenko, the man who had tried to abduct her the first time, and a man called Mitkin who had orchestrated it all on behalf of his father-in-law, a man called Lemtov, she couldn't get her mind off her phone. Something was niggling her in the back of the brain. It was important.

"Ivan has gone off grid," Lite said. "We last saw him come out of his house on Monday." Another picture flashed up on the wall, and pain ripped through her at the sight of the man she'd once trusted. It didn't make her feel any better to see that he looked incredibly gaunt, stress or guilt or some other emotion having weighed heavily on him in the six days since she had seen him.

"We no longer have the element of surprise with Lemtov," Mac said. "He's bound to know we took in some of his guys. Lite, did we learn anything new?"

Lite twirled a pen around on the tips of his fingers. "Lemtov grew up with Ivan's deceased father. Went to school together. So there is a real connection between the two families. Lemtov is Ivan's godfather. Not sure as of yet whether the main connection is through Vasilii or Ivan."

Vasilii. His call. That was what had been bugging her. They'd forgotten to tell the others about it. "Vasilii called me," she said quickly. "The night you all met with Mitkin. I almost forgot to mention it because Six came home hurt." She looked over at Six, who suddenly sat up and leaned forward, folding his arms on the desk. Thankfully he didn't disclose what had her so distracted that night. Memories of the way he'd taken her made her shiver.

"What happened? What did he say?" Mac said.

Louisa recounted the conversation to them all. "It struck me as odd, because it started apologetically. But somehow it sounded . . . I don't know . . . it lacked authenticity if that doesn't sound too hokey. Then he gave me excuses, about the reputation of the lab and our security. Knowing what Aiden told us, he'd already had visits from the police and the FBI before he called. And then he ended by telling me I was paranoid."

Cabe swore.

"And where's the phone now?" Lite asked. "You wondered how they found you last night, Six. There could be a tracker on it. We should check for that first, then get rid of the phone."

Panic choked her. "If they know where I am because of my phone, what's to stop them from coming here to get me?"

Gaz laughed. "They'd have to be suicidal to come try to get you here. Weapon count, boys?"

All of them suddenly began to pull weapons. From holsters, belts. Louisa looked around the room. To a man, they were armed to the teeth, and not just with small handguns. There were big guns that could do a lot more damage. And knives. Suddenly she felt overwhelmed.

"He's right," Cabe said. "They'd be idiots to try to come in here."

"So what do we do now?" she asked.

"Lite is going to deal with your phone and try to find Ivan, among other things," Mac answered. "Buddha, Gaz, and I are taking a trip to LA to catch up with Lemtov. He's likely being cautious right now, but we'll get eyes on him, who he's meeting with."

Six tapped the table with his fingertips. She could feel the tension rolling off him. A small muscle twitched by his jaw. There was obviously something on his mind. She tapped his foot under the table, but he didn't look up. This time, she kicked it, much harder than the first time.

"Give me a minute with the guys, would you, Louisa?" he said. "Let me talk business for a minute while you get your phone."

They were supposed to be past this, him keeping her out of the process. "Whatever it is you need to discuss, you can say it in front of me. I'm—"

"Please." His eyes met hers. "I just want to tell them what we talked about this morning." His tone was soft.

She'd convinced him to let her give them more so they could honor the bookings they had while taking care of her. "Sorry," she said. "I'll go get my phone."

The air in the locker room was stagnant. It was probably some kind of safety feature that the place in which they slept had no other exits than the door, but they could certainly do with better ventilation. She reached for her phone and turned it on. The eighteen-percent battery was better than nothing but had no signal. She wandered out into the training area to find one and several notifications began to appear, including several missed calls from Vasilii. Dialing her voice mail, she sat down on a chair by the large doors.

"Louisa. It's Vasilii. I'm sorry about the call yesterday. But I need to speak to you urgently. Please call me back."

She saved the message because from now on she intended to keep a complete record of all of her interactions with Vasilii. There was no telling when she might need that information again. She pressed the right button to continue.

"Louisa. It's Vasilii again. Please, I need to talk to you."

His voice sounded strained, frantic even.

"I have sent you a photograph, Louisa. I hate to do this to you, but I need you to see this and return my call."

Louisa pulled her phone away from her ear and opened her email. There was a message with an attachment from Vasilii. When she opened it, there was no text, and for a moment she wondered whether or not she should open it with Six. But he was busy with his men, and she wasn't such a coward that she couldn't open an email in a box of a room where nobody could get at her.

She tapped the little attachment icon, and the several seconds it took to open felt like a lifetime. For a moment, it was all Louisa could do to keep down the food she'd eaten so hungrily earlier. Her mother sat in a place she didn't recognize. The cast on her foot told Louisa that the photo was recent. She didn't look injured, but she *did* look terrified.

Her phone shook in her hand, and she was glad she was seated. There was a garbage can within arm's reach, but Louisa breathed deeply and slowly until she had her heart rate under control. The image changed everything she thought she knew. There was no length too far for Vasilii. He wanted the formula badly enough that he would take her mother. She knew what she had to do. She had to go to him, offer to re-create it in the lab. But there was no way she was going to do something as stupid as sneak out the side entrance and do this alone. Not when there was a room full of men more than qualified to help her scour the earth for her mother. All she had to do was buy them time while they did it, perhaps throw in a couple of missteps along the way to kill time.

Either way, she knew what she held in her hand was crucial information, and it certainly explained where Ivan had disappeared to.

Once she felt under control and able to walk on legs that were shaking, she hurried back to the meeting room. As she hit the hallway, she could hear Six.

"And I say we hire three more right now. Harley could be back here by tonight, and according to Gaz, Jackson is doing little more than screwing around in Tijuana. The guy is thirty minutes away. There's got to be a third that we can find." He'd finally gotten his head around her offer. It had taken an hour of convincing, and when she'd finally made him see sense, he'd insisted on treating it as a loan. Even insisted they pay her back interest.

"I'm on it," Cabe said as he grabbed his phone off the table. "I'll go make those calls."

Despite the shot he'd taken to his side, Six was on his feet, ready to fight on her behalf.

Without overthinking it, she walked around to Six's side of the table. Gently, she placed her hand on his shoulder, encouraging him to sit. Muscles strained beneath her fingertips as he lowered himself to his seat. She knew she'd never convince him to stand down, to let the others help her while he healed. Nor would she want him to. She trusted her life in his hands. But she could get him to rest when it was possible.

"Cabe, you should stay just for a moment," she said with as much authority as she could muster. "I think it's about to get worse." She placed her phone into Six's hands.

"What the . . . ? Who sent you this?" he said, handing the phone to Mac.

"It's from Vasilii. They have my mom." She looked at Six. "And you aren't going to like what I'm going to suggest we do to save her."

CHAPTER THIRTEEN

"Louisa."

The way Vasilii drew out her name in some sicko pretense of being friendly made Six want to punch the guy in the throat, right before he carved out his vocal cords with a blunt fishing knife.

"Where is my mom? Let me speak to her. I need to know she's okay." Louisa moved to pick up the phone, but Six stopped her. They were recording the call. Her hands were frozen.

"You have something I want. I have something you want. A simple exchange is all that is required to put this all behind us. I will send a car for you. Be ready within the next hour. I know where you are. The driver will not be told where to take you until you are safely on your way. He also does not know where my guest is. Don't test me, Louisa, or the thing I have of yours may become . . . damaged. Oh, and as much as I hate to sound like a cliché, if anybody tries to interfere in any way, like follow you or call the police, or attempt to hold the driver hostage, the damage will become permanent, so please, come alone."

The phone clicked silent.

"I should have gotten security for my mom. I've got to . . ."

Six turned to her. "You aren't seriously thinking of going, Lou?" His head had been filled with other options, but none of them involved her getting in that car. The idea of her anywhere other than in his sight freaked the shit out of him.

"It's not like I have a lot of choice," she said, her eyes focused on the phone.

"We need eyes in the sky," Buddha said. "No one ever looks up. We can follow the vehicle that way. Let me see how quick I can be airborne." He grabbed his phone and stepped out of the room.

"He's not going to do anything to me until he has the formula," Louisa said. She placed her hand on his shoulder. It felt tiny as she dug into his muscles. "And you'll get me before then. I know you will."

Cabe coughed. "What she's saying makes sense, Six. We can track the shit out of her. Put a vest on her. The question is where would they take her?"

"Aiden told us Vasilii is distracted by a property he's buying. Could it be there?" Louisa offered.

It was a crapshoot. They could take her anywhere. *Wait.* The photo of her mom. "Lite," he said, turning to the resident tech guy. "If he just bought the property, there'd be a listing, right?"

Lite's face brightened with a smile. "If it was a public sale. But even if it's somewhere else, I got you. Louisa, can you send me the photo from Vasilii?"

Louisa listened as he spelled out his email address, then forwarded the photograph to him. "What are you going to do?"

"Use an image-matching app. See if we can't get a fix on where your mom is through what's in the background of the picture." Lite typed away on his laptop furiously. The energy level in the room was rising as people hurried around, falling into old military habits.

"I called some of the guys to come over and give us a hand. Play decoy, watch the pickup. They're going to expect us to follow Lou. So we should leave now. Get out ahead of them. Let the driver think we all stayed behind."

Louisa moved closer to him and he slipped his arm around her, even though they didn't have much time.

"I'm out, man," Buddha said as he pushed the door open. "Buddy of mine runs the helicopter school north of Serra Mesa. I'll be there in ten, up in fifteen. He's getting it ready for me now." Buddha grabbed Lou from him and hugged her. "Avoid looking up for me," he said. "It kind of ruins the element of surprise. You'll hear me. Most people don't look up anymore when they hear a helicopter or plane because they are so commonplace. But I'll be there, and I'm really good. See these hands?" he asked.

Louisa nodded.

"Good. Well, you're safe in them. I promise." Buddha saluted her and jogged out of the room.

Six let out a breath. "Give me your right shoe," he said as Louisa watched Buddha leave.

"Is this for the tracker? And are you guys always that

cocky?" she asked, putting her phone down to unlace her sneakers.

"Yes, and yes," he said with a wink. He hurried to the cupboard, grabbed a pack of something from one of the shelves, and threw the pack at Bailey. "Set her up, Bailey."

Bailey ripped it open and held out what looked like an insole for a shoe.

"It may look like a sole, but it's got a GPS tracker in it. If anything were to happen to you, if they take you for any reason, they'll pat you down and probably take your phone and anything else they think looks suspicious. But rarely do they take your shoes," Bailey said, sliding it in her sneaker. He messed around on his laptop for a little while, and then handed her shoe back to her.

"Reassuring thought," she said. "I seem to recall someone else telling me the same thing on a beach once."

Despite all the activity going on around them, Six smiled. Their walk on the sand felt like an age ago, but was probably the day he'd begun to fall for her.

"Get ready to move out, guys," Mac said.

"I don't like this," Six said minutes later as he fixed the bulletproof vest on Louisa's shoulders. What were they thinking, letting Louisa go off alone to Vasilii? Once they were en route, he was going to call his contact at the CIA. Hell, they should call in every brother, active or not, to circle the perimeter. But Vasilii had refused point-blank to tell her where her mother was.

"It's okay," Louisa said, looking up at him through those dark eyelashes. "I have faith in you to keep me safe, even though you should be lying down in bed."

"It's just a scratch," he said, pulling on the front of her vest to make sure it was secure. The vest didn't seem like enough protection. Parts of her were exposed. No matter how many times Mac had reminded him that they wanted to take Louisa alive, no matter how much intel they'd already gained about the lab, it didn't seem like enough.

"It was a gunshot wound." She took his wrists in her hands and stilled them. "I'm going to be fine. At least, I hope I am. You and your men will make sure nothing happens. There is no way this is going to stop until they have the formula. We can't let them get that, Six. It's too important. Even if it came down to Mom or me, even."

Six tilted his head from left to right, loosening the muscles. Going in tight was stupid, but he couldn't relax. "We could just go somewhere else. I don't give a shit about Ivan Popov or his grandfather, and please, don't take this the wrong way, but I don't even give a shit about your mom or the medicine you are trying to create." He placed his hands on Louisa's cheeks. Why did she have to look so fucking perfect and fragile today of all days. "*You* are the only thing that matters to me. None of that other stuff. We could get a flight out of here today and disappear."

"You don't mean that. I doubt you've ever backed down from a fight in your life." She turned and pressed her lips to his palm.

She was right. Of course she was right. She was always fucking right. And hopefully it would be that way for at least the next twenty years.

"I haven't. But for you, I'd do it in a heartbeat."

"There is so much more at stake here than me, and you know it."

He did. It was the only reason he hadn't bundled her into his truck and driven away east, back to where he'd be protected by his old team for a while as they figured out what to do next. For the first time in his military life, he was conflicted, torn between his sense of duty and his love for Louisa.

A series of loud bangs came from outside the dorm area and Six flinched.

"It's just the rest of your team getting ready," she said, and wrapped her hands around his waist. "But at some point, you're going to have to unpack what makes you react that way and deal with it."

Six nodded, letting her comfort him as much as he hoped he was comforting her. He'd realized the same thing. No matter how hard he tried, it wasn't going to go away on its own.

He pressed his lips to hers in the hope that she would understand that they were telling her everything he couldn't.

"We gotta go, guys," Cabe shouted.

Six pulled away and tugged on his body armor. He hated wearing the fucker as it constricted his breathing, but the people they were up against had already proven that they would shoot to kill every person who stood between them and Louisa. There was no fucking way he was going down and leaving her unaided. He loaded up his primary and secondary weapon systems and as many magazines as he could fit on the fucking thing. He packed in a couple of charges. There was no way of knowing where this property was or what it looked like yet, but he'd have no issue blowing the fucking doors off, literally, to get Lou out.

Shit. He needed to focus on the mission. Not her.

"Did you know Sar-i Sang in the Badakhshan Province in Afghanistan contains one of the most famous lapis lazuli mines in the world?" he asked her. "It's been mined for over six thousand years." He wanted to hold her hand but didn't.

Cabe looked over and raised an eyebrow at him, and Six shook his head subtly. No, he wasn't going to tell her what had happened while they were there. But he needed to get a lid on his emotions. He'd seen so many jewelry and boxes made of lapis while he was there, and it was a beautifully carved box made of lapis that he imagined now as he tucked his feelings for Lou inside it. He needed to stop thinking about her and start thinking about *them*, the ones who dared to do her harm.

"I *didn't* know that," she said. "See. You taught me something new."

For the briefest of moments, he stopped loading his vest to hold her hand and she grabbed it, her fingers icy cold against his. "We're going to teach each other all kinds of new things when this is over, Lou. I know we're stuck in the middle of some seriously fucked-up shit, but this will always be the period in our lives when we started dating. It's meant to be the period in our lives when we can't take our eyes off each other and the only thing we can think about is the quickest way to get from where we are to being naked on any kind of surface, which is never far from my mind."

Louisa smiled as he'd intended.

"I mean it, Lou. When this is all over, we're holing

up somewhere, my place or yours, I really don't give a shit, and we're getting in bed and staying there for at least forty-eight hours so I can make a concerted effort to thoroughly take care of every single part of you." He brushed his lips against hers, but after the briefest moment, as much as it hurt more than a thousand paper cuts against his heart, he stepped away, let go of her hand, and returned to his weapons. He could soothe her, hold her, warm her later. Now, his primary objective was to keep her safe while they rescued her mom and took down those who'd harm Lou.

Cabe threw him his com equipment, and he slotted it into place on his left ear. He checked his pockets. Multi-tool. Shears. A breaching tool. Extra rounds. A couple of flash-crash. Double-ended flex cuffs so he could tie people up, assuming he didn't kill them. And his tactical gloves.

He helped Louisa slip her sweater over her vest and took hold of her hand.

A crackle came over the radio. "Confirmation that Buddha is airborne and has eyes on our location."

With Buddha in the air and Bailey staying behind to man coms, the remaining men began to pile into two trucks headed for the ranch house Lite had confirmed Vasilii had bought outside of Jamul. They could be heading to the absolute wrong location. Buddha would let them know that. They'd research the area on the drive over.

"Is it right that military guys say *I've got your six* when they mean that they have your back?" Louisa asked as he led her to the door.

He stopped by the doorway and looked over his

shoulder at her as the double meaning in her words hit him. She looked so fucking cute in the gray hoodie, and her words were so sweet, that on any other day he would have stopped what he was doing, lifted her up, and carried her back to bed to show her just how much he had her back covered. Instead, he nodded and swallowed hard.

Their eyes held for a moment that felt like forever.

“Good,” she said with a nervous smile.

Louisa’s first thought was that she’d obviously drunk too much. Her head spun and her stomach clenched. In fact, she wasn’t entirely certain that she wasn’t going to throw up. The details were hazy. Had she and Six been out celebrating?

She struggled to open her eyes. They burned the way the chlorine in her pool burned them if she stayed in the water for too long.

Holding her head, Louisa tried to sit up and look around. She was on a metal-framed twin bed draped in a plastic cover in a bedroom with old pine wood furniture and an overabundance of floral fabric and lace. It most definitely wasn’t like any emergency room or hospital ward she’d seen before. Dread started to fill her. Something had happened, but she couldn’t remember what or how. Everything was muddled. She put her hands to her face. A sweet scent lingered around her. The sample. The car. Six and his team and helicopters.

Fuck. The guy used something on me in the car.

Her heart raced as her chest tightened, making the pounding in her head worse. Louisa pressed her fingertips to her temple.

She leaned forward, clenched her stomach, and looked down at her feet quickly. Thank God. Her sneakers were still on her feet. *They never take your shoes.* She remembered his words on the beach. *Always keep your shoes on. You need to be able to run, should you have to.* Six had been right. Which meant if the GPS that Bailey had installed in her sneaker was working, and Buddha had confirmed the location, Eagle Securities had the place surrounded.

Her skin peeled away from the plastic mattress as she stood. Dizziness overtook her, and she threw her arm out toward the wall to gain her balance. Her limbs felt . . . disconnected. They weren't doing what she told them. Sweat clung to her body, her damp T-shirt confirming that she'd been there for a while. How long, she wasn't certain. There were shutters covering the windows, but there was a door at the other end of the room from her cot. With the way her legs were shaking, the ten yards could have been a hundred miles.

Water.

She could barely swallow but gave herself a few more moments to find her composure and stop the room from spinning.

Six.

Nothing would stop him from finding her. She knew it. She just needed to stay alive long enough for him to get to her. The words he'd said to her in the gym before they left came back to her. *Operative teams have a reputation for being rapid response . . . not the preferred way . . . have time to build a foolproof plan.*

While he was close by, it might be a while until he came. Her initial thought had been to scream and yell, to overcome the fear she had of whoever was on the other side of the door and demand to know where the hell she was. But now she thought it would be better to simply pretend she was still sleeping in case anybody came by to check on her. Anything that would bide time.

She crossed her fingers and prayed that this was Vasilii's new home and that he and Ivan were both here.

Louisa scanned the room, anxious to see if there was anything she could use as a weapon, but with the exception of a small bronze paperweight next to the bed, there was nothing in there. Six had said they wanted her alive, and she hoped that was true.

She curled back up on the bed, the ache in her head dulling as she lay down, but turned so she could see the door. If someone came in, she'd study them carefully before jumping to her feet. Now was the time for her to be clever. Not reckless.

Moments dragged by endlessly. Occasionally, a dull thud or the sound of metal banging against metal would sound in the hollow space.

When the door finally pushed open, Ivan walked through it. A man with a gun stood behind him and yelled something in a language she assumed was Russian before slamming the door shut.

When Ivan finally looked at her, all she could see was a broken man. Whatever had happened, Ivan wasn't the mastermind. Or if he had been at one point, he wasn't any longer.

"Louisa," he said, his voice hoarse. "I'm sorry." Tears filled his eyes as he spoke.

"Who are they? What do they want?" she asked quickly, her eyes flitting between the door and Ivan.

Ivan sat down on the edge of the mattress. "They want the drug we created."

Aware that they wouldn't have long before somebody came to get them both, she hurried on with her questions. "But who are *they*, Ivan? And what do they want it for? How did they even know about it? Are they a rival drug company?" She knew they weren't. There was a huge difference between intercompany espionage and kidnapping. But she wanted to keep him talking. Six's words from their day on the beach came back to her. *If you're alive, you can fight, you can think, you can even wait for someone to come get you. You'll come back from anything they can put you through. But there is no coming back from dead. That's as final as it gets.*

Despondently, Ivan shook his head. "If only . . ." he said.

She needed more information, not abbreviated sentences. "Who *are* they, Ivan?"

He sighed. "I screwed up. And everything got so out of hand. Vasilii arranged it to get me out of trouble. I have money problems, and he was overleveraged. Development of our drug and others was taking too long."

She played along, pretending like she didn't understand. "I don't get it. Did he think somebody else could take the research and then get there faster?" she said, her voice rising in feigned frustration. "We'd only just started animal testing. It could be years before we had the formula right and got it FDA approved."

Ivan looked frantically at the door and shushed her. "They don't want the formula we hoped to create. They want the one we did. They want to weaponize it. Do you think Vasilii wants to be here?"

Louisa sat up and ignored the way her head spun again. Nausea roiled through her like waves, and she swallowed deeply. "You still haven't answered who they are."

"It's such a mess, Lou." His hacking sob echoed off the walls.

All out of patience, she stood and stumbled across the room to Ivan. "First, don't call me Lou." Six was the only person she would allow to call her that, and the man in front of her didn't deserve an ounce of her sympathy. The mess was Ivan's, even if it was now bigger than he'd ever intended. "You and I are not on the same side, even though we are in the same mess. Second, pull yourself together. And third, start from the beginning. Who is behind this and what do they want?"

Ivan started as if she had physically slapped him. As if it were a shock that she'd be so angry.

"What?" she asked. "Don't look so surprised. You have cost me my job, my sanity, and depending on how this all plays out, possibly my life, so stop being pathetic."

"Don't you see, Lou? We *are* on the same side. I'm up to my eyeballs in gambling debt at Lucky Seven Casino. I've been playing their high roller tables for a while, but it's way over my head, Louisa. Vasilii wanted to cut me off, stop fixing my screwups. Said I needed to stand on my own two feet and accept some responsibility for my actions."

Louisa's stomach flipped, and she wasn't sure she wasn't going to be sick. Whether it was the drugs or the pitiful look on Ivan's face that caused her to feel so ill, she wasn't sure. "So, what did you do?" she asked.

"Vasilii refused to bail me out this time. So what was I supposed to do?"

"I don't know," Louisa muttered. "Sell your house, your cars. Cash in some stock. Sell shares in the lab. Sell one of the patents the lab owns."

Ivan stood and paced, tugging his hands through his hair. "I knew the formula could be weaponized . . . so I . . . Well, I knew we weren't in need of it . . . and you are usually so focused on getting the next test ready that I dispose of the old samples."

"So you attempted to sell it?" she asked.

Ivan nodded, and created a small gap in the curtains to peer out of the window into the darkness. Terrified that Ivan would spot Six and his team and alert whoever else was in the house to their presence, Louisa made a pretense of standing and knocking the bronze paperweight to the floor as she stumbled. It was feeble, and she was no actress, but it worked. Ivan dropped the curtain and looked back at her as she picked it up again and returned it to the table.

"I did and I took the money and cleared off my debts. And when you reported the sample missing, Vasilii questioned me about it. Hated me for doing it. Even offered to pay the money back to the buyers to make everything right, but by then it was too late. The Russians I had offered to sell it to through my godfather threatened us. They told me to re-create the sample."

For a moment she contemplated telling Ivan that help was on its way. Though she was pissed that he'd gotten them into this mess, the guy looked more terrified than she felt. But desperation could cause a man to do strange things, so she kept the information to herself.

"So, what happened?" Louisa asked.

"You are meticulous in recording the details, but we must have missed something because no matter how hard I tried, I couldn't re-create it."

The scientist in her balked at his comments. She *was* meticulous. There was no way they had written it down incorrectly.

"So I tested the sample I gave them and recognized straightaway that it wasn't the sample they were after. But I didn't tell them at first. Where is the real sample, Louisa? Because I know it must be you who switched the labels."

"The sample is long gone down the lab drain in a five-part sample, one-part bleach solution, safe from their eager hands."

Ivan's shoulder slumped. "You shouldn't have done that, Louisa. It could have saved our lives. I don't think we'll get through this."

Louisa looked toward the curtained window. She *would* get through this, because somebody was waiting for her outside. *Scratch that.* Someone was going to come and get her. "Where is my mother, Ivan? I want to see her and check that she is okay."

"She's in another room in the house with Vasilii. A different wing. But she's safe, for now. I'll try to arrange for you to see her before they move you."

"Move me? Where am I going?" she asked.

"To a different lab. If you don't cooperate with them, I can't say what will happen. And this has all become too much for Vasilii . . . He seems . . . unhinged." He stood and moved to the door. Knocked on it, then stepped as if to walk outside.

"I hate you for this," she whispered, meaning every word.

"I know. I hate me too," Ivan said as the door closed behind him.

A breeze rustled through the trees that bordered the rear of the old ranch house. Six fixed his night goggles and focused on the rear door, the one that Gaz was going to pick in about six minutes. He looked down at his watch again. As the SEAL who'd always been a fan of direct action, and as the man in love with the woman trapped inside that ugly fucking ranch house, Six was struggling to find the calm he usually found ahead of a mission. He'd promised he'd find her, and it hadn't occurred to him to tell her that it might not be immediate. He glared over at Mac who'd made the call to wait until the hours of the night, when their assault on the house would create shock and awe, and shook his head to clear it. If he didn't get his head in the fucking game, he'd probably lose it. Plus, being the experienced tactician that he was, he knew it was the right call, even if it hurt more than the gunshot wound to his side to know Lou was in there, scared for her life.

"We're going to get her back, Viking," Cabe whispered.

"I know," he said. He believed it. There was no way this was going to end any other way.

"I'm sorry I've been a prick." Cabe rubbed his hand along his jaw. "Losing Jess . . . well . . . fuck. And it's nearly a year."

Had it been that long? Six remembered the call from Cabe that his fiancée Jess's vehicle had hit an IED. He remembered the way his stomach had dropped at the choked sound of his best friend's voice. And fuck, he remembered the funeral and the speed with which Cabe had had to return to his *own* tour.

Cabe's concerns hadn't been about the money, or the job, or even Lou. It had all reminded him of Jess.

"Cabe, I'm . . ."

"Yeah. Don't, man. You found yours. So let's go get her," he said. He forced a grin onto his face. "Just like old times."

Lite was in the barn, up high looking down from his observation post through the sight of his M24 sniper rifle. His favorite kind of concealed spot and weapon. Between Lite, and Sherlock and Cabe in their ghillie suits, they had a full 360 of the property, and a pattern of life on the ranch had revealed that six armed men were keeping Louisa and her mother company. Plus, that fucker, Vasilii, and his grandson were both in there too. He thought about the conversation they'd had earlier trying to figure out the tactics. For the first time in his life, he wanted to annihilate, not capture.

"Okay," Cabe said. "This is from a realtor website so we need to take the layout with a grain of salt. Everyone knows what Lou looks like, but this is Ivan Popov."

"No." Six slammed his fist on the table. "Lou and her mom are our only targets."

Mac slung his pack over his shoulder. "We'll get her out, but despite evidence to the contrary, we have to assume Ivan and Vasilii are innocent until proven guilty."

"No, we don't. Assholes got her into this shit. Our job is to get in and get Lou and her mom out. Everyone

else is under arrest unless they resist, then we do what we have to do."

Cabe sent Mac one of those looks. The one where he clearly didn't agree with Six but was waiting for Mac to interject.

"I'm not fucking kidding, Cabe. I see you lift a fucking finger to help those shits beyond getting cuffs on them, I'll kill you myself."

"Fine," Cabe said. "Now can you rein yourself in? We need the Viking. Not the lovesick fucking puppy."

Six checked his M4A1 5.56 mm with short barrel again. It was perfect for close-quarters battle inside the ranch. The screwed-on suppressor was tightly secured . . . just like it had been the last time he checked three and a half minutes ago. And as he aimed it at the tree to his left, the infrared laser was just as clear as it had been back then too. He checked his vest. Six magazines of thirty rounds ready to go do his bidding at the double tap of the trigger and a handful of flash-crash grenades.

Mac gestured to them it was time to go. Night vision goggles on and their M4s at the ready, they made their way silently under cover of darkness to the rear. Gaz pulled out his lockpick key set. Covert for as long as possible was the plan. Silently, he picked the lock until, with a muffled click, he stepped back and pulled the door open. Out of the corner of Six's eye, he saw Sherlock, ghillie suit gone, moving into a better position to cover the rear exit and the trucks parked around the side of the building. He felt better knowing that if the hostage takers did get Louisa out of the house, they weren't going to get too far.

In the formation they'd agreed on, Mac led and Six followed. Ryder and Gaz brought up the rear. As they entered, Cabe looked left, Six, right, as they took in the open great room. A hallway led off in one direction, a staircase in the other. Suddenly footsteps sounded in both directions. A target appeared in the stairwell, gun aimed at them as he ran.

"Down on the floor," Six yelled, firing a warning shot. "Slide your weapon toward me."

Realizing he was completely outmanned, the guy dropped to the floor and did as Six said. Cabe ran over, kicked the weapon away, and cuffed the man while Six provided cover.

All thoughts of covert action now gone, Ryder pulled the pin of the flash-crash and threw it in the direction of the two men who were hurrying down the hall. Bullets were sprayed in the confusion, piercing the drywall to their right. Six and Mac peeled off left as Ryder and Gaz took the battle forward into the living room.

They took the stairs two at a time, ready to shoot to kill if need be. But despite his earlier feelings of wanting to hurt each and every person who had done Louisa harm, Six knew the more suspects they took out alive, the better chance of someone turning state's evidence. Rapid gunfire sounded from the direction of the kitchen, and both Ryder and Gaz's voices carried over the noise.

The upstairs hallway was deserted, but several doors were closed. Mac threw the first door open.

Six did his ninety-degree sweep to the right of the room. "Clear right," he called out.

"Clear left," Mac said, and they went back to the hallway.

They headed to the next door. Intermittent gunfire and the sound of another flash-crash grenade began in another part of the house. Six's senses told him that Louisa was up here. Mac threw the door open and they repeated the process. Two more doors to go.

As they reached for the third door, bullets flew alongside him and hit the drywall to the side of his head, and he dropped to the ground and crawled a little way along the hall. The bullets had come from the room opposite. Whoever was in there was scared and had started shooting through the walls before they even reached the door.

Both Six and Mac crawled to the other side of the hall and stood. When the firing stopped, Six kicked the door down. He scanned the room. Three people. Antonia, Louisa's mom, had her cast rested on the bed, and a man stood in the dark room backed up into the corner, his arm tight around Louisa's neck, pistol to her temple. His finger squeezed the trigger in preparation for firing. "Do anything to me and I'll—"

Despite the way the sight of her trapped there ripped his heart to fucking pieces, Six didn't wait for him to finish his sentence. Years of training had prepared him for this very moment. He double tapped the trigger and watched dispassionately as both bullets exploded into the man's forehead, covering Louisa in blood.

Louisa screamed as the man fell down behind her, and Six hurried over to her.

"Targets safe," Mac said. "Repeat, targets are safe."

"Getting slow in your old age," Lite said through their earpiece.

"Says the man two hundred feet away in a barn making out with a fucking chicken," Mac replied.

Louisa threw her arms around him. "I knew you'd come," she said.

"You got to keep it together for a little while longer," he said as the gunshots continued elsewhere in the house. Beneath the sour, pungent scent of gunfire that hung in the back of his throat, he could smell burning. Something was on fire, and he prayed it wasn't their exit. He pulled the shutters open and looked outside. It was a straight two-story drop to the ground, which on a good day he'd do, but not with two women, especially when one already had a cast on her leg.

Fuck.

"All clear," Ryder shouted. "But we need to get our asses in gear. We got a fire."

Mac lifted Louisa's mom off the bed, and Six took Louisa's hand, pulling her out into the hall. Smoke had started to fill the stairwell, and Six, still in his goggles, lifted Lou. "Close your eyes and take a deep breath."

He hurried down the stairs, heard Mac's footsteps that told him he was right behind them. Six could just about make out the back door and he ran toward it. The thick, acrid smoke was beginning to burn his lungs as he ran through the open door into the rear yard and didn't stop until they were well clear.

Tears trickled down Lou's face as she blinked furiously. He placed her on the ground and raised his goggles.

He reached around in his pack and pulled out some water. "Here, drink some of this," he said gently. She took it from him and sipped on the cool liquid.

Ryder and Gaz hurried out the door. Pulling two men behind them. They laid them out on the dirt, then shouted to Mac to cover them before they jogged back inside.

"Thank you," she said as he pulled the long sleeve of his tee over his hand and used it to wipe her face.

"Did they hurt you, Lou?" he asked, his voice strained.

She shook her head, desperate to reassure him. "I was out of it for a long time, I think."

Six nodded and then grabbed her. He pulled her into his lap and hugged her tightly, pressing kisses to her hair and face.

Cabe hurried out with Vasilii over his shoulder. The man's hands were tied behind his back, and once Cabe dropped him to the ground, Six could see Vasilii was crying. The flames were beginning to rage harder in one side of the old building.

Two men stumbled out of the door, coughing and spluttering. They fell to their knees, their arms bound behind their backs.

It was a matter of a few moments before two dead bodies were lined up out of sight.

"Anybody see what happened to Ivan?" Cabe asked.

Ryder shook his head as he gulped down some water after running out of the house. "No sign of Ivan."

Six looked back over to the house. It wouldn't be long before it would be razed to the ground, but it would take forever to erase the image of a gun against her temple. He pressed his lips to Lou's neck, squeezed her tightly. "Thank fuck you're safe," he whispered over and over again. "I don't think I would have survived if anything happened to you."

She pressed her hands to either side of his face. "I

knew you'd come for me," she said, looking him squarely in the eye.

Six swallowed deeply and picked her up to take her to the truck. "Always. I'd come get you a thousand times over because I love you."

Lou ran her fingers along his jaw. "And I love you too."

EPILOGUE

SIX MONTHS LATER

"We have to get ready." Louisa giggled as Six turned her around and placed her palms firmly on the new side table she'd bought for the hallway that had been delivered less than twenty minutes earlier. She'd put a giant mirror behind it, something to do with it making the hallway appear wider. If he was honest with himself, even when she'd been explaining it to him before he'd gone away, all he'd been thinking about was taking her in front of it.

"It's an hour before we have to leave, and I promise you this won't take long," he said as he slid the hem of the cute red dress she was wearing up her thighs. Plus, he was prepared. He dropped the condom onto the table.

"You should go away more often," she said breathlessly, and he laughed. Twenty-one long days away from her was just about his limit these days. He'd been down in Colombia on a CIA-related case, offering clandestine cover for an operative who had infiltrated a major cartel. It had been long and exhausting, and since he'd arrived at his home . . . now *their* home . . . he couldn't get enough of Lou.

"No," he said, flipping her skirt over her ass and sliding her underwear down her thighs. Her ass looked so fucking delicious that he bent down and bit it playfully. "Three weeks is my limit without access to this," he said, running his fingers between her legs, delighted to find her already wet for him.

Louisa widened her stance, and he stood to his full height behind her. She looked at him in the mirror, all of her hair up and off her face, offering him the double benefit of seeing those beautiful eyes of hers and giving him something to hold on to once he began to fuck her in earnest.

"Six," she breathed as he slid his fingers into her gently and scissored as he pulled them out. Her hips rolled against his hand, searching for what he was going to give her. She took a step away from the table and arched her back, which gave him the most fantastic view down the front of her dress. He could see the white lace he'd bought her that he knew she wore just for him. While he was away, she'd reverted back to her simple cotton underwear, which he was coming to love just as much as the silk and satin he enjoyed stripping her out of.

In fact, there were lots of things they tried together. Some worked, some didn't. But the simple truth that they were in it together, to grow together, was all he needed.

He shucked his shorts and T-shirt so he was naked. It was hot, with her still clothed and him not, and Lou grinned in response.

"Keep your hands right where they are," he said as she went to hand him the condom, and she stuck her tongue out at him playfully.

Louisa wiggled her hips and straightened her legs, giving him a view guaranteed to make any man hard in zero point five seconds. Quickly, he ripped open the condom and slid it on.

"Hold still, sweetie, just for a minute," he said as he lined himself up against her.

He groaned as he felt her tightening against him. It was crass, but she really did have the sweetest pussy on the earth. She was wet, and warm, and most importantly, she was waiting for him with eyes so hungry they would have devoured him if they could. He looked down at her hands, her knuckles white as she gripped the edge of the table.

Pressing his nose to the side of her neck, he inhaled deeply. She smelled faintly of lavender, and it made him smile. Before he left for an away mission, Lou took the time to spritz the T-shirt he took with him to sleep in. It was an odd thing, but to slip into it on that first night away and smell her was just the boost he needed to get on with the work he was there to do.

He eased farther into her and watched the way her mouth formed a small "o" when he was pressed deep against her.

"Shit, Lou," he said, holding on to her hips as he slowly pulled out. God, he loved that view. He watched his dick, coated in her wetness, and wished he'd taken a moment to taste her. But he was a greedy man, and there would be time for finessing later. Easing back in, faster this time, he wrapped his hand in her ponytail. It had surprised him when it had been one of the things that worked. Careful never to pull so it hurt, he loved the feel of her hair wrapped around his hand.

"Please," she cried. "Faster."

Her wish. His command.

"Like this?" he said, speeding the pulse of his hips and savoring the way she began to tighten around him.

"Yes. Just like that," she said, keeping her eyes focused on him.

Dear God. She was going to kill him.

With one hand on her hip, the other wrapped tightly in her hair, and his eyes on the two of them in the mirror, the telltale tightening of his core warned him he was going to come soon. He stepped his legs a little wider, changing the angle, and Louisa gasped.

"Oh, please. Yes," she said, her movements changing from smooth and controlled to jerky, as they always did when she came. He loved to make her lose control that way.

When she clamped down around him, he was lost. His balls tightened, as did his abs, as he pressed down on her hips and came deep inside her.

"Lou," he cried out, moving back and forth, working every ounce of sensation from his body.

He fell forward, leaving a trail of kisses along her shoulder blades. "I love this mirror, Lou."

Lou laughed. "Well, it's going to be here for a really long time."

"Good. Because I intend to take you in front of it often. I love you, Lou."

She turned her head and he kissed her deeply, softly, at peace with her, his life, and where he was going.

"I love you, too," she replied.

He slipped out of her and dealt with the condom while she hurried along to clean up. Part of him wanted to join her, but part of him knew they'd never make it over to Mac's for dinner if he did.

Life had never looked better, although they were both busier than ever. He'd had his final session with his therapist before he'd left on this job. It had taken months to pull apart everything he thought he knew about himself and war. And Louisa had been there every step of the way, even as she'd busied herself establishing True North Industries, her own research laboratory. And they were still unraveling everything to do with Vasilii.

When Cabe had walked out with Vasilii over his shoulder, Six had been torn between staying with Louisa and storming over to Vasilii to pound on the other side of his face. But the guy had been a sniveling wreck. Vasilii had turned himself into the police and given evidence against the men. After the fire had been put out and investigators had been allowed back inside, they had conducted a thorough search of the building for Ivan, but no remains had been found.

Six hoped that if the guy was smart enough to get out of the house in the chaos, he was now very far away.

By the time they arrived at Mac's, Cabe and the rest of the guys were already there. Lou greeted Mac and Cabe warmly. A by-product of her ordeal seemed to be a new resilience to being around people, but only those she knew well. It still wasn't easy for her, and the rest of the team, especially the new hires who brought Eagle Securities' personnel up to twelve in total, were treated to a wave. But the small increase in newfound confidence looked good on her, even if she still stacked shit and alphabetized things when she was out of her depth.

Louisa had insisted on making the birthday cake for Cabe, and while Six would never admit it to another soul, especially not one of the guys he served with, he kinda liked the quiet domestication of carrying it into his friend's home for her.

Once the food and cake had been eaten, Six made himself at home and grabbed a beer from the fridge, and when Mac's cell phone rang, he left him to it.

Less than a minute or two later, Mac hurried back into the room and waved to him, signaling to grab Cabe.

"What's up?" Six walked into his room and eyed the bag on the bed. "We got a job?" He hated the idea of leaving so soon.

"I gotta go," Mac said. "Delaney is in Landstuhl." He unplugged his chargers from the wall and shoved them into the front pocket of his pack.

"What the hell?" Six tugged his hand through his hair. "The place or the hospital? What happened?"

Mac shook his head and stopped what he was doing for a moment. "Hospital. I don't know how she ended up there, but she isn't fully lucid. All I know is that she's been asking for me. I'm sorry guys, it means we're going to be short for—"

"Shut up," Cabe said. "You need to go. And we've got your back. Don't worry about tickets. I'll find you a flight while you are en route to the airport. I'll text you details, okay?"

Mac nodded and shoved his coat into the top of his

backpack. "Thanks, guys. I'll let you know what's what as soon as I get there."

Cabe stood and slapped him on the back in a hug. "Take care, man."

Six repeated the action.

"Lock up for me?" Mac said to Six, but he didn't wait for a response.

"What do you make of that?" Cabe asked as the door to the condo slammed shut.

Six shook his head. "I don't know, but I'm going to wrap the party up."

When at last he had everyone out of the door, Six wandered to the kitchen and found Louisa wiping down the counter. He wrapped his arms around her waist and pulled her back against his chest. Something about Delaney being injured had caused image after image to appear in his mind of what could have gone wrong in their rescue of Louisa. What if they'd hurt her? What if she'd been killed in the cross fire?

Louisa dropped the wet cloth into the water in the sink and placed her damp hands over his. Neither of them said a word, instead they stood in silence and looked out over the bay. Just being next to her calmed him.

"I'm sorry about Delaney," Louisa said finally. "I hope she's okay."

Six pressed his nose to the soft skin of her neck and then kissed her just behind her ear. "From your lips to God's ears," he said. "I don't know what I would've done if something had happened to you, Lou."

She turned in his arms and placed her hands on either side of his face, a gesture that always warmed him from the inside out. "Well, we'll never need to worry about that, because *you* didn't let anything happen to me. You had my six," she said stepping up onto her toes to kiss him deeply.

Yeah, he did. Having her back was something he intended to do for the rest of their lives. "And I always will. Especially if it's naked."

Louisa laughed as he'd intended, and it broke the mood. She reached forward and wrung the wet cloth, placing it over the faucet to dry, then pulled the plug to let the water drain.

Six handed her the towel to dry her hands, and she looked up at him. "I love you, Six," she said, tilting her head to the side, letting her bangs fall away, a move he'd come to love. Because it meant he could see all of her.

"I love you, too, Lou," he replied gruffly, wishing he had the courage and words to tell her everything she meant to him. "Ready to go home?"

Home.

"With you? Always."

Six threw his arm over her shoulder and led her out of the door.

Don't miss Scarlett Cole's next book

FINAL SIEGE

Mac and Delaney's story

Coming Winter 2018 from St. Martin's Paperbacks